The Madonna of Pisano

A Novel

by

MaryAnn Diorio

"A new twist on *The Scarlet Letter*"

TopNotch Press
A Division of MaryAnn Diorio Enterprises, LLC
Merchantville, NJ 08109

THE MADONNA OF PISANO
by MaryAnn Diorio

Volume 1 of The Italian Chronicles

Published by TopNotch Press
A Division of MaryAnn Diorio Enterprises, LLC
PO Box 1185 Merchantville, NJ 08109

This is a work of fiction Names, characters, places, and incidents either are the product of the author's imagination or are used fictitiously. Any resemblance to actual persons living or dead, business establishments, events, or locales, is entirely coincidental.

Unless otherwise indicated, all Scripture quotations are from the ESV® Bible (The Holy Bible, English Standard Version®), copyright © 2001 by Crossway, a publishing ministry of Good News Publishers. Used by permission. All rights reserved.

Softcover Edition: ISBN: 978-0-930037-22-2
Electronic Edition: ISBN: 978-0-930037-36-9
Library of Congress Control Number: 2015914806

Publisher's Note: This is a work of fiction. Names, characters, places, and incidents either are the product of the author's imagination or are used fictitiously, and any resemblance to actual persons living or dead, business establishments, events, or locales, is entirely coincidental.

While the author has made every effort to provide accurate telephone numbers and Internet addresses at the time of publication, neither the publisher nor the author assumes any responsibility for errors or for changes that occur after publication. Further, the publisher and author do not have any control over and do not assume any responsibility for author or third-party websites or their content.

Cover Deign by Lisa Vento Hainline.

Praise for the Fiction of MaryAnn Diorio

Surrender to Love

I enjoyed reading Surrender to Love by MaryAnn Diorio. It was a short story that packed a powerful punch. Anyone who has ever experienced loss in their life, in any form, can automatically relate to the feelings of Teresa and Marcos in this book. In addition, there were three characters, each who experienced significant loss but also each from a different perspective and this brings even more depth to the book. It showcases how despite knowing "what to do" it's not always easy to tell your heart to do what your head knows it should. And that saying goodbye can feel like a betrayal of sorts…letting go of the old is more than just head knowledge, it has to come from the heart, a full surrender. ~ Cheri Swalwell, *Book Fun Magazine*

I was immediately drawn into the story of this young woman whose future and plans were cut short. The grief that she felt and refused to address applies not only to lost loved ones, but unexpected situations or challenges in life. The discovery of hope is most satisfying, leaving you wanting to share in her new found joy. ~ Deb, Amazon.com

A Christmas Homecoming

Winner of the Silver Medal for E-Book Fiction in the 2015 Illumination Book Awards sponsored by the Jenkins Group

"This short story is a wonderful way to start the Christmas season. It is a story full of human emotion and the struggles this life can challenge us with. The lesson throughout the story is that all things are possible through God's grace. This is a 'feel good' story that lifts the spirits and keeps you encouraging the main character to persevere and not give up. It is a great book for a short respite from our busy lives." ~ Kimberly T. Ferland, Amazon.com

"Well-woven. If only all stories made me sit on the edge of my seat, unsure of the outcome, but desperate for a good conclusion for the characters! ~ Sarah E. Johnson, Poet, Amazon.com

"A great Christian read. A powerful short story packed full of love, hope, heartbreak and a strong message on forgiveness." ~ Jerron, Amazon.com

ACKNOWLEDGMENTS

A book is a joint venture, put together with the help and encouragement of many people. I would like to thank those who worked closely with me on this story, from the brainstorming stage, through the writing stage, and, finally, through the editing stage.

First of all, I would like to thank my God and Father Who gave me both the gift to write fiction and the desire to exercise this gift for His glory. I would like to thank my Lord and Savior Jesus Christ Who first gave me the idea for this story. I would like to thank Holy Spirit for hovering over me with His wisdom and understanding as I wrote this story.

Next, I owe heartfelt thanks to my writing mentor and dear friend, Nikki Arana, who guided me during the initial stages of writing this book. Thanks also to Susan May Warren who offered valuable input along the way.

Tremendous thanks go to my amazing mentors in the Seton Hill University *Writing Popular Fiction* Program, Shelley Adina and Barbara Miller, who guided me every step of the way as I turned my story idea into a full-fledged novel. I owe you both so very much. Thank you also to all of my critique partners in the SHU program who gave of their time and expertise in helping to shape this story. There are so many of you that I hesitate to mention names for fear of inadvertently omitting someone. But you know who you are. Thank you!

Last, but not least, I would like to thank my amazing husband of 46 years, Dominic A. Diorio, MD, who encouraged me along the way and helped me practically by cooking meals and cleaning the house while I worked to meet deadlines. You are awesome!

Special thanks go to my daughters, Lia Diorio Gerken, PhD, and Gina L. Diorio, MA, outstanding writers in their own right, both of whom gave me valuable insights for the plotting of my story. You are the jewels in my crown, and I love you both very much!

Finally, I would like to thank you, my readers, who provide an audience for what I write. May this story bless you and draw you closer to Jesus Christ--the Only One Who gives true meaning to life!

DEDICATION

To my Lord and Savior Jesus Christ . . .
in Whom I live and move and have my being

**To the loving memory of my paternal
Italian great-great-grandmother...**
I wrote this story to exonerate your good name.

**To the precious memory of
Mildred S. Taylor (1932-2014) . . .**
Thank you for encouraging me in my writing journey.

THE MADONNA OF PISANO

"For if you forgive others their trespasses, your heavenly Father will also forgive you, but if you do not forgive others their trespasses, neither will your Father forgive your trespasses."

~ Matthew 6:14-15 ESV

TABLE OF CONTENTS

AUTHOR'S NOTE

The idea for this story stems from a true incident that occurred in my family history. As the first-generation child of an Italian immigrant, I had many questions about my ancestors. When I had the opportunity to live in Italy for a year, many of those questions were answered, yet more were raised. In the process, I came upon an incident in the life of one of my ancestors that struck a deep chord within me. I knew I would have to write a story about it.

This novel is that story.

A word of caution, however. Because this book is a novel, much of the information has been changed to accommodate the story. Names have been altered, and circumstances have been fictionalized. But its essential message remains the same: *Unforgiveness enslaves; forgiveness sets free.*

I trust you will be blessed by reading my story. Most of all, I pray that if you need to forgive someone who hurt you, you would do so.

Jesus says this: *"For if you forgive others their trespasses, your heavenly Father will also forgive you, but if you do not forgive others their trespasses, neither will your Father forgive your trespasses"* *(Matthew 6:14-15).*

The Madonna of Pisano

by MaryAnn Diorio

Prologue

Pisano, Sicily, April 1885

"*Carlo, vieni subito.* Come quickly." Maria Landro flashed a brilliant smile at the handsome young man admiring her from only a few yards away.

In an instant he was at her side.

She pointed to the litter of newly born puppies. "Look! There are six of them. And they are so beautiful."

Maria gazed into the large box at their feet. Nestled in a corner was a lovely female cocker spaniel surrounded by six suckling newborn puppies.

Carlo put his arms around her. "Someday we'll have six of our own." His lips brushing against her ear sent chills down her spine.

She turned toward him and laughed. "Puppies?"

"No, Silly." He took her by the shoulders and turned her toward him. "Beautiful children." He planted a soft kiss on her lips. "Just like you."

How Maria longed for that day! She and Carlo had grown up together, gone to the village school together, and worked together in the fields. Their families had been close

1

and, from their children's earliest years, had assumed that one day they would marry. That assumption turned into conviction as naturally as caterpillars turn into butterflies. By the time Maria was fifteen, she knew without a doubt she wanted to spend the rest of her life with Carlo Mancini. When she turned seventeen, they were formally engaged.

"Will you still think I'm beautiful after we've been married for fifty years?"

He brushed the dark strands back from her forehead. "Each day you will become more beautiful to me than the day before."

She looked deep into his eyes and returned the kiss.

Their wedding was only a few months away. While Carlo continued to work on his family's farm, she'd taken a job as assistant housekeeper at the rectory of her parish church, the Church of the Holy Virgin. There she'd been baptized. There she'd been educated, and there she would soon be married.

Maria's gaze drifted past Carlo to the roughening waters of the emerald blue Mediterranean sea just beyond *Bella Terra*, her family's hillside farm. She'd learned to sense the water's every nuance, every tremor, every slightest change. Today, the Mediterranean seemed tenser than usual.

Her stomach responded in kind.

"Maria." Mama called from the large, two-story stucco house behind them, the house that had belonged to her family for four generations. "*Frappoco si mangia*. We'll be eating soon."

Taking Carlo's hand, Maria gave a flirtatious toss of her long black hair and led him back across the courtyard, past the purple-rose clusters of bougainvillea, toward the house. "I can't wait until we're married." She smiled and gave him a sidelong glance.

"Neither can I." Carlo kissed her again. "Neither can I."

Mama and Maria's younger sisters, Luciana and Cristina, were already seated at the long, oaken table when Maria entered with Carlo. The aroma of garlic filled the air of the rustic Sicilian kitchen. "Oh, Mama. It smells so good."

Mama smiled. "Your favorite, Maria. Linguine with artichokes."

"When are you going to make *my* favorite?" ten-year-old Cristina whined.

Luciana, four years her senior, nudged her younger sister. "Stop complaining. Mama made your favorite last Sunday, don't you remember?"

Cristina scrunched her face into a question mark.

Mama laughed. "Luciana is right, dear daughter of mine. I made angel hair pasta *alla marinara* for you on Sunday."

Cristina's face registered remorse. "Sorry, Mama. I forgot."

Mama blew Cristina a kiss. "I forgive you."

Maria took her usual place at the table. Carlo sat in the empty chair beside her. How good it was to be surrounded by her wonderful family! Soon she would be leaving them to set up her own household and to start her own family with the man she loved. Her life with Carlo would be just as filled with love and laughter as her life at home had been. She would see to it.

If only Papa had lived long enough to walk her down the aisle. His sudden death a year before had rocked her to her core. Thankfully, he'd left Mama and the children with a prosperous family business that would provide for them as long as they continued to build it.

She glanced at Carlo as Mama folded her hands. "Let's pray."

Maria bowed her head with the others as Mama intoned the same prayer of thanksgiving Papa used to pray over every meal ever since Maria could remember. "O God of Heaven and Earth, bless this food that You have provided. Bless us who eat it so that we may continue to serve You in obedience and in health. In Jesus' Name. Amen."

The clatter of dishes being passed to Mama for filling was like the happy refrain of a well-known song. Maria's heart sang as Mama placed generous portions of pasta on each plate then handed it to its rightful owner for the pleasant task of eating its delicious contents.

Maria smiled. If happiness had a pinnacle, then she had surely reached it.

* * *

The daily trudge from *Bella Terra* to the rectory took about twenty minutes on a good day. But the stormy weather this Monday morning made Maria's walk more difficult than usual. She clutched her satchel closer to her cloak and straightened her umbrella. Rosa would be waiting for her with their morning coffee, the way the elderly head housekeeper waited every morning of the work week. Maria had grown fond of the dear woman and their heart-to-heart talks. Rosa was like a second mother to her, and Maria was the daughter Rosa never had.

Maria drew in a deep breath of the cool morning air. The same air she'd breathed ever since her birth seventeen years earlier. Soon, she'd celebrate her eighteenth birthday and, shortly after that, her wedding day.

Her heart surged with longing for Carlo. A longing pure and virginal on both of their parts. After the wedding, Carlo would work at *Bella Terra* as head foreman, overseeing the planting and the harvesting. A very important job, and one he would handle well.

She smiled. Carlo handled everything well. She loved that about him. It made her feel secure and safe. The way Papa had made her feel before he died.

She rounded the last bend in the road before reaching the village. Already vendors were setting up their wares. The smell of fresh squid and mussels from the nearby sea filled the air.

"*Pesce fresco*. Fresh fish. Squid, mussels, clams. Whatever your heart desires." Angelo, the fish vendor, smiled at her as she passed. "*Buon giorno*, Maria."

"Good morning to you, too, Angelo." She laughed. "Despite this rainy mess."

One by one, she greeted the vendors, most of whom sold produce grown on her family's farm. Thanks to their business, *Bella Terra* was thriving. She smiled and waved at each vendor as she passed by.

By the time she reached the rectory, the wind had grown stronger. Closing her umbrella, she left it on the back doorstep and entered the two-story gray stucco house that served as the rectory for the Church of the Virgin. "Rosa, I'm here."

But instead of the older woman's usual greeting,

5

Maria found herself face to face with Don Franco Malbone, her former teacher and the head parish priest. "Oh, good morning, *Padre*. You startled me. I was expecting Rosa." She tried to quiet the uneasy feeling she had every time she was around him.

"Rosa will not be here today. She is not feeling well."

An alarm went off in Maria's soul. "I'm sorry to hear that. I will bring her some homemade soup later today."

"That is very kind of you." He stood there and did not move, a strange look on his face.

Maria removed her shawl and laid it on a bench in the kitchen. "Are you and Don Vincenzo ready for breakfast?"

"I already had breakfast. Don Vincenzo left early to go to Palermo on church business. It is only you and I today, Maria."

The tone of his voice chilled her.

"Well then, I'll be sure not to disturb you, *Padre*. I will go about my duties and then leave quietly."

"Very well. If you need me, I'll be in my office."

She nodded. While still a student under his tutelage, she'd vowed she would never need Don Franco for anything. Not after the way he'd leer at her in a way that made her feel extremely uncomfortable. But when Don Franco had offered her a job as assistant housekeeper at the rectory, she'd decided to take it to save money for her marriage to Carlo. Although Papa had left her family solvent, she refused to take any of her family's resources to set up her own home. Mama and her sisters would need the inheritance for their own future.

Maria nodded.

Uneasy, she watched as he walked away.

When he was out of sight, she turned her attention toward making coffee. Since Rosa had not come to work today, there was no hot coffee awaiting her as usual. Maria filled the little espresso pot with water and then added the dark coffee grounds. She'd miss having coffee with Rosa this morning. Their daily chats about life were the highlight of Maria's day.

While the coffee brewed, she swept the kitchen floor and chopped vegetables for Don Franco's lunch. When the espresso pot began to steam, she removed it from the wood-burning stove and placed it on a brown ceramic tile on the table. She then added four teaspoons of sugar to the pot and let it sit while she took a *demitasse* cup from the cupboard. She then returned to the coffee pot and poured herself some coffee. The aroma of fresh espresso wafting through the air was enough to energize her.

"The coffee smells good."

She startled and turned abruptly as Don Franco approached her from behind.

"Would you like a cup, *Padre*?" Despite her best effort, she could not hide the quiver in her voice.

"Yes, thank you."

Her stomach squeezed at the way he looked at her. It was not a priestly look.

Keeping her eyes lowered, she filled a small cup for him, hoping he did not notice her trembling hands.

"I will be spending the entire morning in my office and do not wish to be disturbed. If anyone comes, please say I am busy. Unless, of course, it is an emergency."

She nodded. "Yes, *Padre*."

Relief flooded her soul when he left the room again.

Although she'd been working at the rectory for three months, she'd never grown accustomed to Don Franco's strange ways, nor his strange looks. He'd suddenly appear without warning, or he'd linger when it was inappropriate to linger. On one occasion, she'd spoken of her discomfort to Carlo.

"You're just imagining things, Maria. He's a priest for heaven's sake! What harm could he do? He was probably encouraging you in your new job. There's nothing to worry about."

But she wasn't so sure. A woman sensed a man in a way another man did not. Although only seventeen, she was old enough to recognize the look of lust in a man's eyes. Village-born and bred, she'd seen enough men—both those who lived in the village and those who passed through—to know what was on their minds when they looked at her.

But a priest? The very thought repelled her.

She brushed all negative thoughts aside and began her daily chores. First on the list was making up the beds and straightening Don Franco's and Don Vincenzo's private quarters. Both bedrooms filled the entire upper floor. Normally, Rosa did this with her, but today she'd have to do it alone. Fortunately, the sleeping quarters were on the second floor, where she could work quickly and quietly while Don Franco remained in his office on the first floor.

She entered his bedroom and opened the large window to let in some fresh air. The rain had stopped, but the sky was still a dark gray, portending another storm. Tropical mid-day storms were common in this area of southwestern Sicily.

For a brief moment, she stood at the window, gazing at the expansive Mediterranean Sea in the distance. Often

—

she'd wondered what lay on the other side. Many from Pisano had already left the tiny village to find out. Would she one day be among them?

She turned away from the window to make Don Franco's bed. As she leaned over to tuck in the sheets, the door opened.

Her heart froze at the sight of Don Franco standing in the doorway.

She straightened and moved to leave.

Don Franco held up a hand. "Sorry to disturb you, Maria. No need to leave. I'll be only a moment. I just came in to get some papers I'd left on the dresser."

She lowered her eyes. Heat flooded her face as she continued to make the bed.

Don Franco rummaged through the pile of papers on his dresser. Then, he turned toward her.

"Maria." His voice was husky.

She stopped short and looked up at him. "Yes, *Padre.*"

"I have something for you."

She immediately straightened, smoothing the front of her apron. "What is it, *Padre?*"

Extending his hand, he showed her a gold ring. "It's beautiful, is it not, Maria?"

There was that strange look again. Did she not know better, she'd think him delirious.

"Something I purchased several years ago, before I entered seminary. I intended to give it to a woman I loved and wanted to marry."

She tensed. His words were inappropriate. His eyes, faraway.

9

He held up the ring between his thumb and index finger. "But she refused me, Maria." He laughed a laugh marked by madness. "Imagine that! She rejected me."

Maria's heart raced. She inched backward toward the door.

He extended the ring toward her. "I thought you might like to have it."

She recoiled. "Oh no, *Padre*. I cannot take it." She pressed her hand on her throat. "I *must* not take it. It would not be right."

His face contorted, and his eyes ignited with angry flames. "You would dare reject me, too?"

She eyed the door. "*Padre*, you are not well. I will fetch Doctor Gandolfo."

She moved to go, but Don Franco raised a palm. "I am quite well. No need to fetch the good doctor."

Maria bolted toward the door. But before she could escape, he caught her by the hair and threw her down on the bed.

The ring fell to the floor, clanging as it rolled across the room.

With one hand, Don Franco muffled her screams while with the other, he threw up her skirts. Her violent struggle was no match for his unbridled power.

Her female body no match for his male fury.

Threatening her and her family with death if she divulged his identity, he ordered her to silence her screams.

When it was all over, he fled from the room, leaving her utterly alone with the taste of death in her mouth.

* * *

Three Months Later . . .

"The test is positive." Doctor Gandolfo's face was grim. "You are with child, Maria."

"But it cannot be, *Dottore*! I am innocent!" Hot tears stung her eyes. "Please believe me! I am innocent!" Under penalty of death, she dared not reveal the child's father.

Doctor Gandolfo patted her trembling shoulder. "Perhaps you should go to your confessor."

She recoiled at his cruel words. He did not believe her. Why should he in a village where men were always right and women were treated as inferior creatures?

The thought of revealing her condition to her family filled her with dread. What would her beloved Mama say? The one who had spent her life training her to live in holiness before the Lord? Thank God Papa had not lived to see his daughter in such a state. And Carlo? What would he think? What would he do? Surely she would have to tell him. Even if she did not, he would find out the truth when she delivered her child fewer than six months into their marriage.

She had no choice but to tell the truth.

Or else run away.

But where would she go? Where could she hide from her shame?

Where and how could she safely raise a child born out of wedlock?

To confront Don Franco would be to place herself in grave danger. Rumors of his Mafia connections had long floated around Pisano. Were he to discover she was with child—*his* child—both her life and her baby's life would be endangered, not to mention the lives of her mother and sisters.

No. She must not tell the priest she was with child. She must not tell anyone. She must bear the ignominy alone and carry it to her grave.

As the doctor left the examining room, she buried her head in her hands and wept.

* * *

Hands stuffed in his pockets, Carlo stood with his back to Maria and stared out the large kitchen window of her hilltop home. The distant fields, ripe with wheat and corn, glowed in the warm September sunshine. Soon, together with many of the other villagers, he would be setting his hand to the harvest. On a nearby branch, a sparrow sat poised with purpose, intent on his next destination.

Carlo's shoulders shook. Maria's shocking news had knocked the wind out of him. Anger at her betrayal wrestled with compassion for her plight. How could she have done such a wicked thing? And with their wedding day so close at hand? Could she not have withstood her attacker's advances? Could she not have run away?

Or maybe she'd seduced him.

Carlo cringed. To think such a thing of the woman he was planning to marry was nothing short of abominable.

He wiped a trembling hand across his forehead. The thought of losing Maria forever was more than he could bear. They'd known each other since childhood. Even at the tender age of nine, he knew he'd marry her one day. "At least tell me who he is."

She grabbed him by both arms. "I am sworn to

secrecy under penalty of death, not only my own, but that of my mother and sisters."

His gaze searched her eyes. Was she telling the truth? "But I'm your fiancé. Surely you can tell me. I will not betray your secret." Bitterness tinged his voice.

Maria let go of his arms. "Carlo, more than anything in the world, I want to tell you. But I can't. He will kill me and the baby--or have us killed." She lowered her head and turned away. "Besides, you wouldn't believe me anyway." She covered her face with her hands. "No one would believe me."

He reached for her but then withdrew. His stomach was a cauldron of fire. His blood, a river of ice. "What do you mean no one would believe you?"

She lifted her head. "I mean just that. No one would believe who it was who raped me."

"And why not?"

"If you knew who it was, you would understand what I'm saying."

Carlo placed his hands on her shoulders. "I want to understand, Maria, but I can't unless you tell me who raped you."

She looked at him with pleading eyes. "If you truly love me, you will never again ask me that question."

"Could you not have resisted?"

She stiffened under his touch and blinked back hot tears. "Carlo, I tried. Believe me I tried. He was physically stronger than I. I could not free myself from his grip."

Carlo's stomach knotted. "Maria, stop, please. I cannot endure the thought. It drives me mad." He thrust nervous fingers through his black, wavy hair and began to pace around the room.

Maria lowered her head. "I have caused you shame and humiliation, but I have not been unfaithful to you in my heart. You must believe that."

"Where will you go?" Suddenly he regretted the words. What kind of man was he that he would not try to keep her from leaving? How could he say he loved her when he was willing to let her go?

She burst into violent sobs, his words obviously confirming her worst fear.

In an instant, he took her into his arms. "Oh, Maria! What am I thinking? I can never let you go. I am worse than a coward for even thinking it. You and I are one soul. To let you go would be worse than dying." He stroked her long, silky black hair and pressed her close to his heart, but she resisted.

"You've made known your true feelings. If you cannot accept my child, you cannot accept me."

Carlo scowled at her passionate expression of love for her illegitimate child. He drew back. "How can you love a child conceived against your will?"

Maria's eyes flamed. "How can a mother not love her own child, no matter how the child was conceived? It is impossible."

Carlo turned on her in rage. "I cannot love a child conceived in sin."

Maria grabbed him by both arms. "I did not sin! I was raped!"

Carlo stood motionless, his arms hanging at his sides.

Maria pulled back, her eyes indicting him. "I thought you loved me."

"I do love you, but . . . ."

"*But*? So, there is a condition on your love for me?"

His silence spoke volumes.

He pulled away from her and returned to the window. For a long moment, he remained silent while rage and love warred within him. He gazed at the graying Mediterranean in the distance. "It is better that we not marry. For your sake, and for that of your child."

Still staring at the darkening waters, he heard the wrenching sob that rose to Maria's throat. Without looking back at her, he turned and stalked out of the room.

Pisano, Sicily, September 1891

Six years later . . .

Chapter One

She had no other choice.

Maria Landro led her little son by the hand as they hurried down the winding road from *Bella Terra* toward the village. Distant, dark clouds gathered in the morning sky. Looked like a storm coming. The anxiety that had been churning for days in the pit of her stomach now spread to chill every part of her body. It was all she could do to keep herself from turning back.

Nico tugged on her wrist. "Are we almost there, Mama?"

She squeezed his hand in return, the hem of her skirt rustling against the pebbles as it swished along the cobblestone road. "Almost, darling. Are you all right?"

He looked up at her. He had her father's eyes. Kind, deep, and probing. They always made him so easy to love.

"I'm well, Mama." But his fingers fidgeted in her hand.

His nervousness only fueled her own. She squeezed his hand more tightly. Please let the village be kind to him. Regardless of what they believed about her.

A sudden gust of wind caught the edge of her

headscarf, pulling it back past her temples. "My, the wind is getting stronger. Let's hurry before the storm breaks. We don't want you to arrive at school soaking wet on your very first day, do we?"

"No, we don't, Mama. I would look silly." He laughed, and an arrow pierced her heart.

If anyone hurt him . . .

A hay-filled wagon rumbled past them, its wooden wheels creaking against the pebble-strewn road. The driver turned his face away as he passed.

She winced, pulling her son closer to herself to hide him.

"Will the storm carry us away, Mama?" Nico laughed again. "Maybe the wind will pick me up, and I'll fly like a bird and land on the school windowsill, and my teacher will laugh."

She tensed. Nico's teacher. No, Don Franco would never laugh. If only she could have chosen someone—anyone—else to be his teacher.

But not in Pisano.

The tiny village had only one schoolhouse and one teacher.

As they turned a bend in the road, she caught a glimpse of her family's large tan stucco house. It sat majestically atop the hill, like a queen on her throne, surrounded by sloping fields of fragrant orange and lemon groves, purple-red vineyards, and golden wheat fields. Nestled among a cluster of tall poplar trees, would the queen soon be forced to give up her throne?

Was the farm's failure Maria's fault as well?

She looked down at her little boy, all dressed up for

his first day of school. She'd made him the pair of navy-blue cotton britches the school uniform required, topped by a white, short-sleeved shirt and navy-blue ascot. His new black leather shoes, though a bit too big, would soon fit his rapidly growing feet.

As they approached the village, she recoiled at the sight of the medieval church steeple reaching toward the gray morning sky. The church stood in the middle of the village as a sign of God's central position in the lives of the villagers.

She hadn't stepped foot in it for nearly seven years.

Pinwheeling out from the church, little pastel-colored stucco houses lined dirt roads framed by borders of yellow pansies and russet daylilies. Next to the church stood the rectory, its burnt orange tile roof in much need of repair.

She averted her eyes.

A few drops of rain splashed against her kerchief and sprinkled her face. She looked up just as a streak of lightning slashed the eastern sky. Then, with a loud clap, the clouds broke loose, dumping their reservoir of rain. Why hadn't she brought an umbrella?

Gripping Nico's hand, she started running. The rain pummeled her head and her back as she tried to guide her little boy around the puddles.

"Oh, Mama. My new shoes. They're covered with mud."

So much for showing off her son. After six years of hiding him, she would see her bold, triumphant moment ruined by mud. "Don't worry. As soon as we get to the school, I'll wipe them off for you."

Just as quickly as it had started, the rain stopped. She took out the handkerchief she'd shoved into her large canvas bag, next to the fresh fruit and nuts she'd brought for Nico's snack, and wiped her son's wet face. Wet from the rain, she hoped, and not from tears.

She couldn't take tears. Not from him. Not from herself.

As they entered the village square, shouts of haggling customers caught her ear. Young mothers with babies on their hips bargained with shopkeepers over the price of peppers, eggplant, and squash. At the far end of the square, old women dressed in black shuffled out of the Church of the Holy Virgin, fresh from hearing daily Mass.

Nico pulled at her hand. "Mama, so many people. I never saw so many people."

He seemed like a new puppy let loose from his cage. "Yes, my son. The village is full of many people."

Her eyes scanned the bustling square where she'd once spent many happy moments at Luigi's outdoor café, eating pasta and sipping espresso in the company of family and friends.

Deftly skirting farmers pulling wobbly carts laden with lemons and oranges, she guided her child through the market crowd. Small groups of old men, their heads covered with flat-topped *coppola* hats, huddled at little round tables, chewing on long pieces of fennel while playing chess. A young mother, dressed in the black attire of year-long mourning for a deceased loved one, held onto a toddler with one hand while, with the other, she sorted through artichokes, cucumbers, and leeks. The smell of freshly caught tuna, squid, and mussels, fruit of the nearby sea, turned Maria's empty stomach.

She led Nico through the square. Her face grew hot as

neighbors and one-time friends raised their eyes to her. Old women shook their heads, while younger ones scanned her from head to toe, then turned away with uplifted chins. Men of all ages scraped their eyes over Nico then leered at her.

The skin prickled on the nape of her neck. "Come, Nico. We must hurry so we won't be late."

"Yes, Mama."

Wide-eyed, he drank in the new sights. Poor child. He'd been sequestered on the family farm his whole life. He knew nothing of this world beyond *Bella Terra*.

Whispers grew into mumbles and then into shouts, roaring in her ears as she hurried through the gathering crowd.

"Can it be? Maria Landro? And that must be her bastard child."

She stiffened.

"What are they saying, Mama? What does 'bastard' mean?"

Keeping her eyes straight ahead, she guided her child toward the school just beyond the square.

"Bastard! Bastard! Bastard!" The word echoed after them.

"Mama, what does 'bastard' mean?"

Her stomach tied itself into a tight knot. Lowering her head, she quickened her pace. "I'll explain at another time. Right now we must get to your school, or you will be late."

* * *

Don Franco Malbone froze as he read the name on the student roster. Nicholas Joseph Landro. First Grade. Born

21

January 13, 1886.

Impossible.

He rose to open the large casement window to the right of his desk. Perhaps some fresh air would clear the sudden tightening in his chest.

A sparrow landed on the window ledge, startling him. The little brown-headed creature stared at him for a moment then flew away as quickly as it had come.

Taking a deep breath, Don Franco returned to his desk. He read the name again. Nicholas Joseph Landro. Unless adopted, an illegitimate child always bore the mother's name. And Maria had no brothers. A cold sweat seeped through his pores as his mind performed the mental calculations. Yes. A child conceived that fateful day would now be of school age.

He dragged trembling fingers through his hair. Perhaps she would not come.

No. Maria would come. She would want her son educated, despite her shame. Her own education at the very school where he was now headmaster had opened her eyes to the world beyond Pisano. A rare privilege afforded to few girls.

His hands shaking, he withdrew his pocket watch from a fold in his cassock. Seven thirty. In one hour, the students would arrive.

He leaned his head against the back of the chair. If only he could turn back the clock. If only he had not succumbed to her beauty.

If only he could undo what he had done.

* * *

22

Luca Tonetta took his place of daily prayer by the window of his tiny bedroom. The early morning rain danced on the rooftop as he knelt and raised his hands in worship. There was nothing more wonderful than basking in the presence of God's love. He knelt for several moments, praising his Lord. Casting his cares upon Him. Asking Him for His help for the new day.

Then, rising and taking up his worn leather Bible, he sat at the small walnut desk by the window and opened the pages to the tenth chapter of the Gospel of John. His eyes fell on the tenth verse: "The thief cometh not, but for to steal, and to kill, and to destroy: I am come that they might have life, and that they might have it more abundantly."

He raised his eyes from the page. Why was he not enjoying this abundant life? He certainly didn't want for any material thing. And it wasn't for lack of trying to enjoy life. Did he not faithfully follow the rules of discipline he'd set for himself? Time with God each morning. Study of the sacred Scriptures. Boundaries regarding his relationships with women.

His shoulders rounded as the guilt of his reproach settled over him once again. He hadn't meant to exchange his virtue for shame.

The words of the Scriptures fell lifeless on his soul. He closed the Holy Book, then walked to his small kitchen overlooking the main street of Pisano and gazed out the window. Already sounds of a new day stirred in the square below as merchants set up fruit stands, vegetable bins, and fish stalls. The aroma of freshly caught squid mingling with that of vine-ripened oranges filtered through the slightly open window. Soon customers would be arriving at his door, needing the town tailor. His father would have been proud of his twenty-five-year-old son's success. God had made him prosperous, and he lacked no good thing.

Except a good wife.

His three-room, second-floor apartment needed a woman's touch.

Luca took a pale-green ceramic bowl from the cupboard, the one that had belonged to his father. He filled it halfway with freshly brewed coffee then poured milk over it. He added a tablespoon of sugar and stirred the ingredients. As was his father's custom, he took a chunk of day-old bread, broke it into small pieces, and carefully dropped them into the hot liquid. Then he sat down and gave thanks.

Suddenly it seemed as though his father were sitting there with him once again, as he used to do every morning, enjoying his *caffelatte* from this very bowl. Luca ran a finger over its chipped edge. Seven years had gone by, and still he could hear his father's laughter, smell his clothing, see him smooth his moustache.

How he missed Papa!

The bell hanging over the front door clanged in the shop below. Luca glanced at the ornate German wall clock, a relic of his only trip outside of Sicily. Quarter to eight. Someone must be in a hurry—the shop didn't open for another fifteen minutes. He grabbed his black leather apron, and, running down the steps, tied it securely behind his back.

He unlocked the narrow wooden door. As he opened it, a blast of humid air filled the little shop. He drew back. "*Buon giorno.*"

"Good morning." A man in his late thirties stood at the door, holding a canvas bag. "I'm looking for Luca Tonetta."

Luca smiled. "I am Luca Tonetta. How may I help you?"

"My name is Giulio Genova. I'm sorry to have disturbed you. I thought you opened at seven thirty."

"Come in, *Signor* Genova." Luca motioned the man into the shop, closed the door behind him, then opened the shutters on the front window to let in the light. "Maybe we'll get some sun later on, I hope."

Luca walked past the two brown leather chairs in the customer waiting area and took his place behind the counter. "What can I do for you, *Signor* Genova?"

"I have come all the way from Trapani on business and heard of your fine reputation. Would you have time to alter this suit for me by this afternoon?"

Luca smiled. "Trapani. That's a long way."

The man smiled in return and pulled a suit from his canvas bag and laid it on the counter. "I need this suit altered for my upcoming move to America. I will be leaving in one month."

America. The word tugged at Luca's heart. Although he loved Pisano, for a while now he'd wondered if his destiny lay elsewhere. Several men from Pisano had already emigrated to what was being called "the new Promised Land." Reports were trickling back of the unlimited opportunities available for those who were not afraid of hard work.

"Where are you going in America?" Luca studied the knobby texture of the gray woolen suit.

"Philadelphia." Giulio's eyes widened. "My cousin is already there and doing quite well. From what he tells me, it's a worker's paradise. The hourly wage is ten times what it is here." He chuckled. "In fact, my cousin says that tailors are doing especially well and are in great demand."

Luca lifted his gaze and focused on the man before him. "Is that right?"

"Yes." *Signor* Genova laughed again. "No one knows the tailoring business like the Italians."

Luca smiled. "You're right, my friend. God has especially gifted us with this art." He handed Giulio the suit. "I'll need you to put this on so I can take your measurements." He pointed to a small dressing room to the side of the counter area. "You may change in there."

"Thank you." Giulio took the suit behind the curtain.

The shop bell sounded again.

"Good morning, Luca." Teresa Monastero's bright cheery voice burst into the room, followed by its owner, the woman who couldn't seem to understand that no, he would not marry her.

Despite the fact she was, indeed, an exquisite specimen of feminine beauty and a woman of impeccable taste, as revealed by her finely tailored linen dress.

Setting her richly textured tapestry bag squarely on the countertop, she gave him a sidelong glance. "Well, how is my favorite tailor today?"

He didn't miss her emphasis on the word *favorite*. "I'm well, thank you. And you?"

His question was like a magnet that drew her to his side. She tilted her head. "I'd be a lot better if you would come visit my parents sometime. After all, our families have known each other for generations." She curled her lower lip downward and batted her eyelashes.

Giulio emerged from the dressing room, his eyes

focused on his pant cuffs. "*Signor* Tonetta, you'll notice these are much too long for . . ." He looked up and stopped himself. "Ah! I'm sorry. I didn't know your wife was here." Giulio extended a hand in greeting. "It's a pleasure to meet you, *Signora* Tonetta. I . . . uh . . ." He looked down at his baggy pants then back up at Teresa. "Please forgive my appearance."

Beaming, Teresa gave Luca a quick glance.

Luca's jaw clenched. "*Signor* Genova, this is not my wife but *Signorina* Teresa Monastero, a longtime friend of the family."

"Oh, I'm sorry again. You two looked as though you were married."Teresa grinned. "Why thank you, *Signor* Genova. That's quite a compliment."

Luca pushed a stack of fabric between himself and Teresa. "I'm working on several urgent projects at the moment, so a visit will have to wait until later."

"Very well, then." She removed a garment from her bag. "I'll just leave Papa's coat here. Since he's already spoken to you about it, there's no need for me to wait. You can bring it by this evening."

"I'm going to church this evening."

The familiar pout appeared on her lower lip. "You're always at church. You spend so much time at church, you will never find a wife."

He grabbed his tape measure. No wonder the serious young men of the village avoided her. Who wanted a wife as brazen as she?

"Please tell your father he can pick up his coat late this afternoon." Luca knelt to measure Giulio. The customer stood ready, his arms outstretched to the sides as if he'd done this many times before.

Teresa cleared her throat. "Of course, you could always deliver it to him and get a good meal in the process."

Luca held his tongue. "Your father's coat will be ready late this afternoon."

"Very well. Good day, Luca. And good day to you too, *Signor* Genova."

The shop bell clanged a little more loudly as she pulled the door after her.

Luca sighed in relief then redirected his full attention to his client.

Giulio chuckled. "I think she's in love with you."

Luca spoke around a pin in his mouth. "I know she is. But I am not in love with her."

"Ah, one of life's greatest tragedies. When one loves another and that love is not reciprocated."

"True. And it's also a tragedy for the one unable to reciprocate the love of another."

"Well, you make a good point. I imagine the pain, although different, is on both sides."

"Yes, it is, especially for the one in love, I suppose." Placing a pincushion bristling with straight pins on the floor beside him, Luca measured the proper length for Giulio's trousers then inserted pins to mark the hems. Next, he stood and measured the sleeve cuffs. Satisfied, he looked up and smiled. "There. All finished."

While Luca filled out a work order, Giulio returned to the dressing room to change back into his street clothes. When he came out, he removed his wallet from his back pocket.

Luca raised a palm toward him. "Pay me when you pick up the suit."

Giulio replaced his wallet. "Now I know why you have an excellent reputation."

Luca smiled. "Perhaps you will think differently when I tell you that I won't be able to have your suit ready until late tomorrow afternoon."

"No problem. I'll be leaving Pisano tomorrow evening. I can pick up the suit on my way to the train station." He put his wallet back into his pocket. "You're quite a busy man, I see. Perhaps you need to get yourself some help."

"Actually, I've been looking for help, but I haven't found the right person."

Giulio winked. "You need a wife and a seamstress. Too bad Teresa is not to your liking."

Luca's cheeks warmed. "She's just a family friend. Besides, she can't sew." He chuckled then grew serious. "I want a wife who is—"

"Beautiful? Smart? Patient?"

Luca handed Giulio his receipt. "Forgiving." He laughed, his chest tightening. "But beautiful would be nice, too."

Chapter Two

"Mama, I'm scared."

The tremor in Nico's voice caught Maria by surprise. She stopped at the bottom of the schoolhouse stairs. "But you've been talking about school for days." She stooped and took hold of his hands. "Darling, there is nothing to be afraid of. You will have lots of fun. Wait and see."

But he did not seem convinced. Instead, he buried his face in her shoulder.

Two students walked around them, one of them snickering. "Baby. Baby."

The other shouted, "Hurry up, Chicken-Heart, or you'll be late."

Nico backed away, his face tight. "I'm not a baby, am I, Mama?"

"No. You are not a baby. You're a brave big boy, and I'm proud of you. Now, let's wipe those tears and walk into this school as though you own it."

He nodded. "I'm big and brave. I'm big and brave. I'm big and brave."

"That's my boy. Big and brave." Perhaps she'd made a mistake enrolling him in the village school. Her muscles tensed. "Let's go in, shall we?"

He did not respond. She took his hand once again and

led him up the flight of steps. Her heart raced as she opened the heavy oak door into the large single classroom. Once upon a time, she'd entered these doors as a student herself.

Entered an innocent. Full of hope and anticipation. Until . . . .

The door's loud creaking made her shudder.

At the sound, every eye turned toward her.

Including Don Franco's.

Maria stopped short, her skin turning to ice. Every bone in her body screamed escape, but she refused. No matter what, she would hold his gaze and advance.

With Nico's hand firmly in her own, she proceeded toward the front of the classroom, her heart pounding wildly as her feet did violent battle with her will.

Her head began to spin. She took a deep breath and led her child forward, all the while keeping her eyes fixed on Don Franco's steady gaze.

The silence of the classroom crowded in on her, threatening to shake her resolve. She straightened her shoulders and, step by strenuous step, she advanced toward Nico's teacher.

The man who'd raped her.

Lifting her chin, she stopped squarely in front of him. "Good morning, *Padre*." A different epithet would be more appropriate, but there were, after all, students present.

His once black hair now held tufts of gray along the temples. Deep furrows lined his once smooth brow. His jaw, taut and square, resolved into a tentative smile.

A cursory glance was all he gave the child, but in that glance she saw a mingling of anguish and delight. Now that Nico stood by him, she was amazed at the resemblance. The boy's face was his. Round, with a square chin and a strong nose. The build of his body, just like his father's. Even the thick shock of hair on his head mirrored the priest's.

"Hello, Maria." His eyes pierced hers.

Was it hatred she read in them, or fear?

Don Franco took a deep breath and kept his gaze fixed on her. "I saw the boy's name on the roster, but I did not think you would come."

She threw back her shoulders and lowered her voice to a whisper so that Nico could not overhear. "Or is the truth that you were afraid we *would* come?" She laced her words with venom.

His gaze turned into steel, but he remained silent.

Maria steadied her soul against his piercing eyes. "Perhaps contrary to my better judgment, I am entrusting the child to you. Rest assured that I will know if you do not take care of him."

Franco's jaw twitched. He turned his eyes toward the child. "And you must be Nicholas."

The child stood to his full height. "Nico. My name is Nico." He tightened his grip on Maria's hand.

She could still turn back.

Don Franco extended his hand in greeting. "I am happy to meet you, Nico."

The child took Don Franco's extended hand. "Me, too." He gave Maria a cursory glance, as though seeking her approval.

The priest's eyes were on her once again. "I will take him under my wing, I promise you."

I promise you. Why should his promise mean anything to her? She'd just as soon trust a rattlesnake. "It's

33

the least you can do."

She stooped to eye level with her son. "Don Franco will take good care of you, Nico. Be obedient and learn well."

"I will, Mama." He threw his arms around her neck and kissed her cheek.

She then removed the fruit and nuts from her bag and handed them to him. "Be sure to eat your snack."

The child nodded.

Maria stood and faced the priest. "I will return promptly at the close of the day's session." With a last glance at her son, she moved toward the door.

"Maria—"

Raising her eyebrows, she turned toward Don Franco.

He followed her toward the door and lowered his voice. "This is our secret, and ours alone. Is that understood?" His eyes on hers were cold.

"I've kept it this long, haven't I?"

She flinched as he drew closer.

"And you will keep it forever." His voice was a hiss. "Or else."

Or else. He knew he held her in the grip of fear. A fear she endured only for the sake of her son. Were it she alone, she would proclaim Franco's guilt from the rooftops.

She clenched her jaw to squelch the hard words on her lips. To protest would endanger her son. She would remain silent.

At least for now.

Withholding her burning reply, she turned on her heel and left just as a flash of lightning streaked across the darkening sky.

* * *

Wiping away her tears, Maria set her jaw and pushed into the menacing storm. What had she expected? To walk into the schoolhouse and face Don Franco without reopening the wound? Impossible. Yet she couldn't allow herself to nurse her wounds, not with *Bella Terra* slipping out of her hands. The past was past. Now she must think of her future.

And Nico's.

The storm released its full fury as she entered the square. Wrapping her shawl more tightly around her shoulders, she lowered her gaze to avoid nosy stares as she hastened toward the road on the opposite side that led to *Bella Terra*. Vendors hurriedly covered their stalls with awnings to protect their wares, while mothers with toddlers in tow scurried to find refuge from the tropical storm. The smell of squid and eel hung heavy in the humid air.

She was glad for the rain. It kept impertinent eyes from staring at her as people focused on finding shelter.

By the time she reached home, the rain had subsided. But there'd been enough to soak her to the skin.

An unfamiliar wagon stood at the back door, its horse tethered to a wooden post, while the driver lay across the bench, fast asleep under the canopy. Voices came from the veranda. Gathering up her drenched skirts, she climbed the few steps to the landing then stopped short at the sight of her mother wringing her hands. A wide-set man leaned against the wooden rail with his back to Maria, his arms crossed.

Maria released her gathered skirts. "Mama?"

The man turned, and Maria's eyes narrowed. "Uncle Biagio."

35

He'd aged a good deal since she'd last seen him at her father's funeral, eight years earlier. His gray hair was shorn close to his scalp, and salt-and-pepper whiskers now framed his square chin.

To think he used to be her favorite uncle. Until the day he'd learned she was pregnant. Then he'd turned against her, accusing her of destroying the family's good name.

Of course, she had. She'd grown accustomed to the stain of her alleged sin.

Still, she paused on the steps, shrinking from him, even as she had a few short years ago.

"*Buon giorno*, Maria." He approached her, took her hand, and planted a kiss on each of her cheeks.

She recoiled and withdrew her hand from his. There was only one reason he'd come. To wrench *Bella Terra* from their hands.

Her uncle cleared his throat. "Your mother and I were just discussing the future of *Bella Terra.*"

An alarm sounded in her heart as she shot a questioning look at her mother. Deep furrows lined the older woman's brow. She sat, hands clenched, in a rocking chair that swallowed her small frame. Next to the chair, a potted red geranium brightened the otherwise drab veranda. On a little bamboo table lingered the remnants of an early morning repast—an empty demitasse, a crumpled napkin, and a crumb-littered plate. At the far corner of the veranda, a statue of the Blessed Virgin stood guard, like a confidante privy to family secrets.

Her mother motioned her toward an adjacent chair. "Sit down, Maria."

"I'm comfortable standing, Mama." She wanted to

maintain equal footing with her uncle. He was so different from his older brother. It was no secret her uncle had hated her father and envied him his good fortune. Papa had once spoken of the intense rivalry that had existed between them as boys. A rivalry her father had often attempted to erase, even on his deathbed, but to no avail.

Her uncle's hard voice pierced the late morning air. "You and I both know *Bella Terra* is in serious financial trouble and, as your closest male relative, I've come to offer to take the farm off your hands."

Maria gritted her teeth. "But we are unwilling to give up the farm. My father left *Bella Terra* to my mother and to his children, and we intend to keep it."

Her uncle's eyes became slits. "You are wrong, Maria. Or should I say partially wrong. Yes, your father left *Bella Terra* to your mother and his children. But on his deathbed, he asked me to sign a document stating that should you and your mother be unable to maintain the farm, I would have first right of purchase."

Maria felt the blood drain from her face. She turned to her mother. "Is that true, Mama?"

"I'm afraid so." Her mother's voice drooped.

Something wasn't right. "Mama, did Papa tell you about this document?"

"No. But I'm sure he simply did not want to concern me."

"That doesn't sound like something Papa would do. He always let you know what was going on."

In the distance, the sky braced for another storm as heavy dark clouds moved toward them. She faced her uncle. "Where is this document?"

He pulled a paper from a pocket inside his jacket, unfolded it, and then handed it to her.

She scanned the crumpled paper. Surely enough, the statement read just as her uncle had said. And the signature looked like her father's. But her father never would have left his wife in the dark about so serious a matter. Maria raised her eyes. "I would like to keep this document."

Her uncle scowled. "Whatever for? It's of no use to you."

"Oh, you are quite wrong, Uncle. It is of much use to me. I plan to check it against the municipal records."

Her uncle snatched the document out of her hands. "This is the only copy. Besides, I think your mother has a say in the matter. Wouldn't you agree?"

She looked at her mother.

"Your uncle is right, Maria. Since we can no longer keep the farm, he has the first right of purchase."

Had her mother gone mad? "But, Mama . . ."

Her uncle interrupted her. "Maria, you fail to realize that no court of law will contradict your father's wishes. It is obvious that you cannot pay for the upkeep of the farm. Your creditors have already begun to file suit for payments long overdue. Rather than have the property fall into the hands of strangers, I will take it off your hands as your father desired and keep it in the Landro name."

Maria bristled. What Uncle Biagio wanted was to wrest his brother's land out of the hands of its rightful heirs. *Bella Terra* was prized property, and he knew it. The estate would sell in no time, and for much more than he would offer them. But they did not want to sell it. It had been in the family for four generations, and Maria and her mother wanted to keep it that way. But clearly her uncle hated the fact that it belonged to his brother's wife and children, and not to him.

Biagio stood directly before her, his towering presence threatening to diminish her slender frame. "And since I am in a position to—"

She raised her chin. "To what, Uncle? To steal our property? I'm sorry, but *Bella Terra* is not for sale." She tempered her voice even as she wanted to rip his eyes out. She'd had enough of men stealing from her. Of dominating her.

Of humiliating her.

She glared at him. "If you are so kind and loving, why not give us a loan that would allow us to remain on the land as we pay off our debts?"

The look he gave her proved the arrow had struck its target. His face grew dark and his voice tight. "I see you have become quite the rebel, my dear niece. Were your father still alive, he would never have tolerated such behavior on the part of his daughter."

She kept her voice low and lethal. "If my father were still alive, he'd drive you off his land with one swift kick. You're nothing but a liar and a thief. "

"Maria!" Her mother leaped to her feet and waved a hand at her. "That is no way to talk to your uncle."

"Perhaps not, Mama. But his actions are certainly no way for him to treat his brother's widow and children. That document is a forgery, and I will prove it."

Her mother faced her brother-in-law. "Biagio, I'm sorry. Perhaps I should discuss this with Maria privately first."

He glowered. "Very well. As you choose. But let me remind you that if your creditors are not satisfied within the month, your property will be seized, and you and your children will be forced to leave. And, if that happens, don't look to me for help."

Document in hand, he stormed off the veranda to his waiting horse and wagon.

Maria gripped the railing as she watched him leave. "Mama, I don't trust him."

"Maria, I am appalled at your behavior. You may dislike your uncle, but he is, nonetheless, your uncle."

"Uncle or not, he's up to no good."

The older woman placed an arm on her daughter's. "We are no longer in a position to negotiate. If we don't do something immediately, we will go bankrupt unless we sell the farm. And since your uncle has the first right of purchase, we cannot sell it to anyone else."

"Mama, I think you know as well as I do that the document is a forgery."

"But how can we prove it? Unless we can prove it, we have no choice but to recognize it if we want to sell the farm."

The wheels of Maria's mind spun as she paced the floor. "I am convinced the document is false. I just know it in my bones. But be that as it may, we still don't have to sell *Bella Terra*, because I'm going to get a job."

Her mother raised an eyebrow. "And who is going to hire you?"

Maria flinched at the unintended blame in her mother's question. "Someone will hire me."

"Well, you'll have to travel outside the village,

possibly to the next province, to find someone who doesn't see you as a criminal." Her mother's face softened. "I love you, Maria, but we both know that your reputation has been ruined beyond redemption."

Mama's words were rocks thrown at Maria's heart. She turned to face the distant hills. Was her mother right? Was there no hope left for her?

The answer resounded within her. As long as there was life, there was hope.

She would not give up. She would make a way.

She would save not only her family's farm, but her good name as well.

* * *

Luca put the finishing touches on *Signor* Monastero's coat. Teresa would return shortly to pick it up. Luca tensed. Despite her exquisite beauty, he found her pursuit of him annoying. Over the past five years, her constant desire for his attention had worn him down. Why didn't she get the message that he simply wasn't interested in marrying her? Perhaps he'd have to tell her point blank. But, determined as she was, even then she'd probably not give up.

He exhaled a long breath. Women. The bane and joy of man's existence.

He stood and took the coat to the pressing table where he gave it a final pressing before placing it on a hanger. Then, after wrapping it in brown paper, he hung it on the rack of completed orders.

His muscles relaxed. Another project finished. Yet, a huge pile of garments still awaited him on the work table. Business was booming. Both a good thing and a bad thing.

He'd have to hire some help soon in order to meet customer demands. Men were leaving Sicily in droves, headed for America, the Italian mainland, and England. Most of them needed old suits altered or new suits tailored. While he was thankful for the business, he was having a difficult time keeping up.

Maybe he shouldn't even consider going to America. There was enough work for him here.

As he retrieved Giulio's suit from the pile of waiting jobs, the clang of the shop bell interrupted his thoughts. It must be Teresa.

He lifted his gaze toward the door.

At the sight of the unfamiliar young woman, his heart caught in his throat. A newcomer to Pisano, obviously.

Composing himself, he laid aside the suit and moved to greet her.

She had an unusual beauty, midway between simple and stunning. Her deep brown eyes, sad yet strong, magnetized him. Her skin was the color of fresh cream and just as flawless. Nor did the shapely beauty of her well-proportioned body escape him. She carried herself with an air of royalty bathed in gentleness and the fragrance of lavender.

His senses stirred.

As she approached, he noticed the exquisite tailoring of her white ruffled blouse and the textured fabric of her fine finished linen skirt. Her delicate gold drop earrings bespoke an understated elegance he found appealing.

"*Buona sera.* How may I help you?"

She smiled. "Good afternoon. I am a seamstress by trade and am looking for work. I thought perhaps you might be in need of some help."

It took him a moment to register her words. "Work?" Did that mean she was without a husband?

She shrank back at his question, and he had the oddest desire to reach out, to tell her not to leave.

She nodded in reply, as if horrified by her own words, and averted her gaze.

"Of course—yes." Luca fumbled for the right words. "What kind of sewing do you do?"

"Mostly simple alterations, but I am also skilled at making men's shirts."

His mind raced. "Perhaps . . . Why don't you bring me a sample of your work?"

To his surprise, she removed a folded garment from her bag and placed it on the counter, unfolding it to reveal a boy's white shirt. "This is a shirt I recently finished for my son. Of course, it is for a child, but at least it will give you an idea of my ability."

His heart plummeted. She was already married. Which was probably for the best, since his personal code of ethics would not permit him to have a single woman in his employ.

He took the shirt from her hands and studied it. Clearly she knew how to sew. The seams were straight and precise, and of just the right tension. Not too tight. Not too loose. Taking the tape measure from around his neck, he applied it to the shirt. All parts of the garment were well proportioned, with both sleeves of exactly equal length and the back slightly longer than the front to accommodate for the slight curve in the shoulders. The buttonholes were evenly spaced and their edges finished with smooth precision. He looked up and smiled. "You are a very talented seamstress."

She smiled in return, a slight blush coloring her cheeks. "Thank you. I owe it to my mother. When I turned twelve, she insisted I learn a trade. She said a girl never knew when she might need one."

"And you need one now?" Instantly he regretted the question, fearing he had embarrassed her.

She looked up at him. "Yes." Her voice held a hint of shame. "Yes, I do."

"How soon would you want to start?"

"I could start today if you have the work." She hesitated. "But there is one thing."

"And what is that?"

"Would it be possible for me to work at home?"

It was not an unusual request. Over the years, he'd hired tailors and seamstresses to help him during especially busy seasons, and all but one of them—an elderly gentleman— had worked from home. Besides, having a woman work with him alone in his shop would violate another rule he'd established for himself about never being alone more than a few moments with a woman who was not his wife.

"That would not pose a problem at all, as long as you live close by. Occasionally, I may need a quick turnaround of a project, and I would not want distance to cause any delay in delivery."

"Of course, I certainly understand. I live just outside the village, on the hillside overlooking Pisano." She seemed to want to say more but, instead, smiled at him. "So, I have the job?"

"Yes, you have the job."

Her eyes lit up. "Thank you very much."

Perhaps her husband had been injured, or lost his business. Whatever the case, it was not Luca's right to probe.

He turned toward a table behind the counter and picked up a pile of folded garments. "You can start with these. All of them need simple alterations. They have already been pinned and marked. The only thing you have to do is sew them. I will need you to return them by three o'clock tomorrow afternoon."

"That will work perfectly for me, since I fetch my son at school every afternoon at three- thirty. In fact, I'm headed there now. I will deliver each day's work on my way."

She gathered the garments into her canvas sack and turned to go.

Luca came forward. "Oh, by the way— I never got your name."

Her shoulders slumped slightly. "My name is Maria. Maria Landro."

Landro. He'd heard that name before, but it was so long ago he couldn't remember how or where. "Pleased to meet you, *Signora* Landro. "

Her face reddened. "Pleased to meet you too, *Signor* Tonetta."

The smile she gave him stirred an untouched part of his soul. He fought to swallow the lump that rose to his throat.

Chapter Three

As Maria turned to leave, the shop bell sounded with a loud clang.

A beautiful young woman entered with a flourish, her long brown muslin skirt making a swishing sound as she circled to close the door behind her. "Dear, dear Luca." Her lilting voice rang through the air. "I've come for my father's coat." She stopped short and gave Maria a questioning and comprehensive head-to-toe look, then turned all of her attention to Luca. "So, how is my favorite tailor today?"

Maria's gaze flew to Luca's face then back to the woman. From the intimate way she spoke to Luca, it was obvious the woman was in love with him. She was probably his sweetheart.

"Teresa, I'd like you to meet Maria Landro, my new assistant seamstress. Maria, this is Teresa Monastero, a family friend."

A frown instantly clouded Teresa's face. "Oh?" Her lips quirked into a pout.

Her face hot with embarrassment, Maria nodded. The girl was beautiful. The most beautiful woman she'd ever seen. Her fine features and olive skin posed a sharp contrast to Maria's own larger features and fair complexion. "Pleased to meet you, Teresa."

Teresa's black eyes narrowed. "Landro? Where have I heard that name before?"

Every bone in Maria's body turned to ice. She could not afford to lose her job. Not now. Not with *Bella Terra* on the verge of bankruptcy. "I'm afraid I don't know."

Teresa pursed her lips, her eyes fixed on Maria's as though searching them for hidden information.

What if Teresa knew more than she was letting on? Would she reveal everything to Luca as soon as they were alone?

Teresa wrinkled her nose. "I know I've heard your name before. I don't often get out of Pisano, except to visit my married sister in the next province." She emphasized the word *married* and gave Luca a sideward glance.

So, Maria was right. Teresa had her eye on Luca. Why did Maria find that surprising? He certainly was quite a catch.

She bit her lower lip. "I think I'd better be going. I will get these things back to you tomorrow, *Signor* Tonetta."

"Thank you. And please call me *Luca*."

She hesitated for a moment. "Uh, yes. Luca." Then, giving Teresa a cursory nod, she made her exit. As she closed the door behind her, the look of consternation on Luca's face did not escape her.

Nor did Teresa's finger wagging in his face.

Maria's stomach churned. The last thing she needed now was to lose her new job.

* * *

Luca took a step back as Teresa sidled up to him.

48

"She's a very pretty woman."

"Yes, she is." Luca's muscles tensed as he tried to think of a way to get Teresa to leave. "Teresa, I really need to get back to work."

"How long have you known her?"

"Known whom?"

Hands on her hips, Teresa planted herself squarely in front of him. "You know exactly whom I mean. That loose woman who just left your shop."

Blood rushed to his face. "How dare you call her a loose woman? You don't even know who she is."

"I know more about her than you do." She took him by the hands. "Luca, the name Landro. Doesn't it mean anything to you?"

He withdrew his hands from hers. Frantically searching his mind, he found a vague memory of a Landro involved in some sort of scandal. But he would not admit as much to Teresa. After all, if it were not true, he did not want to be involved in any form of gossip. Such behavior was forbidden by God. "I vaguely remember the name, but I am not certain in what context."

Teresa lowered her voice almost to a whisper. "Luca, she's no *signora*. She's a whore. If she told you she's married, then she lied to you."

Blood bulged the veins of his neck. "How can you say such a thing? Don't you realize you could be defaming an innocent soul?" He forced himself to calm down. "Besides, she never said she was married." He lowered his eyes. "Only that she has a son."

"Oh, really? Well, that proves my point."

Luca raised his eyes. "What do you mean?"

49

Teresa sighed. "About seven years ago, the whole town was astir with the news that a daughter of the family that owns *Bella Terra* sold herself to a visiting merchant and disgraced her family name. That girl was none other than Maria Landro. The same woman who is now working for you."

Luca's blood froze. If what Teresa said were true, he'd placed himself once again in the direct path of temptation. But if what she said were false, Maria's reputation was in grave danger of being severely maligned.

"I will not believe it until I have proof. " He took a deep breath. "I'm sure you're mistaken, Teresa. The woman you're talking about cannot possibly be the same woman I've hired."

Teresa folded her arms. "Very well, Luca. Think of your business reputation. You have worked hard to become the top tailor in the province. Are you going to let a tainted woman ruin all you've worked so hard to build?"

His head spun at her harsh words. "But you have no proof."

She stood before him. "I will get you all the proof you need. You may be unwilling to face the truth now. But be careful. One day soon you may have to." Her gaze pinned him in place. "And by then, it may be too late."

* * *

Don Franco could not remove his gaze from the little boy sitting quietly in the front row. Gripping the thick pencil in his plump little right hand, the child carefully formed each letter of his first name, looking up, as he completed each one, at the alphabet charts posted along the front wall of the classroom. His nose wrinkled as he concentrated.

Don Franco's chest tightened. The boy possessed his mannerisms, his pensive demeanor, his smile. Even the shock of thick black hair that grew low on his forehead mirrored his own. But his eyes definitely favored Maria's family. Thank God for that, or someone might easily notice the resemblance.

He swallowed hard and walked over to Nico. "Would you like some help?"

The boy looked up and smiled. 'Yes, *Padre*."

Don Franco took the pencil from the child. "Like this, Nico." He curved his fingers into the proper position, repeating the gesture and showing the boy all angles. Then, placing the pencil in Nico's hand, he covered it with his own and gently guided him as the child formed each letter of his name. N-I-C-O. His son's soft skin against his own awakened unfamiliar paternal feelings.

Don Franco withdrew his hand.

"What's the matter, *Padre*?"

He shuddered. What an observant little chap!

"*Padre*, look. I did it. I wrote my name."

"*Bravo*, Nico!" A rush of anguish filled his soul.

"What's the matter, *Padre*?"

Don Franco stumbled for an excuse. "Uh . . . oh, nothing, my son. I must go help the other students."

With clenched throat, he resumed his walk around the classroom, stopping to check on each pupil's work. The first day had passed quickly. Soon, Maria would be returning for her child.

Their child.

He stiffened.

After completing his rounds, he called the class to order. "Boys and girls, I have a surprise for you. The bishop will be paying us a brief visit this afternoon to celebrate our first day of the new school year."

A collective gasp rippled throughout the classroom.

"Please clear your desks. We want to show the bishop what an orderly classroom we have, don't we?" He looked over at Nico. The boy's face glowed with anticipation.

The classroom bustled as students began closing books, collecting pencils, and packing notebooks. After the desks were clear, Don Franco stood before the class. "Now, remember. When the bishop arrives, we will all stand to welcome him. Remember also to call him 'Your Excellency.' If he asks you a question, stand up to respond. If you want to ask him a question, raise your hand, and the bishop will call on you in turn. Then, when he does call on you, be sure to stand up." He glanced around the classroom. "Are there any questions?"

Nico raised his hand. "Is the bishop your daddy?"

The whole classroom burst into laughter—and a sword pierced Don Franco's heart. He ordered the class to be silent.

"Actually, Nico, that is a very good question." Don Franco swallowed hard. "In a sense, the bishop is my daddy. He is my spiritual father because he has spiritual authority over me and watches over my soul. I must answer to him for my actions both in the school and in the church."

A stirring at the front door interrupted him as everyone turned around.

Don Franco squared his shoulders. "The bishop has arrived, class. Please stand."

He walked toward the door to greet the bishop. "Your Excellency."

A tall, muscular man, Bishop Armando Fumo looked more like a warrior than a clergyman. His left hand bore the signet ring of the bishopric. His right hand, raised in blessing, formed the sign of the Cross over Don Franco.

"Franco, I greet you in the Name of Jesus."

"And I, likewise, Your Excellency." Trembling, Don Franco bowed to kiss the ring of his immediate superior, the man to whom he was accountable on this earth.

Don Franco led the bishop and the young priest who accompanied him to the front of the classroom. "Class, I present to you His Excellency, Armando Fumo, bishop of Agrigento."

In unison, the students greeted him. "Good morning, your Excellency."

Don Franco signaled them to be silent. "The bishop has a word for you, so please be seated."

When the bishop finished his message on the value of learning, Don Franco invited questions.

Nico raised his hand.

Don Franco tensed. "Yes, Nico. What is your question to the bishop?"

Nico stood. "Hello, your Ex-ex-ency."

Snickering laughter floated across the classroom.

Don Franco gently corrected the boy. "Excellency."

Nico nodded. "Your Excellency, my name is Nico, and my question is, 'Do you know a lot of people?'"

The bishop chuckled. "Yes, Nico. I know many people. Why do you ask?"

"Do you know who my daddy is?"

Don Franco's heart stopped. Blood rushed to his face.

The bishop furrowed his brow. "I'm afraid I do not know your daddy, Nico. I have never met him."

Nico lowered his gaze. "I don't know him, either."

From across the room, a student shouted. "That's because you're a bastard."

"Silence!" Don Franco's voice boomed, startling even himself. "There will be none of that kind of talk in this classroom."

The room began to spin. With trembling hands, Franco grabbed hold of his desk to steady himself. His breath came in short gasps as perspiration dripped from his brow.

In an instant, the bishop was at his side. "Franco, are you all right?" His superior's curious and concerned gaze settled upon him.

Don Franco struggled against the tightness in his chest. "Yes, your Excellency. I simply will not allow such language in my classroom."

"You are right not to allow it, but boys will say such things from time to time. Do not take it so hard, or it could ruin your health."

Don Franco took a deep breath. "You are right, your Excellency. Boys will say such things from time to time."

The bishop's hand weighed heavily on his shoulder. "Is it possible you could find out who the child's father is?"

Panic clawed at Franco's heart. "I will do my best, Your Excellency." He drew in a deep breath then whispered, "I will do my best."

Chapter Four

Maria quieted the unexpected stirring that Luca had engendered within her. She slung the canvas garment-filled bag over her right shoulder and, despite her misgivings about Teresa, exhaled a long sigh of relief as she left the tailor shop for Nico's school. Mama would be overjoyed she'd found work and found it so quickly. The job would bring in enough money to hold them over for a few more months. At least until she could stir up enough courage to convince Don Franco to exonerate her and clear her good name.

But his threatening words that fateful day still rang in her ears even after seven long years.

"If you dare breathe a word of this to anyone, I will see to it that you and your family are destroyed forever."

She shuddered at the memory. So far, the truth remained hidden. But now she'd reached the point of no return. She could not go on living a lie. A lie that was destroying not only her, but Nico and her family as well. Either Don Franco would tell the truth, or she would.

Even if it meant risking her life in the process.

She analyzed the plan that had been formulating in her mind for a long time now, especially since her family's financial situation had taken a drastic turn for the worse.

Their having been forced to let go of most of their hired farmhands shortly after Nico's birth had only increased the urgency of the dilemma. A few loyal men had stayed on, accepting lower wages in exchange for work. The land still had to be tilled, the seed planted, and the crop harvested. In order to pay them, she'd had to tap into the family's savings.

But now their savings were nearly gone. She'd reached the point where confronting Don Franco seemed inevitable if her family were to survive. Unless he cleared her name, no produce vendor would ever buy from them again.

She bristled at the unspoken code of honor that had kept her family a prisoner of her shame.

And her son's father a mystery to all but her.

Ever since Nico's birth, business had gone downhill as, one by one, vendors turned to other farms to supply them with produce. She'd even tried lowering prices to the bare minimum, but it made no difference. For a while she'd managed to acquire vendors from adjacent provinces, but even they, when they'd learned of her disgrace, took their business elsewhere. Finally, she'd had to halt the planting altogether.

The price of honor, it seemed, was non-negotiable. Despite the vendors' lame excuses, she'd read the scorn in their eyes. No matter that many of them were themselves guilty of worse sins. Pointing the finger seemed to be a favorite pastime in Pisano. Although they refused to admit it, their allegiance had shifted. No one wanted to do business with a family of ill repute.

Nausea shook her stomach at the depth of their hypocrisy.

But now *Signor* Tonetta—Luca—had given her a

chance.

How kind he was—and how sincere his handsome smile! Rumor had it that he was the most eligible bachelor in all of Pisano. Unless, of course, Teresa Monastero had already hooked him with her subtle bait.

Which seemed to be the case.

His kindness had been like a balm to Maria's wounded soul. There was something in his manner that was deep and clear, with no trace of guile. When she looked at him, it was like looking into deep waters. Waters that, years ago, she might have been tempted to plunge into and explore. But what right had she to think that Luca Tonetta—or any decent man—would ever look at her twice? At least not as a man would look at a prospective wife. A tainted woman would remain such for as long as she lived. And even thereafter, her memory would reek with the stench of her shame.

But only if she did nothing. And doing nothing was not an option.

Dodging the stares of leering men, she hastened out of the square toward the schoolhouse. The palm trees swayed in a light breeze that played at the edges of her dark hair. She brushed back a wisp that had broken loose from the pile atop her head and tucked it neatly behind her ear. Shifting the garment bag from her right to her left shoulder, she turned her thoughts toward Nico. How had he fared on his first day of school? Had she made a mistake leaving him with the guilty priest? Had her son felt rejected or alone?

She reached the schoolhouse just as the children were leaving in a rush of laughter and cheers. The older children ran out first, followed by the younger ones. She looked for

Nico, but he was nowhere in sight. Quickening her step, she approached the building but stopped at the sound of her son's voice coming from behind a tree.

"I don't have a daddy." His words shook with emotion.

"You're right. You don't have a daddy because you're a bastard." An older boy shouted the ugly word. "That means you're a nobody. A big fat nobody. No daddy wants you."

Flinging her bag to the ground, she shouted at the bullies. "Stop! Stop right now and get out of here!"

Nico ran to her arms. "Mama! Mama! They called me that word again." He sobbed, his breath coming in short gasps. "What does 'bastard' mean?"

She gathered her son into her arms and pressed him hard against her pounding heart. Blinking back angry tears, she gently stroked the back of his head. "Everything will be all right, Nico. You are strong, my son. Don't let cruel words hurt you."

"I—I'm—a—big—brave—boy." Wracked with sobs, he struggled to repeat the words.

Maria held him close. "Yes, Nico. You are a big, brave boy."

Tears sprang to her eyes. She must not cry. Whatever she did, she must not cry.

Releasing him, she took his hand and, after picking up her bag, she led him toward the gate. "Let's go home. You'll feel much better when we get home."

As they crossed the schoolyard, he pointed. "Mama, look."

Her eyes turned toward the schoolhouse. There, on

the top step, stood Don Franco. The expression on his face revealed he'd seen everything. He descended the steps and came toward her. "I'm sorry, Maria."

Bile rose to her throat. "Not as sorry as you should be." She spat the words then watched him retreat into the schoolhouse.

* * *

Still enraged by her encounter with the bullies, Maria led Nico up the hill to *Bella Terra*. The afternoon was hot, and the air thick and oppressive.

She brushed a mosquito away from her face. Only the blessing of her new job mellowed her anger. With Nico in tow, she entered the kitchen via the back door. Mama and her sisters were busily working in the kitchen.

"Mama, I've taken a job as a seamstress at the tailor shop in the village."

Her mother stopped washing the dishes and broke into a broad grin. "Thank the good Lord." She made the sign of the cross. "This is a miracle. Tell me more."

Her younger sisters, Luciana and Cristina, gave a cheer.

Luciana hugged her. "Maria, that's wonderful news!"

Towel in hand, Maria took a dish from the drain board and wiped it dry. "This morning, after leaving Nico at school, I stopped by Tonetta's Tailor Shop to inquire about work. It so happened that *Signor* Tonetta needed someone right away. He said there are so many men leaving Pisano for a better life in America and other parts of the world that he has more work than he can handle. It seems as though everyone needs clothes mended or tailored. So he hired me."

Her mother's eyes widened as she resumed her dishwashing. "Just like that? On the spot?"

"Yes. Fortunately, I had thought to bring a sample of my work with me. So he didn't hire me without knowing the kind of work I can do." Maria smiled at the memory of Luca's face. "And he was pleased with what he saw."

Cristina gave her a hug. "I am not surprised. You're not only a good sister, you are a good seamstress, too."

"Thanks to Mama." Maria passed the hug on to her mother. "I'm so glad you taught me how to sew."

Her mother laughed. "Despite your resistance." She took another dish out of the soapy water. "So, tell me. What is this *Signor* Tonetta like?"

"Yes, tell us, Maria." Luciana chimed in with a clap of her hands.

Heat rose to Maria's face. "He seems to be a very nice man."

Her mother gave her a probing look, as though sensing her daughter's emotion. "Is he married?"

Maria took another dish from the drain board. "Oh, Mama. Is that the only thing that mothers who have marriageable daughters think about?" She put the second dried dish atop the first. "To answer your question, he's not married."

Her mother smiled knowingly but changed the subject. "O, *figlia mia*, this job of yours is indeed good news." She joined her soapy hands as if in prayer and raised them toward heaven. "Now, perhaps, we can pay off our debt and keep *Bella Terra*."

"That is my goal, Mama. To get us out of debt."

"Yes, but we must move quickly. Your Uncle Biagio

will not rest until he owns this farm."

Maria's muscles stiffened. "He will not have this farm, Mama. I will fight for it until my very last breath if I have to."

Her mother washed the final dish. "Well, I hope, my dear daughter, that the fight doesn't last that long."

"Whether it does or not, I am up to it."

The old woman dried her hands on a dish towel and wrapped an arm around her daughter. "You are a good girl, Maria. A very good girl."

A warm sensation flooded Maria's soul. She hoped Nico was as encouraged by her approbation as she was by her mother's.

Yet, there was one whose approval would mean a lot to her as well.

And that was Luca Tonetta.

* * *

Luca knelt at a side altar of the empty church, his mind reviewing the events of the long, busy day. A ray of evening sunshine filtered through a large stained-glass window, casting a long shadow on the simple wooden crucifix before him. Vases of white lilies graced the small alcove, their sweet perfume rising like incense, while old women shuffled through the Stations of the Cross, black rosary beads dangling from their calloused hands.

As much as he tried to pray, he could not get his mind off Maria. Her visit to his shop earlier that day had felt almost supernatural—as though God had sent her to him. He leaned his elbows on the cold marble railing, a strange ache tugging at his heart. His eyes steadied on the figure of Christ, arms outstretched in the greatest act of love the world had ever known.

Luca swallowed hard as he remembered the day he'd encountered his Lord. It had happened a week after his parents' death and only a day after his sexual impropriety with a young girl from the nearby town of Ribera. He'd gone there after his parents' funeral, alone and shaken. The sudden tragedy of losing both his mother and his father simultaneously had left him reeling in grief and loneliness. An only child, he'd had no siblings with whom to share his grief, no relatives to comfort him.

She was a servant girl in the inn where he'd spent the night. The one who'd made up his room. She'd entered unannounced, with lust in her eyes. The softness of her face and the roundness of her arms had darkened his reason. Before he knew it, he'd succumbed.

Afterwards, guilt mingled with shame, suffocating him as he rode the snail-like train back to Pisano. He hadn't loved her. That was the worst of it. He'd only sought solace in her arms for his unbearable grief. For all of his pride about being so holy, he was as wicked as everyone else.

Across the aisle that day, a young man had studied him. He'd seemed out of place in the third-class train, overrun with cackling chickens, swarming flies, and screaming children. His long-sleeved white shirt and his blond hair marked him as a foreigner.

"Excuse me, is this the train to Secca Grande?" His heavily accented Italian confirmed Luca's suspicion.

"Yes. Secca Grande is two stops ahead."

"Thank you."

Luca was curious. "Are you English?"

The young man smiled. "American. I'm a missionary." He extended a friendly hand.

A conversation had ensued, during which Luca repented of his sin and surrendered his life to Jesus Christ. By the time the young man got off at Secca Grande, Luca had become a Christian.

The memory overwhelmed him with a profound sense of God's love. For the first time in his life, he'd understood that Christianity is not a religion but a relationship. The revelation transformed his life. Even now, that momentous decision to accept Christ sustained him in difficult times and guided his every step.

Christ would guide him regarding a wife as well.

He rose to leave, his footsteps echoing on the marble tiled floor. The sun had dropped beneath the level of the windows, leaving the sanctuary in shadows. In front of the main altar, candles flickered fervent prayers to the Almighty.

Luca pushed open the heavy wooden door and walked into the balmy evening air. A beggar sat on the church steps, his eyes hollow with hunger. He extended a gnarled hand holding a rusted tin cup. Compassion clutched at Luca's heart. Digging into his pocket, he withdrew several coins and dropped them into the cup. "God bless you."

"God bless you, too." The voice reminded him of his father's, soft-spoken and kind.

Dozens of pigeons strutted along the plaza in front of the ancient church. Here and there, children chased them or picked them up to stroke their heads. An old woman, bent with age, sat on a bench and fed breadcrumbs to a lone pigeon that had left the flock for better fare.

Luca's stomach growled. As he headed toward Gino's

Trattoria, images of Maria haunted his mind.

Chapter Five

Drawing the blankets up to Nico's neck, Maria tucked her little son into bed. His eyes were still red and swollen from the tears he'd shed all the way home from his first day of school that afternoon. Despite her attempts to comfort him, he would not be consoled.

"I'm never going back to school again," he blurted.

While she wanted with all her heart to shield him from future hurt, she knew she must not. Nor could she. "Nico, I will talk to Don Franco about what happened in the schoolyard, and he will punish the boys who hurt you. So you have nothing to be afraid of."

"But what if they hurt me again? Or say that *bastard* word. I still don't know what it means, Mama." His voice trembled.

She searched her heart for the right answer. "If they try to hurt you again, stand up to them. Do not allow them to push you around. They are nothing but bullies, and bullies will back off if you show them you are not afraid of them."

He squirmed under the blankets. "But I *am* afraid of them, Mama. They're bigger than I am."

She sighed. Had she not been afraid of the bullies in her own life as well? The vendors who had destroyed her family business by their boycotts? The villagers who had destroyed her reputation by their gossip? And Don Franco himself, who had kept her a prisoner by his cowardly deception and threats of harm?

How could she ask Nico to do as she said when she herself was afraid to do as she preached? "Bullies seem bigger only on the outside, my son. On the inside you are far bigger than they."

He looked at her with his big dark eyes. "So, I could make the bullies afraid of me?"

She tousled his hair and smiled. "Yes, Nico. You can make the bullies afraid of you."

"But how, Mama?"

Stroking his brow, she pondered his question for a long moment. "By not letting them know you are afraid of them, even though you are."

He looked at her, his little mind obviously racing. "All right, Mama. Tomorrow if they try to hurt me and I'm afraid, I'll pretend I'm not."

Like mother, like son.

She kissed him on the forehead. "And I will, too."

* * *

Dawn's first gray light edged the sky as Don Franco hurried from the rectory to the Church of the Holy Virgin to say the six o'clock Mass. Today he would confront the boys who'd bullied Nico and aroused Maria's wrath on the first day of school yesterday. Appeasing her would be his biggest challenge. If he didn't continue to keep her quiet, she'd expose his sin.

So far, his original threat of harm seven years earlier had kept her silent all these years. She'd done nothing to

66

avenge herself. Of course, who would have believed her anyway? At least he had that on his side. No one would believe a parishioner over a priest. Otherwise, he would have been defrocked long ago.

A familiar sense of failure gnawed at his stomach. Nico had been in his class for only a day, and already things had gone wrong. To make matters worse, the bishop's question about the identity of Nico's father had sent shock waves through Don Franco's system. He shivered. And, perhaps worst of all, against his better judgment, he'd allowed the child to capture his paternal heart.

A heart that, for the first time, ached with a profound sense of loss.

A slight chill, a remnant of the previous night's thunderstorm, lingered in the air. Its damp breath penetrated the thick cotton fabric of his cassock. He thrust his hand into his pocket and fingered the worn rosary, an ordination gift from his mother. Since her death two years earlier, he'd carried it with him wherever he went.

He let the beads slide to the bottom of his pocket. What if his assignment at the parish school ended like everything else in his life? With rejection and defeat? He'd spent the last ten years taking the school to a higher level of excellence. It was the only thing he'd ever done of which he was truly proud. He'd worked too hard for Maria to destroy it now.

A shiver ran through him as he approached the medieval village church. A sudden gust of wind snatched at the wide brim of his black hat. He grabbed it and held it firmly against his head.

The ancient edifice, though in need of repair, stood

proudly at the far end of the village square. A bastion of piety and virtue, over the centuries it had witnessed hosts of weddings, funerals, baptisms, confirmations, and first holy communions. He'd grown up in its shadow, been nursed on its liturgy, and launched into ministry in its sanctuary. But unlike the stones that made up its structure, he'd never felt like an integral part of it.

He suppressed the painful truth.

He was a misfit.

The church bell tolled the half hour. Soon the first parishioners would be arriving, in time for the daily recitation of the rosary prior to Mass. Mostly old women, with a few old men among them, they comprised the core of the faithful. The matriarchs and patriarchs of Pisano. People he'd known all of his life. They'd watched him grow up. He'd played kickball with their children. Attended the same school. They'd cheered him off to seminary in Rome and then welcomed him back with the highest respect. Now they had become his flock. Those for whom he would be held accountable before God.

His chest tightened as he pictured himself giving an account for Maria one day. His blood ran cold at the image of the Almighty, with finger pointed in wrath, condemning him to hell for all eternity.

A rooster crowed in the distance, sending a shiver through his veins.

His heart pounding, he wiped the sweat from his brow and quickened his steps toward the private entrance at the rear of the building. The sacristan had already unlocked the door in anticipation of his arrival.

"Good morning, *Padre*." The old man smiled and

bowed slightly as Don Franco entered the large room.

"Good morning, Gennaro. How are you today?"

Gennaro chuckled. "At my age, I'm grateful I woke up this morning."

Don Franco forced a smile. "That's something to be grateful for at any age, my good man." Taking a cotton handkerchief from his pocket, he wiped the beads of perspiration that slicked his forehead.

"Your garments are ready for you, *Padre*."

"Thank you."

Gennaro left, closing the door behind him.

Don Franco ran trembling fingers over the priestly garments laid out before him, symbols of holiness and moral rectitude. The ritual of donning them each day had dulled his heart to their symbolism. Yet today, because of Nico's intrusion into his life, the garments spoke to him more loudly than ever. Sharpening his sensitivity to the virtues they represented. Accusing him of violating those virtues.

Just as he had violated Maria.

A knock at the sacristy door jolted his nerves.

"Come in."

A young altar boy opened the door and poked his head in, a questioning look on his face. "*Padre*, it's time to begin Mass."

Don Franco turned toward the boy. "Thank you, my son. I'll be right there."

The boy nodded and left.

Don Franco rubbed his fingers across his aching forehead. Then, with trembling hands, he lifted the square white amice, placed it over his head, and dropped it to his shoulders. He crisscrossed the laces behind his back, bringing them forward again to tie in front. Next, he donned the alb, the long white linen tunic signifying purity of heart. He shuddered as the clean garment touched him. Taking the cincture in both hands, he hesitated at the sight of the tasseled cord, symbol of sexual purity. By donning it, he proclaimed to the whole world his obedience to his vow of chastity. Eyes closed, Don Franco tied the cord around his waist.

He leaned momentarily against the table, steeling himself to become the priest the spiritually hungry parishioners awaited on the other side of the sacristy door. What did he have to offer them? His stomach churning, he put on the stole, maniple, and chasuble, then walked to the full-length mirror at the far end of the sacristy. He stopped short. Who was this stranger? He studied his face, once ruddy with the manliness of youth, but now old and worn. His hair, once rich and black, but now streaked with gray. His eyes, once bright and clear, but now darkened under the weight of fatigue.

He was only thirty-four.

He drew in a deep breath. Like a nervous actor preparing to walk out on stage, he wondered if this would be his last performance.

* * *

Maria quickened her pace as she approached Tonetta's Tailor Shop to drop off the day's work before picking up Nico. She'd worked late into the night and all that morning on the first batch of alterations, more demanding of herself than any customer could be. Now she hoped her work would earn Luca's approval.

She took a deep breath. Her angry interchange with Uncle Biagio the day before had left her more determined than ever to keep him from taking the farm. But it had also left her more anxious than ever about paying off the outstanding debt in time to avert bankruptcy.

Quickening her pace, she shielded herself from the growing wind that whipped around the vegetable stands lining the square. Soon the *scirocco* season would begin. The hot wind that swept over the island each year from North Africa brought with it severe dust storms that sometimes covered the villages for days on end. Dust in their food, grinding between their teeth. Dust in their drinking water. Dust in the bath, so that she never felt clean. Perhaps this year it would last only a few days.

The shop bell clanged softly as she opened the door. A rustling sound came from the back room, followed by Luca's appearance in the doorway.

He burst into a wide grin. *"Hello."*

She smiled, wishing she could stop her face from burning. "Hello, *Signor* Tonetta. I've finished the first batch of work for you."

He strode toward the counter. "Luca. Please call me Luca."

"Yes. I'm sorry. I forgot." Warmth rushed through her as a flutter skimmed her heart. He grew more handsome each time she saw him. His strong forehead framed translucent blue eyes filled with peace.

For the past day, he'd been at the forefront of her mind. It wasn't physical attraction that drew her, although he was certainly a handsome man. No. It was a light that shone through his eyes, from someplace deep within him. Like an oasis that invited one to rest by its quiet waters and drink.

Holding her breath, she opened her bag, pulled out the neatly folded garments, and laid them on the counter.

She studied his strong hands as he unfolded the first piece, a man's jacket. He carefully examined the seams on the sleeve cuffs and the buttonholes. Next, he opened the jacket and ran his expert fingers along the edges of the lining. Her muscles tensed as she awaited his verdict.

Finally, his deep blue eyes rose to meet hers. "Excellent work, *Signora* Landro. I am very pleased."

Relief flooded her soul as her face grew even warmer. She did not correct his referring to her as *Signora*. "Oh, please call me Maria."

He smiled. "Yes. I, too, forgot. Excellent work, Maria."

"I am so glad you are satisfied."

"Very satisfied, indeed."

Her pulse quickened as his eyes briefly lingered on hers. Her gaze followed the sculpted muscles of his forearms as he picked up the completed garments and placed them on a table behind him. His broad shoulders exuded strength.

He returned to the counter and withdrew an envelope from a drawer. "Here is your first paycheck." He handed her the envelope. "For the first batch of alterations."

Her heart soared. Every cent would go toward paying off the debt on *Bella Terra*. "Thank you. You are very kind."

"It has nothing to do with kindness, but everything to do with your hard work." He smiled. "There is an unspoken rule in life: labor produces fruit."

His compliment brought tears to her eyes.

"And now I have more work for you." He slid a pile of men's shirts from a shelf behind him and placed them on the counter. "These shirts require alterations. I've marked them and pinned them in the right places. I'll need these by tomorrow. The men who ordered them are leaving for America shortly."

She glanced down at the pile of linen and cotton. The one on top might have been the man's best shirt, though it had a coffee stain on the cuff. "Yes, you'd mentioned that many men from Pisano are leaving to make their fortunes in America." Her mother had told her of a family friend whose husband had gone to America and never returned.

"That is so. In the last year, dozens of men from Pisano alone have ventured across the seas in search of a better life."

She detected a wistfulness in his voice. "And have they found what they were looking for?"

He smiled. "From what I'm told, they have." He hesitated, as though distracted by a thought. "Anyway, I will need these by tomorrow afternoon."

"Of course." Her face flushed at the impropriety of engaging him in conversation other than that related to business. Perhaps she'd offended him. But he showed no signs of displeasure.

She found herself wanting to stay longer, wanting to know this man better. Who was he? Why wasn't he married? "Well, I must go now to fetch my son at school."

"Then I shall see you again tomorrow. Same time."

"Yes. I'll be sure to get these back to you then."

She lingered for a brief moment more then left against her will.

73

Chapter Six

Nerves taut, Don Franco sat at his classroom desk the next morning pondering the bishop's visit the day before. Soon his superior would be contacting him regarding the results of his research on Nico's paternity. A leaden weight lodged in Franco's stomach as perspiration slipped down the side of his face.

Maria.

She was never quiet inside his head. The very thought of her name brought back bittersweet memories. His mind drifted back to the first day she'd stepped into his classroom, her cautious nature stirring his senses against his will. And again his senses had stirred when, on her first day of work at the rectory, she'd emerged from the kitchen like an angel of light to serve the priests their lunch. Her quiet demeanor reminded him of Silvia, his first love. Fresh with the bloom of innocence on her cheek, Maria had demonstrated a reticence he'd found attractive. Challenging, even. The sensuous tilt of her smile, the sweet fragrance that emanated from her shapely body, and the self-conscious way she leaned over him to place his plate before him aroused feelings he'd thought were long dead. There was a shyness about her that drew him, making him feel needed. Safe in her presence.

Accepted.

Unlike the way Silvia had made him feel.

Whenever he saw Maria, he felt a weight lift off his soul. Soon he found himself looking for ways to be with her. At the end of each meal, he'd linger, despite her obvious diffidence, while she cleaned off the table. He'd even taken to helping her carry the dirty dishes into the kitchen with the excuse that a servant of Christ must be a servant of men.

Being in her presence filled a part of him that had remained empty and barren for far too long. The part of him that craved approval. Acceptance.

Affirmation.

Innocently and unknowingly, she'd given him all three. It wasn't long before he'd realized he was in love with her.

Yet, all the while, his conscience had convicted him. He was a priest after all. A man forever forbidden to form such a relationship with a woman. He'd been treading on dangerous ground, and he knew it.

Each time he'd see her, he'd whisper incessant repetitions of rote prayers under his breath, hoping to quiet his conscience. But those prayers had done nothing to subdue the longing within him. In the midst of desperately fingering his rosary, thoughts of her bombarded his mind. To his shame, even as he said Mass, her image would rise before him, beckoning him in her innocence. Her eyes drew him like onyx magnets, seducing him to the point of sacrilege. Torn with guilt, he'd used every ounce of strength to keep his relationship with her solely one of pastor and parishioner.

But that fateful day, when he'd come upon her making his bed, something had snapped inside him. Finding

Maria there, he'd stopped short, overcome by her unexpected presence in his private quarters. When it was all over, he'd felt no relief, only loathing and self-hatred.

Now, alone in his classroom, he shuddered at his utter depravity. Somehow, in that blinding moment, the festering wounds of past rejection had broken the dam of tormenting rage and finally unleashed its violent waters in a horrific act.

He rose from the chair and walked toward the window. A strong breeze blew through the open sash, filling the room with the fragrance of orange blossoms. He rubbed his hand over his face and sighed.

A few children straggled into the classroom. *"Buon giorno, Padre."*

He only nodded, unable to form the words of greeting. Under the guise of fetching supplies, he retreated to the closet in the far corner of the room, locked the door, and wept.

* * *

Maria struggled to contain her anger as she entered the schoolhouse. She'd arrived early to have a few moments to talk with Don Franco before classes began.

After leaving Nico at his desk, she approached the priest at the front of the classroom. "I must have a word with you. In private."

Deep wrinkles edged his tired, reddened eyes, making him look old before his time. If she didn't know better, she'd think he'd been weeping.

"Come this way, Maria."

He led her to a far corner of the room, by the window, where they would not be overheard.

A gray sky loomed overhead as a chill swept through her.

"What is it?" The edge in his voice made her shiver.

"What have you done to discipline the boys who called Nico a b—?" She could not bring herself to say the dreadful word. "Called him a horrendous name? Upon seeing me, they fled. I do not know who they are, but I demand that you reprimand them severely."

He lowered his eyes. "I saw them running off just as you arrived."

"And you did not try to stop them?" A knot formed in her stomach.

He lifted his gaze. "I was not quick enough for them. But I know who they are. And I assure you they will be disciplined today."

Although his words took the edge off her anger, she still feared he would not follow through. "Listen, *Padre*." The title stuck in her throat, too sacred to be applied to the man standing before her. "I will hold you accountable for what happens to my son." *Our son.* The very thought of their common parenthood sickened her. "If those boys do not pay, and pay well, I will report the incident to the bishop." It was a warning. A dose of Franco's own brand of medicine that might do him good.

His face contorted with panic.

Threats seemed to work with him, as long as they weren't empty ones. Perhaps demanding he publicly exonerate her would not be so bad.

Without offering a thank-you, she walked over to Nico and hugged him good-bye. "Now remember what we talked about last night. Stand up to bullies, and they will back down."

"Okay, Mama." He hugged her, nearly ripping the heart out of her.

She leaned over and whispered in his ear. "You're a big, brave boy."

He grinned. Then he whispered in her ear, "I'm a big, brave boy."

Tears stung her eyes. She left quickly so he would not notice she was crying.

A sultry heaviness hung in the air as she hurried across the square on her way home. Despite the earliness of the day, the sun beat down upon the little village with the unrelenting heat of the tropics, while palm trees drooped their branches in languid surrender. An old beagle lay asleep on the sidewalk ahead of her, mosquitoes buzzing around his black snout.

As she approached Luca's shop, she hesitated. Although her last batch of work was not due to him till that afternoon, she'd worked late into the night and had already completed every garment but one. And that one would not take her long. She would finish it this morning. Perhaps he had another batch she could get started on early. She needed all the work she could get.

Besides, it would be nice to see him.

She wrestled with the decision only briefly.

The clang of the shop bell sounded her arrival. In a moment, he appeared from the back room. "Maria." His face reddened. "I'm surprised to see you so soon. Have you finished your batch already? I'm so busy—the days sometimes run into one another."

Perhaps she should not have come. "Oh, no, Luca."

His name sweetened her tongue. "I just dropped Nico off at school and thought I'd stop by to see if you had any pressing work." Her cheeks flushed. "Except for one small alteration, I've finished the last batch and thought I might get a head start on the next one."

He hesitated. "Well . . ."

"Of course, if I've offended you, I'm sorry."

His eyes mellowed. "Oh, no. No, you haven't offended me at all. As a matter of fact, a large project came in just this morning. Three suits and two coats to alter, plus an order for five new shirts." He smiled. "So it is fortuitous that you came."

"Oh, good. I was hoping you wouldn't be upset with me. I don't ever want to presume on your kindness."

"Not at all. In fact, I am pleased at your foresight. A day of work is a day of work, and the sooner I can fill these orders, the better." He hesitated again then disappeared into the back room.

Despite his objection, she was sure she'd offended him. She should have never requested more work. She'd made herself look too eager. Too presumptuous.

Too desperate.

No wonder he'd hesitated.

Her pulse raced. What if Teresa had divulged her identity to him? Maria closed her eyes with a mental wince. No matter what, she must keep her job. She would prove herself faithful and diligent.

As she waited for Luca, she studied the shop. Adequate in size, it held a small sitting area to the right of the counter. Two armchairs flanked a wood stove that sat empty in the far corner. Next to the wood stove stood a pile of small logs nestled in a large cylindrical bin, ready for rare chilly days. On the wall hung a framed sepia photograph of a man and a woman, probably in their early forties. Luca bore a striking resemblance to the man—very likely his father or grandfather. But his eyes were like the woman's.

Maria wished she'd known them.

Behind the counter, sturdy shelves lined the walls on both sides of the window. Piles of fabric filled the far shelves. On those closest to the counter were stacks of folded garments. In the back part of the room a doorway led to a back room, probably an office. From this room, Luca presently emerged, carrying an armful of clothing.

"Here are the three suits and two coats. I think this will give you enough work for a little while."

She took them from him. "I think so, too."

As he handed them to her, her hand brushed his. A spark of fire coursed through her veins.

Luca's gaze softened. "If not, you can always come back for more."

Did she only imagine that his tone of voice held the promise of a more personal invitation? Perhaps he wasn't upset with her after all. Her muscles relaxed. "Only if I need to."

He laughed nervously. "Of course."

Placing the garments in her canvas sack, she nodded and bid him good day.

* * *

For several moments after Maria left, Luca fought the longings that assailed his soul. She was off limits. A married woman. And the mother of a child.

God, help me.

And if what Teresa had told him were true, he had even more reason for questioning his judgment in hiring his new employee. Yet, he didn't feel right about dismissing her. Not just yet, at least. She didn't at all fit the description of a loose woman. On the contrary, she seemed a paragon of purity and virtue.

Something inside him told him to investigate further. He dragged his fingers through his hair. Perhaps he was just making excuses for the troubling feelings within him. Feelings he'd never experienced before.

No woman had ever stirred him as she had. The first day she'd walked into his shop, she'd caught him off guard. Like a butterfly alighting on a leaf, she'd shaken his composure, and he had not regained it since.

He returned to his workroom, his soul filled with the fragrance of Maria's presence but also with the guilt that her presence had engendered. She'd been here for almost fifteen minutes. He'd been so caught up in her he hadn't noticed the time.

He fidgeted in his work chair. Teresa's words about Maria played over and over again in his mind. Had he really made a terrible mistake? Although Maria's work was outstanding, had he placed himself in a position that would ultimately compromise not only his personal standards but also his reputation? He should have asked about her first. Learned about her background. But at the time, God had not prompted him with a warning.

He glanced at the clock. *Signor* Genova would be returning shortly to pick up his suit. Luca put the finishing touches on the hems of the sleeves. After carefully pressing the jacket, he hung it with the already finished trousers. Taking a long sheet of brown paper from the roll he kept under the counter, he covered the entire suit and hung it with the rest of the altered garments. He then pinned a copy of the order on the top edge of the paper.

At the clang of the shop bell, he turned to see a smiling *Signor* Genova enter. "*Signor* Tonetta."

Luca returned the smile. "I was expecting you. In fact, I just put the finishing touches on your suit. It's all ready for your trip to America."

Giulio extended a hand. "You are amazing." He let out a long breath. "I leave in one week. I must confess I am a bit nervous. I hear that the voyage across the Atlantic can be rough at times. But the worst part will be leaving my wife and children. I hope to earn enough to have them follow me in a year or two."

"I wish you Godspeed." A thought crossed Luca's mind. "Why don't you leave me your address in America? One never knows what life will bring. I may get there myself some day, Lord willing."

Giulio chuckled. "If you come to America, I will cook you the best Italian meal on the other side of the Atlantic."

Luca laughed as he placed a sheet of onionskin paper, a bottle of ink, and a quill pen on the counter. As Giulio wrote the information, Luca prayed a silent blessing over him.

Giulio blew on the ink to dry it. "There. Look me up when you come to America. " He pushed the paper toward Luca. "And now, I must pay you for your services."

After completing the transaction, Luca came around to the front of the counter and shook Giulio's hand. "God go

---

with you, my friend."

"Perhaps when I next see you, you will have a wife."

Luca hesitated then plunged in. "Giulio, I know you are not from Pisano, but have you by any chance heard of a family named Landro?"

Giulio's face darkened. "Why do you ask?"

"I just hired an assistant seamstress named Landro. Maria Landro. An excellent worker." Luca studied his reaction.

Giulio leaned toward him, as though confiding a dark secret. "If I were you, Luca, I would have nothing to do with the Landro family."

"But her work is excellent."

Giulio lowered his eyes. "Her work may be excellent, but her reputation is not. It is rumored that she spent an entire summer as the mistress of a Mafia don."

A cold chill coursed through Luca's body. Impossible. Yet Teresa had accused Maria of consorting with a traveling merchant.

"Are you sure? Rumors are often unfounded."

"Indeed, they are. But all I can tell you is that a friend of mine from Pisano—a produce vendor—used to purchase produce from the Landro farm. *Bella Vista*, I think it's called—"

"*Bella Terra*."

"Yes, yes. That's it. *Bella Terra*. Anyway, as I was saying, my friend used to be a big customer of the Landro family. But when he learned of Maria's behavior—or I should say, *mis*behavior—he wanted nothing more to do with the family."

Luca's muscles tensed. "So, you have this information on good authority?"

"On excellent authority. I have known my friend for twenty years."

Luca shook his head. Despite Giulio's conviction, he still could not bring himself to accept that the young woman he had recently hired was the mistress of a Mafia don—or of anyone, for that matter.

"Thank you, Giulio. I will look into the allegation further."

"It behooves you to do so, Luca. You would not want your long-established good reputation to be ruined by the likes of a whore."

Luca cringed at the word. Indeed, he would not. But the question still remained.

Was Maria truly a whore?

Chapter Seven

Maria breathed a sigh of relief as she reached the veranda. It wasn't easy carrying a heavy bag of garments up a hill on a hot day. The comforting aroma of freshly baked bread filtered from the kitchen, causing her mouth to water. After her strenuous walk, she needed something to eat.

Her mother sat in a rocking chair, a large basket of ripe green beans snuggled at her feet. In steady rhythm, she snapped off the ends one by one as she hummed an old Sicilian folksong.

Maria's heart swelled at the memory of the song. It was one her father used to sing when, as a young child, she labored at his side in the fields. How she longed for his comforting embrace! Whenever she cried, her father would take her in his arms and tell her he saw the sun in her eyes.

How she missed him!

She swallowed hard, lowered her bag to the floor, and let out a long sigh. "Luca gave me more work today." She dropped into a chair across from her mother.

Her mother looked up. "I thought you weren't due to pick up new work until tomorrow."

Maria's face warmed. "I wasn't. But, except for one alteration, I finished the last batch early, so I stopped by this morning to get an early start on the next batch." Even as she spoke them, her words sounded hollow. An early start on the next batch was only part of the reason she'd stopped by Luca's shop. A very small part. Truth be told, she'd wanted to see him.

Plain and simple.

She felt the depth of her mother's discerning gaze. "Tell me more about this Luca."

Maria shifted in her chair. "There's not much more to tell, Mama. He is a very nice man who is also a very good tailor."

"Good tailors need good wives."

"Mama, I can't believe you! Is getting me married all you think about?"

"Well, do you blame me? After all, you have a son to raise. And it's not easy doing it alone."

Maria rolled her eyes. "Millions of women have done it before me, Mama. I'm certainly equal to them."

Her mother paused and looked at her with loving eyes. "Not only are you equal, my child, but you far surpass them."

Tears welled up in Maria's eyes. Despite her mother's many flaws, her love for her daughter was unconditional. Maria softened. "I guess I would like to be married someday. Especially for Nico's sake."

"Speaking of marriage, Lorenzo Mauro stopped by this morning."

Maria smiled. "His year of mourning for his wife must be over, then. How nice he came to visit you! I've often thought you two would make a good match."

Her mother gave her a sidelong glance. "Don't fool yourself, Maria. He came to talk about you."

Maria recoiled in horror. "What do you mean?"

Her mother continued her bean snapping. "I mean he came to talk to me about marrying you."

"That's ridiculous. He's twice my age." She rose. "I'm sure you must be mistaken."

"I'm not mistaken at all." Her mother picked up another handful of beans and placed them in her lap.

Maria's muscles tensed. It wasn't that Lorenzo Mauro was a repulsive man. On the contrary, he was nice-looking, kindhearted, and a perfect gentleman. The kind of man worthy of a good woman his age, like her mother. Plus, he was financially prosperous. But as for marrying Lorenzo herself, that was simply out of the question. He was twenty-five years her senior.

"You know, Maria, there are few men who would be willing to marry a woman with an illegitimate child. I know Lorenzo is not a young man, but he is kind and loves God. And he would love Nico, especially since he never had children of his own. Besides, he is wealthy and would be able to support you and a child in comfort."

Maria turned toward her mother. "But, Mama, I don't love him."

Her mother stopped snapping and looked at her, compassion filling her eyes. "There are times, Maria, when love must be put aside for a greater good."

Maria reeled in disbelief. Surely she'd misheard. "A greater good. What greater good is there than love?"

But, in her mother's silence, she heard the reply.

The greater good was her family's survival. The saving of *Bella Terra*. A good name for Nico. She was the one who'd gotten the family into trouble. She must be the one to get them out of it.

She turned toward her mother. "What did you tell him?"

Her mother looked at her. "When he asked for you, I told him you had taken Nico to school."

"And what did he say?"

"He said he would stop by this evening to talk with you."

Maria's heart caught in her throat. "Why don't *you* marry him, Mama? Then *Bella Terra* would still be saved."

Her mother smiled. "He wants children of his own, Maria, and I am past the years of child-bearing."

Maria considered her mother. "You mean you would marry him to save our family?"

Her mother nodded, her eyes filling with tears.

For the first time she saw her mother in a new light. If her mother were willing to sacrifice her happiness for the good of the family, should not she be willing to do the same?

Picking up her bag of garments, she went inside. The hunger she'd felt earlier had left. The aroma of baking bread now sickened her.

* * *

First Teresa, and now Giulio.

Luca rubbed his tired eyes, struggling to concentrate. All he could think about was Maria and the rumors. How could they possibly be true? Was he deceiving himself? Was his heart deceiving him?

But when he looked into her eyes, he saw no evil there. Only kindness.

And deep, deep pain.

She showed no signs of a loose woman. No seductive mannerisms. Her face spoke of purity and innocence.

Yet, did not Satan appear as an angel of light?

He brought his cup of espresso to the table and sat down. Dusk was falling quickly over Pisano. Outside his window, all was quiet. And would be for the next two hours. Then, the villagers would leave their modest cottages and stroll the square in *passeggiata*, stopping to chat with friends, to catch up on town gossip, and to relax after a hard day's work. Tonight he would join them. Perhaps he could find out more about Maria.

After drinking his coffee, he made his way to the square. The evening was mild under a purple-gray sky. The smell of honeysuckle filled the air while, here and there, a lone firefly blinked to him in greeting. In front of the large fountain in the square, old men tossed *bocce* balls while their wives caught up on the latest gossip. Little children, under the watchful eye of their parents, played hide-and-seek among the empty fruit stands. At the far corner of the square, Old Beppo and his accordion drew a small crowd. A legend in the village, Beppo's music had provided joy to nearly three generations of Pisanians. Luca remembered how, when he was a young child, his parents would bring him to the square to hear Beppo play "*'A Luna Ammenzu 'U Mari*" and other well-loved Sicilian folk songs.

Luca sighed. How he loved this little village! The birthplace of his parents. The home of his childhood. Yet, deep inside, he wondered if he would ever leave it for another world.

But now was not the time to think about that.

Waving to some customers along the way, he strode

91

to Domenico's Pizzeria. Nearly every table was already filled with families, some laughing, some shouting, some eating quietly. He sat down, eager for Domenico's famous Sicilian pizza topped with anchovies. In a moment, a young waiter was at his table. "*Buona sera, Signor* Luca. Would you like the usual?"

Luca nodded. They knew him well. "Yes, Tonino. You know how I love your father's anchovy pizza."

The young boy smiled and bowed. "I know I'm prejudiced, *Signor* Luca, but I do agree that my papa makes the best pizza in all of Sicily. I'll bring you one right away."

As Luca glanced around the restaurant, his stomach clenched. Teresa and her family sat at a far table. Fortunately, she had not seen him. But if she did, his evening of relaxation would be ruined for sure. He turned his chair slightly to face a different part of the square.

The aroma of cooking tomato sauce seasoned with basil and garlic floated through the air, mingling with the smell of the salt air that floated in from the sea. A gentle breeze blew through the open windows.

The waiter returned. "Here you are, *Signor* Luca. Sicilian pizza with anchovies." With a flourish, he placed a large round pizza on the red-checkered tablecloth.

"Thank you, Tonino. This is perfect."

The waiter flashed a smile. "Only the best for our customers." He bowed and then left.

As Luca prepared to take his first bite, out of the corner of his eye he saw Teresa approaching. Every muscle in his body tensed.

"Well, if it isn't my favorite tailor." Uninvited, she sat down and leaned into him. "I saw you as soon as you walked in. My parents want you to join us at our table." She gave him a flirtatious smile.

So much for a relaxing evening. This woman was driving him crazy.

She lowered her voice. "But before you join us, have you fired Maria yet?"

Luca nearly choked on his pizza. "What?"

Her eyes widened. "Knowing what you do about her, you don't intend to keep her on, do you?"

He quickly swallowed the morsel in his mouth. "Teresa, listen. I know what you're saying, but I have absolutely no proof that Maria is guilty of your accusations." He kept his voice low. Already people were staring in their direction. "On the contrary, I can find no fault whatsoever in her. She is a diligent and faithful worker and even goes the extra mile. She has never once given me the impression there is something amiss with her."

Teresa raised an eyebrow, and immediately he regretted his words.

She placed a hand on his. "You are so naïve, Luca Tonetta. If you can't find any fault in her, I will simply have to show you myself. Once the truth stares you in the face, you will believe it."

The pizza churned in his stomach. "You talk about truth. Where are you getting your information? From old women who have nothing better to do with their time than to gossip?"

She rose, fists clenched on her hips. "How dare you think that of me? I am only trying to look out for you. If you don't want my help, then fall flat on your face. See if I care." Her eyes flaming, she turned on her heels and returned to her parents' table.

Heat flooded Luca's face as an elderly man at an adjacent table gave him a knowing smile. So what? Let him think it was merely a lovers' tiff. Luca felt a twinge of guilt. Perhaps Teresa did want to protect him. But did he need protection? Was he really blind to the truth?

He took another bite of pizza. Maybe he should pay more attention to Teresa's advice. He would look more thoroughly into Maria Landro's past.

And he would do it before she came back tomorrow.

* * *

Don Franco entered the rectory kitchen and found Rosa, the housekeeper, busily preparing the midday meal.

"There is a letter for you, *Padre*." Rosa removed an envelope from her apron pocket and handed it to him.

"Thank you, Rosa."

The gray-haired woman nodded then resumed her cooking.

He read the return address with a blend of curiosity and dread. It wasn't every day that a priest received a letter from his bishop.

Breathing heavily, Don Franco sought the privacy of his office. He closed the door behind him and moved toward the light of the open window. A gray sky warned of rain, while thunder rumbled in the distance.

With trembling hands, he tore open the sealed flap and unfolded the paper.

My Dear Franco,

I very much enjoyed my visit to your classroom. Since then, however, the incident of the fatherless child, Nico Landro, has repeatedly returned to my mind. The child's plight touched my heart. What, if anything, have you discovered about the boy's paternity? I urge you to do all that is in your power to uncover the details of the child's background so that not only will the boy adjust better, but also that we might allay any hint or accusation of shame upon the school. As for the unkind boys who insulted him, I trust that they have been duly reprimanded.

I solicit your response by return mail. Apart from the boy's unfortunate situation, it is also a matter of grave concern to me that the presence of a potentially illegitimate child not give any license for wrong behavior. Propriety must be maintained for the good name of the parish in

particular, and for the good
name of the diocese at large.
In this vein, therefore, I
urge your prompt attention to
the matter.

Yours sincerely,
Armando Fumo
Bishop of Agrigento

Don Franco dropped the letter onto his desk as panic clutched his heart. Sliding his hands into his cassock pockets, he paced the floor of his office. The oak-paneled walls seemed to encroach upon him like those of a prison. The heavy wall tapestry depicting the Battle of Catania in the fourth century before Christ drew him into its violence, threatening to crush him.

Perspiration dripped from his forehead. The bishop's letter demanded a response. As long as Maria remained silent, he had nothing to fear. He would simply tell the bishop that no progress had been made on discovering the boy's father. Perhaps, then, the bishop would forget the matter and not trouble him about it again. But if Maria continued to grow bolder regarding the child, he would have to find a way to silence her.

Her increasing boldness unnerved him. Perhaps maternity had awakened in her a protective fierceness hidden up until now. Whatever it was, he must be on his guard. Exposure would seal his ruin.

He returned to his desk. His hands shaking, he took his quill pen, dipped it into the inkwell, and proceeded to write.

Your Excellency,

It was with both pleasure and concern that I received your recent missive. I am delighted that you enjoyed your visit to my classroom. The students and I were honored by your presence among us.

You are most kind regarding the matter of Nico Landro. I assure you that nothing has yet been discovered of the child's paternity. As you well understand, it is quite difficult to ascertain such information in matters of possible illegitimacy as no records accrue to the situation other than birth records listing only the mother's name. In any event, should such information about the boy's father come to my attention, I will be sure to inform you immediately.

Yours sincerely,
Don Franco Malbone,
Headmaster
Rector, Church of the
Holy Virgin

His hands shook as he waved the paper, waiting for the ink to dry. He would post the letter himself before the post office closed for the day.

A peal of thunder crashed outside the window. Startled, he turned to look. A gale blew through the tall palm tree, bending it nearly in half. He rose to fasten the shutters.

If only it were as easy to fasten the shutters of his heart against the fury of the storm within him.

Chapter Eight

Maria cringed at the sound of the door chimes on the floor below. Caught up in her sewing, she'd forgotten that Lorenzo Mauro had promised to visit. The blood drained from her face. Perhaps she could feign illness. Indeed, it would not be feigning, for she suddenly felt quite sick. If only she could alert her mother to offer her apologies to *Signor* Mauro.

But no. As much as her heart protested, her conscience insisted on good manners. It would not be right to leave her mother in such an embarrassing situation, especially since Maria herself was the cause of her family's current financial distress. She would face *Signor* Mauro, and she would face him with dignity.

Gathering up the shirt on which she'd been working, she folded it neatly and placed it with the remaining garments from her latest project for Luca. Would that he were the one knocking at her front door!

She dismissed the impossible thought.

Hastening to her dressing table, she subdued some wisps of rebellious hair.

As she smoothed the wrinkles in her muslin dress, a knock on her bedroom door called her to attention. Before she could reply, her younger sister Luciana pushed it open.

The girl's face was flushed. "Maria, *Signor* Mauro is here."

Maria's brows furrowed. "Thank you, Luciana."

The girl tugged at Maria's sleeve. "Are you going to marry him?"

She took Luciana's hands in hers. "Don't ask such impertinent questions, child. His is only a friendly visit, I'm sure."

"That's not what Mama said. She said *Signor* Mauro wants to marry you."

Based on Maria's conversation with Mama earlier that day, Luciana spoke the truth. "Well, I hope Mama is wrong, because I don't want to marry him."

"Then what shall you ever do if he asks you?"

Maria stiffened but did not reply. Her mother had no right to be discussing the matter with Luciana. She would speak to Mama about it later. But for now, she would deal with the situation at hand.

"Run along, Luciana, and tell Mama to entertain *Signor* Mauro for a few moments longer. I won't be long."

The child gave her a squeeze and ran out of the room.

A dark cloud of imminent doom settled over Maria. She walked to her bedroom window and looked out over the land. Despite its lack of care, *Bella Terra* lay before her as majestic as ever. Its tall oaks and expansive vineyards, the fruit of decades of loving and attentive cultivation, spoke of generations of Landros before her. Ancestors who had surely loved the land as much as she and who had wanted to preserve it for their descendants. But now that lineage was threatened with extinction.

All because of her.

She swallowed hard.

Yet, fate had now offered her a way to prevent the loss of that hard-won legacy. Lorenzo Mauro. It was in her power to keep *Bella Terra* in her family's possession. She had only to accept the hand of a man she did not love but who would provide well for her and Nico, for her mother and her sisters.

A man who would restore her good name by giving her his.

She buried her face in her hands. Was she up to the task? Could she sacrifice love for security?

Turning away from the window, she took one last glance at herself in the mirror. Then, with determined focus, she left her room and headed downstairs toward the parlor.

* * *

Don Franco slipped out the back door of the rectory and headed in the direction of the post office. His reply to the bishop had been quick and to the point. He hoped it would also be satisfactory.

Skirting the brilliant red and purple bougainvilleas that lined the front lawn of the church, he entered the square. The storm had subsided and given way to a purple-orange sunset.

The post office closed at seven, so he needed to hurry. A few stragglers remained in the square. Most had gone home for a light supper before returning once again to visit among friends later in the evening.

As Franco approached the little dilapidated building that served as the village post office, he found the postmaster closing the shutters. "Good evening, Bruno. I would like to post this letter."

The clerk smiled and took the envelope. He glanced at the address. "It will go out first thing in the morning, *Padre*, on the six-o'clock coach."

"Very good. And how long will it take to get there?"

Bruno glanced down at the address again. "To Palermo? About two days, barring any adverse weather."

Don Franco furrowed his brow.

"Are you in need of a faster delivery, *Padre*? If so, I could send it by express with a private driver."

Despite his urgent desire that the matter be closed immediately, delaying the bishop's receipt of his letter as long as possible would serve in Franco's favor. It would give him that much more time to avoid exposure. "No. It is not a problem. Two days will be fine."

The clerk nodded. "Very well, then, *Padre*. Your letter is safe in my hands."

"Thank you." He turned to go.

"By the way, *Padre*, my son told me of the bishop's recent visit to your school."

Don Franco started. He had forgotten that the clerk was the father of one of his students. "Why, yes. Yes, we had a wonderful visit with the bishop. In fact, my letter is to thank him for honoring our small school in such a big way. The bishop is a very busy man, you know."

"I can only imagine, *Padre*. In any case, my Marco was enthralled to meet him. He spoke of nothing else for days." Bruno chuckled. "Who knows? My boy may become a priest someday—and maybe even a bishop."

"Your Marco is a good student. Diligent. Always working hard."

The clerk laughed. "He'd better work hard, or else he'll have me to contend with."

"A good father is a great gift to a child."

"And so is a good teacher, *Padre*."

Don Franco smiled, nodded, and left.

On the way back to the rectory, he pondered the clerk's words. A good teacher. He shrank back. A good teacher was, first and foremost, a person of impeccable character.

No, he was not a good teacher. He was not a good priest.

He was not a good man.

Was he even worthy of being alive?

* * *

The chatter of subdued voices greeted Maria as she reached the bottom of the staircase. Stopping to compose herself, she took in a deep breath and braced herself for what lay ahead. Quietly, almost on tiptoe, she entered the parlor. Immediately the chattering stopped as all eyes turned toward her. Her mother was seated on the long sofa with a smiling Lorenzo Mauro at her side. Dangling nervously from his hands was a gray silk *coppola* hat. He smiled when he saw her.

Her back stiffened.

Across from the sofa, Luciana and Cristina sat erect on two straight-backed upholstered chairs, their anxious gazes glued on her. Maria was grateful she'd put Nico to bed early and he was fast asleep.

She sought her mother's eyes and read the eagerness reflected in them.

"Maria, come. We have been waiting for you. Lorenzo is here to see you."

Maria drew in a deep breath and proceeded to take the remaining chair next to her mother.

But before she sat, Lorenzo rose, his face a bright red. "Good evening, Maria." Ever dangling his hat, he withheld his hand, perhaps more out of shyness than out of respect for her.

She only nodded and sat down, briefly catching Luciana's anxious gaze.

For a moment, no one spoke. Then her mother smiled. "Maria, *Signor* Mauro has become aware of our dire situation and has offered to assist us." She waited for a reply.

Maria's mouth went dry. "That is very kind of him."

Lorenzo seemed unable to contain himself. "As an old and dear friend of your father—may he rest in peace—I feel it my duty to help his family in any way I can. Having been made aware of your difficult circumstances, I have come to offer the best that I have. My name and my fortune."

Maria's stomach catapulted to her throat.

"I would like to ask for your hand in marriage." He gazed at her with longing eyes.

She looked at her mother's face and read anguish mingled with hope. Luciana and Cristina both bit their lips in anticipation—or was it dread?

She lowered her eyes then raised them. "*Signor* Mauro, I have always known you to be a very kind and generous man. Once again, you are proving your kindness by your generous offer." She glanced at her mother and swallowed hard. "Although it is very tempting—as it would certainly keep us from losing *Bella Terra*—it is not an offer I can, in conscience, accept." She squared her jaw. "You see, I do not love you in the way a woman should love a husband."

There. She'd said it. A wave of relief washed over her.

"I understand, Maria." Lorenzo's eyes were almost pleading. "But perhaps you could learn to love me."

Her mother intervened, her voice trembling with emotion. "That's precisely what I told her. Just as I learned to love her father."

Maria bristled. Yes. Her parents' marriage had been arranged, and they had learned to love each other. But they were among the few fortunate ones. She knew of many arranged marriages in which the husband and wife spent their lives in misery, despising each other.

Yet, to refuse Lorenzo's offer would seal her family's ruin.

The anguish of indecision tore at Maria's heart. The thought of marrying Lorenzo gave her no peace. The atmosphere hung heavy with anticipation as all eyes were riveted on her.

She lowered her gaze. Was she being selfish? Was she betraying her flesh and blood? Worst of all, was she betraying her son's future?

Suddenly, she knew what she had to do.

"I'm sorry, but I'm not willing to take that risk."

Fumbling with his hat, Lorenzo lowered his head but remained silent. After a prolonged pause, he rose, nodded to Maria, her mother and sisters, and left the room. Maria's mother followed solicitously to show him to the door.

Luciana ran to Maria's side and embraced her. "Oh, Maria, I was so afraid you would accept him!"

Cristina joined Luciana in hugging their sister. "I'm still trembling from the stress of it all. I couldn't bear to see you married to such an old man, no matter how kind and generous he is."

Although glad for her sisters' support, Maria wondered if she'd made the right decision. Her mother's return only increased her doubt.

The older woman stood at the parlor's entrance, her hands clasped tightly in front of her, a scowl on her face. "Maria, you have effectively sent us to the poorhouse."

"But, Mama!"

"And the man is devastated. Have you no heart?"

Maria's blood boiled. "Have I no heart? Have I no heart? What about you, Mama? Have you no heart for your own daughter? Do you really want me to marry a man I do not love?" No longer able to contain her distress, she rushed past her mother and stalked out of the room.

She ran up the winding staircase, careful not to awaken Nico. Her body trembling, she burst into her bedroom and flung herself on her bed.

She had, indeed, effectively sent her family to the poorhouse. Lorenzo had offered her a way out, a way to save *Bella Terra*. And she had refused it. Yes, she still had her job. But what she earned would never be enough to satisfy the family's massive debts. Still, there was one option left. Uncle Biagio. They could sell the farm to him.

She buried her face in her pillow. The thought of handing the victory to Uncle Biagio was almost as repulsive as the thought of marrying Lorenzo. She blinked back hot tears.

If only Luca Tonetta could love her.

But that would never happen.
Saving the farm was up to her.
And her alone.

Chapter Nine

Luca needed a breath of fresh air. For the first time in a long time, he'd lain awake most of the night, tossing and turning. His recent conversations with Teresa and Giulio hammered his mind, especially Teresa's incessant accusations against Maria. Despite their words, he still had a nagging feeling they were wrong. Surely they had confused Maria with someone else.

Unable to concentrate on his work, he grabbed his cap and flipped the door sign to the "Closed" side. Then, after locking the shop door behind him, he headed outside. Maybe an espresso would do him good and help keep him awake for the long day ahead.

The hot, humid air hung heavy over the village, creating an atmosphere of lethargy. A low haze blurred the horizon, filtering the strong rays of an already torrid sun. In the distance, seagulls swooped listlessly across barren hillsides.

He lowered the front of his cap over his eyes to lessen the glare.

The square was more quiet than usual today. Produce vendors had raised awnings over their stalls in order to protect their wares from the hot sun. Fish stalls were bare, the vendors having placed the day's catch in wooden, ice-filled bins. In front of Giacomo's barber shop, two old men sat at a small table, playing cards.

"*Buon giorno, Signor* Luca." With calloused hand, Angelo, the fish vendor, withdrew a baby octopus from the ice bin and waved it as Luca walked by.

"Ah, fresh baby *polpo*. My favorite." Luca waved in return, smiling warmly at his father's old friend. "Looks like the kind of weather before the *scirocco*."

"Yes. You're right. Heard it's going to be a rough one this year."

Luca stopped and walked over to him. "Is that right? How did you hear?"

"My brother-in-law works on the shipping route between Tunisia and Sicily. Sails back and forth. Said the winds have already started there and are moving in our direction."

Luca studied the man's sober face. "Not a good thing, is it?"

Angelo sighed. "Well, it depends on how strong the winds are. Some years they are mild; other years they could blow the island away." He broke into a toothless grin. "Hope my brother-in-law's wrong."

Luca patted him on the shoulder. "I do too, my friend. I do too." Tipping his hat, Luca continued on his way.

In a few moments, he reached Alessandro's coffee bar. A lone young man, deep in thought, sat at the counter sipping an espresso. At a nearby table, two elderly men argued over the *pros* and *cons* of Garibaldi's invasion of Sicily over thirty years earlier. Luca smiled. Sicily always seemed thirty years behind the rest of Italy and at least fifty years behind the rest of the world. No wonder so many were leaving the island.

"The usual, Luca?"

Luca turned toward Alessandro. "*Sí, grazie.* How are you, my friend?"

Alessandro poured rich, black coffee into a demitasse and placed it in front of Luca. "Can't complain. The poor economy hasn't kept people from their morning cup of coffee, that's for sure. So as long as they stay addicted, I stay solvent."

Luca laughed. "You speak truly, Sandro. What would we Italians be without our espresso?"

Alessandro chuckled as he slapped the counter with his hand. "So, what is new with you? Any marriage bells ringing in the near future?"

Luca crossed his arms, trying not to reveal his discomfort. "In the far future, perhaps, but not in the near."

Sandro placed an elbow on the counter and nestled his chin in his hands. "If you're seriously looking, I may have just the girl for you."

Luca laughed. Sandro was the Sicilian male version of a yenta. "Who is it this time, Sandro?"

Sandro leaned into him. "My second cousin Giuseppina is looking for a husband. She's a decent-looking girl, a bit on the plump side, but with a big heart. And boy, can she cook! You'd never have to worry about lacking a good meal."

"Now that's the most important consideration in a marriage, I would say. A wife who can cook."

Sandro looked at him quizzically at first, but then burst out laughing. He punched Luca on the arm. "You're fooling with me."

Luca punched him back and downed the last gulp of espresso. "You're right about that, my friend. Maybe that will teach you not to fool with me next time."

Sandro grabbed Luca's hand and shook it hard. "That's what I love about you, Luca. You're always ready for a good joke."

Smiling, Luca placed two coins on the counter and left.

The sun had traveled a finger's width over the tallest housetop, casting patterned shadows across the red tiled roofs. In the center of the square, the splashing waters of the fountain created a welcoming oasis. Several people sat along its edge, cooling themselves from the intense heat.

As Luca drew nearer, he stopped short. On the far side of the fountain, a slatternly beggar woman sat on the ground. Her outstretched trembling hands matched the trembling cry of her voice. "Help me. Please help me." Her shoeless feet, covered with sores, were partially tucked under a tattered skirt that had surely not been washed in weeks.

Compassion instantly rose in Luca's heart. He advanced toward her, but before he had covered much ground, a young woman approached the beggar and stooped down beside her, wiping her brow with her own handkerchief dipped in the cooling fountain. Enthralled, Luca stood by and watched. Once satisfied that the beggar's face had been adequately refreshed, the young woman embraced her and dropped several coins into her hands. Then, as a last gesture of kindness, she cupped both of her own hands and, dipping them into the fountain, drew up a draught of water and presented her cupped hands to the beggar as a drink offering.

The beggar woman drank voraciously.

As the young woman stood to leave, Luca caught a glimpse of her face.

Maria Landro.

It was Maria Landro.

His heart leapt. He quickened his pace toward her, but before he could catch up with her, she was gone.

Overwhelming joy flooded his heart. What greater proof could there be of Maria's character than her most loving gesture toward the beggar woman? He would tell Teresa at the first opportunity.

With quickened pace, he returned to his shop and resumed his work with a light heart. The riddle had been solved. Maria was a virtuous woman.

There was no need to dismiss her.

* * *

It was after eight o'clock in the evening by the time Don Franco returned to the rectory. Rosa had gone home for the day, and Don Vincenzo was away for a few days on church business. Franco would have the whole house to himself. After the events of the past week, he craved solitude.

As he entered the kitchen, the aroma of fresh tomatoes and basil filled the air. He realized that, in his eagerness to post his letter to the bishop, he had not eaten.

After placing the lantern on the countertop, he took a plate from the cupboard and a knife from the knife block on the counter. He then opened the breadbox and withdrew a large chunk of round bread that Rosa had baked that morning. He cut two thick slices and then reached for a large tomato. It felt ripe to the touch. With the knife, he cut three thick slices and placed them on the bread. He drizzled the tomatoes with olive oil and sprinkled them with basil and salt. His meal ready, he carried the lantern to the table and sat down to eat.

But his appetite was gone.

For a long moment, he stared at the food before him. The bishop's order rang in his ears. *I urge you to do all that is in your power to uncover the details of the child's background.*

A cold sweat erupted on Franco's forehead, and his hands began to shake. Taking the plate of bread and tomatoes, he rose, wrapped the plate in brown paper that Rosa kept in a drawer, and placed it in the outdoor pantry where the night air would keep it cool. Then, returning inside, he fastened the latch on the back door, took the lantern from the table, and walked toward his office.

A sense of foreboding fell over him. He couldn't ignore the bishop's request. To do so would bring a serious reprimand with dire consequences. At the same time, he couldn't expose his sin.

His mind raced.

Perhaps he'd tell the bishop that the boy's father was dead. That the child wasn't illegitimate at all, but merely an orphan.

But with Maria getting bolder, that plan could fail.

As he opened the door to his office, he tensed. What he really needed was to keep Maria quiet. If she remained silent, he could handle the rest.

A knock on the front door startled him. Probably a parishioner with an urgent need. Why else would anyone come to the rectory at this late hour?

He took his lantern and walked down the long hallway that led from his office to the front door. The flame from the lantern cast eerie shadows against the sepia photographs hanging in a row on the wall. For some reason, he felt compelled to stop momentarily before the one of his father. His parent's stern look reminded him of the high expectations he'd had for his son. Franco's heart sank. Yes, he'd fulfilled his father's expectations by becoming a priest. But in the process, the real Franco Malbone had died. He wondered if his father would have been happy about that.

Another pounding on the door startled him back to the moment. He rushed down the hallway and opened the door. A young child, about seven years of age, stood breathless and frightened on the doorstep.

"Don Franco, please come quickly!" the child exclaimed.

"What's happening, Filippo?"

"Nonno is dying!"

Don Franco took a deep breath. Grabbing his black leather last rites bag he always kept ready by the front door, he followed the lad into the darkening night. A brief rain had cooled the air and left in its wake a long string of puddles.

Neither of them spoke as the boy led the way down Via Galileo past Addevico's Bakery toward Via Nazionale. Except for the sound of their footsteps on the cobblestone street, the village lay silent beneath a bank of low-lying, dark clouds. In the distance, a lone wolf howled on the hillsides.

Don Franco hurried after the boy past the familiar houses of his parishioners. He knew every person in every family and had heard the confessions of most of the women and few of the men. In Pisano—as in every other village in

Sicily—the women had a monopoly on religion. The men farmed the land, played bocce, and drank homemade wine. The women kept house, bore children, and knelt at the altar of God.

"We're almost there, *Padre*," the boy said, pointing to a house at the far end of the street.

Don Franco followed Filippo toward the house he'd visited many times as a child. Giorgio Marandino, the boy's grandfather, had been a long-time friend of his own father.

A light shone in a window on the east side of the house. As they drew closer, Don Franco could see through the curtains the shadows of several people standing huddled as though in prayer.

"Don Franco! Don Franco!" A middle-aged woman grabbed his arm as he followed the lad through the front door of the tiny house. "We have been anxiously waiting for you. Papa is dying."

Don Franco reverently nodded and followed the woman into the room where Giorgio Marandino lay pale and motionless. Don Franco opened his bag and took out a small vial of holy oil. There was no time to lose. He removed the top, turned the vial upside down, and emptied a few drops onto a piece of cotton. Then he quickly applied the oil to the dying man's five senses while reciting a prayer of healing. As he finished his prayer with the sign of the Cross, the old man expired.

A cry of anguish escaped the lips of Giorgio's eighty-year-old widow who had been keeping vigil by his bedside. "*Santa Vergine! He's dead!*" she cried as her children, wrapped in their own grief, attempted to comfort her.

Fear gripped Don Franco. Were he to die at that

moment, he'd surely go to hell. Unconfessed sin was a certain deterrent to eternal life.

Yet how could he admit his guilt regarding Maria? Regarding Nico? To do so would be a ruin worse than death.

After feeble attempts to console the family, he took his leave, bag and lantern in hand. A heavy rain had begun to fall over the village. Here and there a candle flickered in a window, but mostly everywhere, darkness reigned. In the distance, a dog howled, while nearby, crickets chirped in discordant song.

He made his way through the muddy streets. The sloshing of his shoes against gravel irritated his sensibilities, like the constant grating of guilt upon his soul.

By the time he reached the rectory, it was after ten o'clock. Letting himself in, he took the lantern and went straight to his office. Despite the lateness of the hour, he must do some research in the church's baptismal records. Perhaps he could make a case for Nico's paternity other than his own.

* * *

The wind picked up speed late the following afternoon as Maria hurried down the road from *Bella Terra* toward the village. Tiny particles of sand whipped around her face and settled in her teeth. She squinted to keep it out of her eyes.

The *scirocco* season had begun, bringing with it hot winds from the Sahara desert across the sea. She'd have to hurry before the winds grew in intensity and made it impossible for her to return home. These sandstorms could last as long as four days, cutting off all commerce and communication.

If only the storm had waited until later to start, after she'd brought Nico safely home from school.

She broke into a run. Along the road, palm trees bent in submission to the whistling winds. Her muscles tensing, she braced herself against their stubborn power. As she reached the square, vendors covered their stalls and shopkeepers closed doors and shutters.

She wrapped her scarf around her face and kept running. As she approached the school, parents ushered their children out the door. She ran into the classroom. Nico stood inside the door, his book bag on his shoulder, waiting for her. Behind him stood Don Franco.

She wasted no more than a glance on the priest then turned toward her son. "Nico, we must leave quickly. The storm is getting stronger."

"All right, Mama."

Taking hold of his hand, she turned to go.

"Be careful, Maria." Don Franco's words rang out behind her.

A strange sensation settled over her at what seemed like genuine concern in the priest's voice. Yes, she would be careful. She had too much at stake to die now.

She nodded toward him and then left.

Pressing Nico close to her side, she pushed against the now violent winds. "Stay close to Mama and walk as fast as you can." She shouted the words above the roar of the storm.

Nico pressed in more closely in response.

She worried that his little legs would not be able to withstand the force of the winds. She could carry him, but doing so would slow them down.

Anxiety gnawed at her throat. It took all of her strength to keep them from being swept away by the storm. Swirling sand filled the air, making it difficult for her to see and to breathe.

A loud crash startled her.

"Look, Mama."

Ahead of them, an empty produce cart had overturned, blocking their path. Veering around it, she approached the edge of the square. Not a soul was in sight. Storefront awnings flapped wildly, while shutters banged against stuccoed walls.

Although *Bella Terra* was only two kilometers away, she feared they would not make it. She could turn back to the school and take shelter there. But the thought of being trapped with Don Franco for up to four days horrified her.

No. She would press forward.

Or . . .

She banished the thought. She couldn't risk tainting Luca's impeccable reputation.

No. She would find another way. But she had to act quickly. A delay of even a few moments could place them in grave danger.

As she passed Luca's shop, she glanced in the window. The lantern was lit.

Should she go in or not? Suddenly, on the opposite side of the square, a statue of San Vincenzo Ferreri, patron saint of Pisano, crashed to the ground, knocked over by the raging wind. If they remained outside a moment longer, they could die.

"Nico, we're going in here."

Turning abruptly, she pushed open the shop door and

gently nudged Nico inside. As the bell clanged, she shoved the door shut against the raging wind.

Had she made a mistake in coming?

If so, Luca's sudden appearance made her question moot. "Maria. Are you all right?" He rushed toward her from behind the counter. Outside, the wind beat against the rooftop, making loud creaking noises.

She lowered the scarf from her face and took a deep breath. "Nico and I were on our way home from school. I thought we could make it, but the wind is too strong for us to walk. May we rest here for a few moments? Just until the storm subsides?"

"Why, of course." Luca motioned toward the sitting area. "Please. Sit down and rest. You must be exhausted."

Heat rushed to her face. "I am sorry to impose on you like this. I did not know what else to do. The winds are so strong, it's impossible for me to make it home now, especially with my little one." The knot in her stomach grew tighter with every word. She'd made a big mistake coming here.

He stooped before the child to help remove his jacket. "My, my, young man. You are a brave soul, aren't you?" Luca smiled. "And a big boy."

"I'm a big, brave boy." Nico lisped proudly between his two missing front teeth.

Maria's heart stirred at the sight of Luca tending to Nico. Wouldn't it be wonderful if—

She pushed away the thought.

"There now. Not only are you a big, brave boy, but you must be a hungry one too, right?"

Nico laughed. "Yes. I'm this hungry." He spread his

little arms wide apart.

"Ah." Luca tousled his hair. "You have the appetite of a giant. Let's go get you something to eat, Mr. Giant Nico."

The boy laughed aloud.

Maria watched with a mingling of joy and sorrow. How easily they related to each other!

Nico grabbed Luca's hand. "Can Mama come, too?"

Luca's gaze upon her was kind and welcoming. "Why, of course she can come. She must be hungry, too."

At Luca's invitation, Maria rose. Although she was glad to be indoors, it was awkward to find herself at her employer's shop on a matter other than business. She hoped the storm would end by evening so she could return to *Bella Terra*. But who had ever been able to predict what the *scirocco* would do?

She left her scarf, shawl, and bag on the chair and followed Luca. The wind raged, rattling the windows and shaking rafters in the roof.

"It's getting quite nasty out there." Luca led them toward the staircase. He picked up Nico and put him on his shoulders then motioned for Maria to go ahead of them. As she climbed the stairs to Luca's private apartment, she had the odd sensation she was exactly where she was supposed to be.

But misgivings assailed her, nonetheless. Had anyone seen her enter the shop? She hushed her runaway mind. No one was out in this weather. Besides, if anyone had seen her, what of it? She worked here.

The top of the staircase opened into a small landing. Straight ahead was a mid-sized sitting room. To the right was the kitchen, to the left, a bedroom. Luca's bedroom.

Her cheeks flamed.

She entered the kitchen, a bright, airy room with a square oak table situated just below a wide window. The window overlooked the square. Through the panes she could see clouds of dust swirling all around. "The wind seems to have gotten stronger."

Luca took Nico off his shoulders and stood him gently on the floor. "I'm glad you decided to take refuge here. It's much too dangerous for anyone to be outside in this storm."

She turned toward him. "It's very kind of you to take us in. I'm sure it will be for only a few hours. As soon as the wind subsides, we'll be on our way."

"But not before you have a meal." Luca put an arm around Nico. "I made some fresh tomato sauce today, so all I have to do is boil the pasta." He leaned toward the child. "Would you like to help me set the table, Nico?"

"Oh, I can do that." Maria's face grew hot. She should have offered to help before he had to ask.

Luca smiled and handed Nico three ceramic plates from the cupboard. "If you don't mind, Maria, you can make the salad." He pointed to the icebox in the far corner. "Good thing I bought some vegetables this morning, before the storm broke."

She opened the icebox and retrieved a head of romaine lettuce, two red bell peppers, a cucumber, and an onion. She placed them on the counter, next to the wooden bowl that Luca had brought out for the salad. Behind the bowl stood two glass cruets, one containing olive oil, the other balsamic vinegar.

"Everything has already been washed." Luca handed

her one of his black leather aprons. "Here. You may wish to use this to protect your dress." He smiled. "It's a bit too big, but it will serve the purpose."

Her cheeks flamed, more from appreciation than from embarrassment. She took the apron and put it on, reaching behind her to tie it.

"Mama, I'll tie it for you. I know how to tie."

Before she could object, Nico grabbed the two ends of the ties and began forming them into a knot. "Look, *Signor* Tonetta, I can tie Mama's belt."

Luca observed the boy's handiwork. "I knew the moment I met you that you were a big boy."

Nico positioned himself in front of his mother. The smile on his face was like sunshine over *Bella Terra*. Tears stung Maria's eyes.

If only . . .

She took the head of romaine lettuce and began tearing it into small pieces that she then placed in the wooden bowl. Next, she cut the peppers into bite-sized chunks and added them to the lettuce. She added thin cucumber slices to the mix and topped it off with chopped onion. She mixed the olive oil and vinegar in a cup, added a little salt and pepper, and poured the mixture over the salad. Finally, she tossed all of the ingredients until everything was well coated with dressing.

Fine sand particles beat against the kitchen window. They sounded like a million pinpricks as the wind hurled them against the glass. Maria's muscles tensed. Instead of subsiding, the storm seemed to be getting worse.

"The salad is ready."

Luca smiled. "And so is the pasta."

"And so is the table." Nico stood proudly by the set table.

Luca brought the large bowl of spaghetti to the table. "You have set a table for a king, Nico."

"And a queen." Nico pointed to his mother.

Maria's face grew even warmer. She glanced at Luca. To her surprise, he was smiling.

"It's time to eat." Luca pulled out the chair to his right for Maria. Nico climbed into the chair to Luca's left.

As Luca settled into his chair, Maria suddenly became aware of a deep sadness filling her soul. This was what normal family life was supposed to be like. The kind of life she would never know.

The window rattled loudly as Luca bowed his head to pray. "Lord God, thank You for this food. Bless it, Father, that it may strengthen us to do your work." He hesitated. "And thank You for bringing Maria and Nico here today. In Jesus' Name. Amen."

"Amen." Nico shouted the word at the top of his lungs.

"Nico." Maria gave him a stern look. "Remember your manners."

He lowered his gaze. "I'm sorry, Mama."

Luca took the large serving spoon and placed a generous portion of spaghetti on Maria's plate. How kind of him to serve her and Nico first, just like a gentleman!

"*Buon appetito.*"

"I wish you a good appetite, too." She fought to temper the emotion in her voice.

The wind rattling against the house overpowered the gentle clatter of silverware against the plates.

"You make an excellent salad," Luca remarked. "I see you are not only an exceptional seamstress, but an exceptional cook as well."

Maria's heart warmed at his compliment. "My mother taught me both."

His eyes were probing, but in a kind sort of way. "So, tell me about *Bella Terra*."

She tensed. How much should she reveal? That the estate was on the verge of bankruptcy? That her Uncle Biagio was trying to wrestle the farm from them? She would certainly not divulge the reason for their financial ruin, especially not in Nico's presence.

But at another time?

Luca was so easy to talk to. There was something about him that inspired her confidence. She could trust him. "*Bella Terra* has been in my family for four hundred years."

He offered her some bread. "Is that right? That's a long time. You must be very proud."

"I am not only proud; I am grateful for my ancestors who preserved the farm." Her voice dropped off as she took a slice of the rich, dark bread.

"There is something to be said about family roots, is there not?" Luca's voice sounded wistful.

"Yes. Yes, there is." Growing uneasy, she turned the conversation toward him. "What about your family roots?"

"Well, as far back as I can remember, my family has been in Pisano. My grandparents and parents were born and raised here. In fact, my father started this tailor shop and built it to be one of the best in all of Sicily." Luca's eyes shone with pride.

He took a generous helping of spaghetti. "I learned

the trade at my father's side. Then, seven years ago, my parents died in a shipwreck off the coast. They were on their way to the mainland to visit my mother's cousin in Calabria."

Compassion flooded Maria's soul. "Oh, I am so sorry."

Before he could reply, a loud crash shook the house. Luca rose and hurried to the nearby window. "A large palm tree has fallen against the shop."

"Oh, no!" In an instant, Maria and Nico were at his side. The village square was a violent blur of swirling sand. Debris flew in every direction as the storm raged in all of its fury. Streetlamps remained darkened against the approaching twilight.

The fallen tree had gouged a deep hole in the tiled roof. Worst of all, it had blocked the entire front of the shop, leaving no way of escape other than a second story window. Panic gripped her as Maria realized that even if the storm subsided, she and Nico would not be able to leave.

"Mama, the tree broke the roof."

She was too stunned to reply.

"Will the tree fall on us, Mama?"

Gathering her composure, she drew Nico toward her. "No, darling. The tree will not fall on us."

She felt his arms tighten around her waist.

"I know why. *Signor* Tonetta will take care of us, won't he, Mama?"

Luca seemed to sense her awkwardness. "Don't worry, Nico. I will take good care of you and your Mama."

The boy disengaged his arms from her waist and wrapped them around Luca's.

Luca smiled. "Now, let's finish eating, shall we?

We're going to need strong muscles to move that tree."

Nico's eyes widened.

Despite the seriousness of the situation, Maria laughed. But no sooner did she return to her meal than another crash sent the dishes flying to the floor.

Chapter Ten

Once back at the rectory, Don Franco fastened his office shutters securely against the raging wind. The growing darkness made the storm even more ominous. His stomach churned. Had Maria and Nico made it home safely? Any other man of God would have advised them against leaving and offered them shelter in the school.

He sat down at his desk and once again studied Nico's baptismal record. He'd found it the night before in a section of the church archives reserved for children of unknown parentage. His own name did not appear on the document. Only Maria's name and that of the midwife who had delivered and baptized the child. A common practice in the case of illegitimate births.

Shame washed over him.

Often illegitimate children were given up to the nuns, who then placed them in families. There was less shame in that.

But Maria had chosen to keep her child.

Their child.

He rose unsteadily. The storm raging outside his window was nothing like the storm raging in his heart. Placing his hands in his cassock pockets, he paced the floor. The bishop's order blared in his consciousness. *I urge you to do all that is in your power to uncover the details of the child's background.*

On whom could Don Franco pin the blame other than himself? Fortunately, his name was not on the document. But what story could he fabricate that would not eventually be proven false? If he said Nico's father was dead, how could he prove it? Did the midwife know the truth? Worst of all, what if Maria exposed his sin?

He placed a trembling hand against his throbbing head. He was trapped in a lie, and there was no way out.

A pounding on the front door of the rectory interrupted his anguished thoughts. Who could it be at this late hour and in this terrible storm? He trudged toward the door and opened it, struggling to hold it ajar. The storm blew in, filling the entry with bits of debris and the smell of seaweed.

"*Padre*, the storm is wreaking havoc on the village." Antonio Esposito, the village carpenter, stood before him, a worried look on his face. "A fire has broken out at the Monasteros' house, and we need all the men we can get to fight it."

"I will come with you immediately."

Grabbing the lantern from the hall table, he forced the door closed behind him and followed Antonio into the raging storm. The blinding sand beat against his face. It seemed as though all air had been sucked out of the atmosphere. He coughed and gasped for air.

They had gone only a short way when the acrid smell of smoke reached his nostrils. As they rounded the bend toward Via Sant'Umberto, orange-red flames licked the sky above the Monastero house. He quickened his pace as he thought of Stefano and Paola Monastero, faithful parishioners, and their only daughter, Teresa. *God help them.*

Antonio turned back toward him. "Hurry, *Padre*. The fire is spreading to other houses."

Laboring against the wind, Franco pushed toward the burning houses, hoping it was not too late. Air thickened with the smell of smoke made it difficult to breathe. He coughed and blinked, his eyes smarting against the sand-charged air. How would they ever put out a fire in this raging wind?

As they approached the burning house, Don Franco spotted Teresa and her mother huddled under a wrought-iron enclosure in the clay-pot garden, supporting each another against the strong wind. *Signora* Monastero, a black kerchief around her gray head, wailed in anguish while her daughter tried to comfort her. Nearby, her husband fought the blaze, while a few neighbors emerged from surrounding houses to offer help despite the vicious storm.

The fine sand scratched Don Franco's eyes, hampering his vision. He squinted as he approached Teresa and her mother. Teresa grabbed his arm. "*Padre*. Please pray for a miracle." Her voice trembled.

He nodded then pushed past her, fighting his own despair.

A long line of villagers, young and old, had formed to convey buckets of water from the nearby sea. The sandstorm beat against their determined faces as they passed bucket after bucket of water down the long line of men. The wind whipped without mercy around the flaming house while fiery tongues devoured the rafters and walls.

Don Franco took a place near the head of the line as a young man handed him a bucket of water. "This one is straight from hell, *Padre*," the grim-faced young man shouted over the winds. "We need a miracle."

Don Franco reached for the bucket just as a blast of sand struck his face. Another request for a miracle. Everyone looked to him, as though he were Pisano's miracle worker. Didn't they realize he was only a man, just like them? What about the miracle he desperately needed for himself? Who was there to help him with that one?

A loud crash startled him, followed by a woman's scream as a side of the burning house caved in. He glanced over to see Teresa's mother collapse in her daughter's arms. His jaw tensed. The chances of saving the house now were nil. He could only imagine the poor woman's heartbreak.

A man's shout jolted him once again. "The fire has spread to the Taorminas' house."

Don Franco looked up. The house to the right of the Monasteros' house was now aflame. Like a starving man, the fire ate at the roof and surrounding palm trees. It seemed like a losing battle. If the wind didn't subside, soon the whole village would be ablaze.

Weary with fatigue, Franco straightened for a moment to wipe the perspiration from his brow. Smoke mingled with sand made his eyes sting. He rubbed them with the back of his hand. Another bucket of water headed toward him, drawing him back to the task at hand. But this time, the line of men diverted the water to the Taormina house.

The task seemed almost impossible as flames now leaped from the Taormina house to the DiMinos' house next door. His muscles ached from the strain of repeated lifting and lunging. The DiMinos' house stood only a few hundred meters from the school. His muscles tensed. With the wind scattering flaming debris all over the place, it would be only a matter of time before the fire spread to the school.

Suppressing a surge of panic, he resumed his task with renewed determination. At whatever cost, the school must be preserved. It was the only penance for his great sin.

Yet, how to quench a blaze fed by voracious winds? The *scirocco* pummeled the tiny village, refusing to back down. Overcome with exhaustion, a few of the men had withdrawn from the line.

A sharp pounding on Franco's back made him turn. He looked into Antonio's terror-stricken eyes. "*Padre*, come quickly. The school is on fire."

* * *

"Mama, what happened?" Nico pressed into Maria and buried his face in her skirt.

She hugged him close, his little body trembling against hers. "The wind shattered the window and knocked our meal to the floor."

"Poor Luca's pasta."

Luca brought in two wooden boards and turned to him with a smile. "What do you mean, poor Luca's pasta? Shouldn't you be saying, 'Poor Luca' instead? After all, I'm the one who has to push this wind back outside."

Nico giggled.

Maria watched as Luca lifted a board and positioned it squarely over the gaping hole where once stood a windowpane. With strong strokes of the hammer, he nailed the wood securely in place and then repeated the process with the second board.

"There. That should keep us from eating sand for a

little while."

His smile was like balm on the anxious places of her heart. Soothing and warm.

As soon as the wind was under control indoors, she set about cleaning up the mess on the floor. Broken dishes lay scattered across the ceramic tile floor, covered by bits of pasta and splashes of tomato sauce. A picture of the broken pieces of her life, splattered with the blood of an unmentionable sin.

Her stomach roiled. If Luca knew the truth about her, he'd never have allowed her to stay under his roof.

Carefully, she picked up the pieces and threw them in the wastebasket. After removing all of the large chunks of broken glass and then sweeping up the remaining slivers, she took a wet cloth and began wiping up the remaining morsels of pasta.

Would she ever be able to clean up the broken pieces of her life the same way?

Suddenly Luca stood beside her with a mop. "Here, let me do that."

"Oh, no, Luca. This is woman's work." She reached for the mop, but he refused to give it to her.

"What do you mean, woman's work?" He leaned on the mop, his chestnut hair falling slightly over his hazel eyes. "A woman's work is to let a man do things for her."

Something gave way inside her, like the melting of ice under a hot sun. For the first time in her life, she found herself speechless.

"Now, please, go sit down. You've been through enough today." He guided her gently toward a chair. "Once I clean up the floor, I'll make the three of us some boiled orzo milk."

"Ooh, orzo milk," Nico shouted. "I love orzo milk."

Maria raised a finger to her lips. "Shh, Nico. Please don't shout."

His brows furrowed."But, Mama. I can't hear myself above the wind."

She glanced out the part of the window that had remained intact. The sand-filled wind gave an eerie, yellowish glow to the atmosphere. The sound of sand pelting against the tiled rooftop was like the constant crunching of gravel beneath one's feet. What if she and Nico weren't able to leave tonight?

The thought raked over her mind with a mingling of dread and desire. Dread at what her staying overnight would do to Luca's reputation. Desire at what spending time with him could do to her impossible hope that she could ever interest him. In the few short hours she'd been there, she'd felt at home. Even more than at home.

She felt she belonged.

A few moments later, Luca brought three small cups of boiled orzo milk on a wooden tray and placed it on the table. As he leaned over, she caught a whiff of the rich smell of his worn leather work apron.

"Be careful, Nico. It's hot." He placed the boy's cup in front of him then took Maria's from the tray and placed it in front of her.

His sinewy muscles stretched the fabric of his short-sleeved cotton shirt, sending a shiver down her spine.

"Sugar?"

She redirected her thoughts. "Uh, yes. *Grazie.*" As she reached for the sugar bowl, her hand brushed his. Her whole body tingled.

She drank the warm liquid in silence. Her father's favorite drink. Hardly a night went by that he didn't have his warm orzo milk sweetened with three teaspoons of raw sugar. When she was a little girl, he'd place her on his lap after drinking his orzo milk and play the traditional Italian hand-threading game where he'd pretend he was sewing his fingers together. How she would giggle! Then Papa would give her a big hug and carry her off to put her to bed.

If only he were still alive.

"What are you thinking?" Luca's question drew her from her reverie.

"I'm thinking that orzo milk was my father's favorite drink. Mama made it for him almost every night."

Luca laughed, a bit too loudly, it seemed. "Is that right? It was my father's favorite drink, too."

"And it's my favorite drink, too." Nico smacked his white-rimmed lips and grinned.

Maria joined her laughter to Luca's. Just at that moment, her gaze caught his, and her stomach twitched. He seemed not just to be looking at her, but into her. Heat rushed to her cheeks.

The wind continued to beat against the house, rattling the shutters. The sand pelted the rooftop in a never-ending *danse macabre*. Her heart in her throat, she glanced at the ornate clock sitting on a credenza in the corner of the kitchen. Seven-twenty. She and Nico had been here nearly four hours. If they wanted to make it back to *Bella Terra* before nightfall, they would have to leave soon.

Suddenly she remembered the fallen tree against the front door. "Luca, is there another way out of here? Nico and

I must go home soon."

The child held his cup in midair with both hands. "No, Mama. I want to stay. I like it here."

"Now, Nico. *Signor* Tonetta was kind enough to give us shelter, but we must go back to our own home. We don't live here."

"But I want to live here, Mama."

Her face flushed.

To her relief, Luca intervened. "Wait just a bit longer. The wind is still strong."

Nico's eyes grew wide. "I know, Mama. We could sleep here and go home tomorrow."

Maria's face burned. "Oh, no, Nico. We must go home tonight. I'm sure Nonna is frantic with worry." By now, her mother probably thought they were both dead or lying injured somewhere along the road. But how could they make it back to *Bella Terra* that evening? The wind showed no signs of abating, and fallen branches covered the square. Yet, spending the night at Luca's was out of the question. Propriety demanded she and Nico leave.

Luca strode to the window and looked out. "There is no way I can have the tree removed from the entrance before morning. It will take two men at least to haul it away. Besides, with the wind blowing the way it is, it would be dangerous to try to move it tonight."

Maria's stomach twisted into a knot. "Perhaps we can leave through a window or a back door."

"There is no back door. My flat abuts on another apartment. And the only first floor window is the one by the front door. So it's blocked by the same tree."

137

Her body tensed. "But we must find a way out. I must get Nico home tonight." She couldn't risk ruining Luca's reputation. As for her own, it was too late to avoid that.

Luca scratched his head. "To venture out now in this storm would be dangerous. Wait another hour. A lot could change by then." He poured her another cup of orzo milk.

As she drank the sweetened drink, she realized how much she really wanted to stay.

Not just for the night.

But forever.

* * *

Don Franco pushed against the raging winds toward the schoolhouse. Billows of dark smoke rose from the rooftop only to be snatched and blown away by the biting sandstorm. Here and there, long, narrow flames sliced through the smoke. Fortunately, the school had a regulation water pump behind it with a long fire hose. The villagers had seen to that when the school was built.

A group of men was already on the scene fighting the blaze. Don Franco battled toward the burning building as fast as he could, shielding his eyes from the flying sand. So far, the flames had reached only the wooden strips under the clay-tiled rooftop. The lower part of the building remained untouched.

"Don Franco, thank God you're here!" Salvatore Pietrosanto, father of one of the students, hoisted the fire hose over his shoulder and joined the line of men. "I was securing the doors to my woodshed when I saw the flames and came over right away."

Don Franco placed a hand on the man's shoulder. "Thank you, Salvatore. How does it look?" His voice trembled.

"If we work quickly, I think we'll be able to save the building. Most of the damage is on the roof. The classroom inside seems to be all right. Problem is, it's getting dark, and the wind is giving us no respite."

"Yes. It's as strong as ever." Don Franco grabbed a portion of the hose and lifted it over his shoulder. The pulsating water powered through the long canvas tubing in rhythm with the rapid pumping action of the man at the well. The water gushed out from the end of the hose in great spurts.

Watching the schoolhouse burn was like watching his soul burn in hell. Maybe this was a sign of his destiny. A sign of God's ultimate judgment.

As water poured from the hose onto the structure, the flames sank, swallowed by the smoke. A man approached him. "We've got the school under control, *Padre*. Just a little damage to the roof, but everything else looks intact."

Don Franco's knees weakened with relief. "Thank you." He blinked against the strong wind and lowered the hose to the ground. Then he picked his way through the debris to the schoolhouse. The main door creaked loudly as he opened it with the key that always hung on his cassock. The classroom reeked of smoke, but none of the flames had reached the books and desks. Except for a few roof tiles that had fallen to the floor, the damage was minimal. As soon as the storm subsided, he'd have the roof repaired. It should take no more than a day.

His gaze traversed the room and rested on Nico's desk. A twitch caught in his chest. Were the boy and his mother all right?

If they didn't make it safely home, he'd never forgive himself.

Again.

Chapter Eleven

Luca nodded at Maria, directed his gaze toward Nico, and smiled. The child was fast asleep on the kitchen floor. Caught up in conversation, neither he nor Maria had noticed him curl up at their feet under the table.

"Oh, my." Maria started to get up.

Luca put his hand on hers. Her soft skin felt so good against his. "Let him sleep. There's no way the two of you can go out in this storm. You will simply have to stay here."

Her lovely face turned a brilliant shade of pink. "But we can't. It wouldn't be right."

He sensed her distress. It was that of a virtuous woman, not the kind of woman Teresa had accused her of being. "It shouldn't be a problem, as long as you leave just before the sun comes up."

She nodded. "Then no one will know we've been here."

Conviction of his hypocrisy overtook him. She understood his distress all too well. "You and Nico can have my bed. I will sleep in the back room of the shop. There's a cot there I use for occasional naps during store hours so I can hear the bell clang if a customer comes in." He smiled. "Not that anyone would be coming in this weather."

He read the conflict in her eyes.

"I . . . I don't know what to say."

"Well, it seems to me the only thing you can say is *yes*—unless you want to spend the night outdoors in a dangerous storm."

"If I didn't have Nico with me, I'd try to make it home." She turned toward the child sleeping soundly on the floor. "But I'm afraid he'd never make it."

"And neither would you." Luca patted her hand. "So there. It's settled. Now, would you like more orzo milk?"

She nodded.

He watched her wrap long, slender fingers around her cup while he poured the milk into it. Deep sadness filled her beautiful brown eyes, a sadness he could not decipher.

Compassion overwhelmed him. "I'll put Nico to bed. The poor boy must be uncomfortable on that hard floor."

Luca stooped down to pick up the child and carried him into his bedroom.

Maria followed close behind.

"Please make yourself at home. I'm going down to my shop to finish up an alteration for delivery tomorrow." He smiled. "If, that is, the storm has ended by then."

As he took the steps down to his shop, he sensed that something far deeper was going on with Maria. He would make it a point to find out before she left.

* * *

Maria gazed at Nico sleeping soundly on Luca's bed. He must have been exhausted, as evidenced by his deep breathing and limp body. When Luca moved him from the kitchen floor to the bedroom, he hadn't even stirred. Thank

God Luca had taken them in. Who knows what would have happened to them otherwise?

But still she worried about Luca's reputation. His words earlier had come from one who had never been shunned or ostracized. He would feel differently if vicious rumors ended up destroying his business, as they had the farm at *Bella Terra*.

But she wouldn't let that happen. She'd stay awake all night if she had to. The moment the storm passed, she'd take Nico and head home. No one would ever know that Luca Tonetta had had a woman in his house overnight. It was the least she could do to repay him for his kindness.

She took a deep breath. It felt strange being in Luca's bedroom. To her surprise, it also felt right. Tonight, they'd interacted like a normal family. For a short time, she'd forgotten her circumstances and played along with the dream growing inside her. But soon it would be time to wake up again. To face the reality of her life.

A reality that never left her, that thrust her into recurrent nightmares no one knew about. Nightmares that had assailed her for seven long years.

She brushed back dark strands of hair from her son's forehead. How could such a precious child be the fruit of such a wicked deed?

A lump formed in her throat.

The wind outside whistled fiercely while the sand hammered against the house like a million tiny nails. She drew the blanket up under Nico's chin.

If only she could get a message to her mother to assure her they were all right.

She looked around Luca's bedroom. Sparsely

furnished, it held the double bed on which Nico slept, with an antique walnut nightstand next to it. On the opposite wall stood a mahogany three-drawer oak dresser, over which hung a small round mirror. Next to the dresser, a matching table held a white washbasin and pitcher. In the far corner stood an ornate single-door armoire with a carving of a horse's head on either side of the base. An oval rope rug lay at the foot of the bed. It was a simple room, yet cozy and peaceful.

As her gaze returned to Nico, she caught sight of the wooden cross hanging above Luca's bed. Her heart warmed. It was plain and simple, much like Luca himself. She stared at the cross for a long time, thinking about her own lost faith. At one time, she'd been very close to God. Or so she'd thought. She'd gone to Mass every morning, prayed the rosary every day, and helped the poor. God was good, and life was good.

Until Don Franco ruined it.

His act of violence had destroyed her relationship with God as well. She no longer trusted Him. How could she trust a God who'd failed her? Who'd not been there for her when she'd needed Him most?

Who'd turned a deaf ear to her desperate cries for help?

The sound of footsteps behind her made her turn.

Luca stood at the bedroom doorway, his back leaning against the doorjamb and one arm raised against the other. His tall, muscular frame nearly filled the entrance. His chestnut hair, usually combed back, fell slightly over his wide forehead and framed deep, penetrating eyes. "He must have been very tired."

"Exhausted." She rested a hand on Nico's leg. "He's

had a long day."

Luca relaxed his stance and straightened. "And so have you. How about a cup of chamomile tea?"

"Actually, I would like that very much."

She rose from the bed, careful not to disturb Nico, and followed Luca to the kitchen. From the back, his broad, sculpted shoulders bore witness to a man accustomed to lifting heavy bolts of fabric. Her mind wandered, but she quickly brought it back. The fortunate woman who married Luca Tonetta would get a man not only strong on the outside, but strong on the inside as well. No wonder Teresa Monastero had her eye on him.

Maria pulled out a chair as Luca placed a kettle of water on the iron stove then took a chair across from hers. "Sounds as though the wind is letting up a bit."

"I hope so. Mama must be worried sick about us."

"I'm sure she must be." He hesitated. "And your husband, too."

She froze. It was an innocent question, but one she hadn't expected. Her body tensed. Sooner or later, she'd have to tell him the truth. It might as well be now. She drew in a deep breath. "I have no husband." Her voice trembled with the shame that twisted her heart.

For a long time he did not reply. What was he thinking? His face looked pained, like that of a man who has just suffered a great sorrow.

The teakettle whistled.

Maria studied Luca as he rose to prepare two cups of chamomile tea. Still he did not speak. At last, he placed the cups on the table and sat down again. "So, tell me about yourself." His voice seemed distant, yet still kind.

A coldness settled in her stomach. She took a sip of hot tea, but it did nothing to dissipate the icy fear that coursed through her veins. How to begin? Where to begin?

"I grew up on *Bella Terra*, the farm on the hill just outside the village. I'm the first of three daughters. My father died eight years ago when I was sixteen. At the time, I was engaged to be married to a young man from the area named Carlo Mancini. We were very much in love."

Luca's wince did not escape her notice.

The memory of her broken engagement to Carlo pierced her soul. "But then something terrible happened that changed my life forever." She felt Luca's eyes on her, intense, probing, yet full of compassion. She took another sip of tea, wavering. How much should she tell him? How much disdain could she bear to see in his face?

"Go on." His gentle voice gave her the courage to continue.

"When my father died right after my last year of secondary school, I took a job at the rectory here in Pisano to save some money for my future married life with Carlo. Although Papa left Mama, my sisters, and me financially well-off, I wanted to be independent of my family's fortune when I married. Carlo and I wanted to make it on our own, without our parents' help. Besides, Mama and my sisters would eventually need the money to maintain the farm and the family business.

His gaze was intense upon her.

"I took a job as an assistant housekeeper at the rectory and worked with an older woman named Rosa who was the head housekeeper."

"I know Rosa."

Although his comment did not surprise her, she hesitated. Everyone knew everyone else in Pisano. If he knew Rosa, he knew Don Franco, too. Should she continue?

Luca waved a hand in dismissal. "No matter. Please go on."

Her heart pounded. She took a deep breath. "One day, I was making the bed in the bedroom of one of the priests—Don Franco Malbone, who had also been my teacher—when he walked in unexpectedly. I turned to leave but he told me he would be only a moment to gather some papers from his dresser. I continued to make the bed when he interrupted me once again. His face looked flushed, and his eyes had a strange gleam in them, almost like the eyes of a madman." She shuddered and blinked back stinging tears.

Suddenly Luca's hand was on hers. Comforting and strong.

"Don Franco showed me a gold ring." Her voice quivered. "A wedding band. He told me he'd bought it for a girl he'd loved before becoming a priest, but now he wanted to give it to me." Spasms shook her muscles. "I was shocked that a priest would want to give me a ring. Of course, I refused it." Her voice cracked as tears stung her eyes once again. "When I did, he became enraged. He grabbed my arm, threw me down on the bed, and—"

Her sobs came in wracking convulsions, as all the pent-up anguish of seven long years burst like a dam. She relaxed as Luca's arm slipped around her shoulders. His head rested against hers. She felt his closeness, the heat of his face next to hers, the warmth of his breath upon her hair. She longed to bury her face in his broad chest.

When she finally looked up, he was weeping. But as

he lifted his head, her heart turned to ice.

Doubt filled his eyes.

* * *

Luca punched his pillow for the third time as he tossed and turned on the narrow cot in the back room of his shop. The tiger of doubt clawed at his sanity, tearing it to shreds. Clenching his fists, he swallowed his despair.

Old profanities he hadn't uttered since he'd encountered Christ pushed their way to his lips. He bit his tongue. "Oh, God, keep me from evil." Flesh wrestled with spirit in a battle of man's will against God's. "Lord, save me."

Despite the coolness of the night, perspiration slicked his shoulders and chest, while his head pounded with unanswered questions. Maria's lovely face dominated his mind. She could not be guilty. She simply could not.

He shifted on his cot. Only a few moments before, the clock in the shop had struck two.

A shiver ran through him.

She'd looked straight at him as she spoke, her eyes clear and transparent. Her words had carved an indelible groove in his mind, like a dark ditch from which he could not escape. As she spoke, they had rung so true. Yet, to think Franco, his loyal childhood friend, capable of rape was like thinking a fish could talk. And how could the woman who'd begun to capture his heart the moment she'd first entered his shop be a whore?

His stomach roiling, Luca threw off the blanket and rose with a start. He could barely hear the ticking of the grandfather clock above the noise of the storm. He raked his fingers through his hair. Whom to believe? His lifelong friend and beloved priest, Don Franco Malbone, or Maria Landro, the woman of his heart?

Teresa's warning echoed in his brain. *Luca, she's a whore.*

He paced the floor. Surely there should be no question between Franco and Maria. He'd known Franco all of his life. He'd just met Maria—and her reputation had preceded her. Yet, despite the accusations against her, he had a gut feeling she was telling the truth. But if she were, then Franco was a monster, not the gentle man he'd known all of his life.

Luca took a deep breath. No matter in which direction his tormented mind raced, it crashed into the horrific pain of either betrayal or loss. If Franco were guilty, Luca would lose the sacred trust of a loyal and longstanding childhood friendship. If Maria were guilty, he'd have to give up the woman whose beauty and grace had captured that part of him no other woman had ever captured.

His mind reeled with confusion as the clock on the back room table ticked away each agonizing second. Outside, the wind beat against the shutters in a violent rattle of wood against stucco, while upstairs, Maria and Nico slept soundly in his bed. Part of him was glad they were safe under his roof. Another part of him worried that his own reputation would now be ruined. He'd worked long and hard to put the shame of his own sinful past behind him. He'd made strict rules for himself and had been faithful in living by them. Now, taking Maria in for the night could undo all the self-respect he'd spent years to re-establish.

He clenched his fists and peered through the dust that

coated the window. Despite the darkness, the sand-filled air cast an eerie glow across the square. The storm continued to rage, with no signs of letting up. Leaning his head against the pane, he exhaled a long, deep breath.

None of this would matter if he weren't falling in love with her.

He shook his head. Although he did not know the truth, there was one who did.

Luca turned away from the window and fell to his knees beside the cot. "Father, I'm about to explode with rage and fear. The torment of not knowing the truth is eating at me. If Maria is telling the truth, then I want to kill Don Franco. But if she is lying, then I have grossly misjudged her and will never trust a woman again."

His heart clutched as a cry caught in his throat. "I'm in love with her, Lord, and I need to know the truth. You are Truth. Show me who's telling the truth, Father."

For several moments, Luca buried his face in his hands, waiting for the answer that did not come.

A rustling behind him caused him to turn. Nico stood in the doorway, his shirttail hanging out from his trousers. A shock of thick brown hair fell lazily over his forehead. Half asleep, he yawned and rubbed his eyes.

Luca studied the child's features. There they were. The same chin line. The same nose. The same low forehead as Franco's. Only his eyes were like Maria's.

A chill ran through him.

Luca rose and walked toward him. "What is it, Nico?"

"I can't sleep."

Luca drew the child toward him in a tight hug. "Why can't you sleep?"

"I want the wind to stop blowing. It makes me afraid."

Luca led him to a nearby chair and lifted him onto his lap. No matter what the adults in his life had done, he couldn't turn the innocent child away. "Why does the wind make you afraid?"

Nico nestled his head in Luca's shoulder. "It's strong and loud and knocks things down."

The smell of Nico's hair against his cheek made him wish he had a little boy of his own. Compassion flooded his soul. There was no shame in being afraid of what could knock you down. "I used to be afraid of the wind, too."

Nico lifted his head in surprise. "But you're big. Big people aren't afraid of anything."

Luca chuckled. "I wish that were true."

The boy's dark eyes widened. "Do you ever get afraid, *Signor* Luca?"

Luca smiled. "Oh, yes."

Nico furrowed his brows. "Where do you go when you're afraid, *Signor* Luca? I go to Mama. Do you have a mama?"

"My mama died a few years ago. So now, when I'm afraid, I go to my Papa in heaven."

"Your papa in heaven?"

"Yes. God is my Papa in heaven." He playfully tapped Nico's nose. "And he's your Papa, too."

Nico questioned him with his eyes as a sad look crossed his face. "But I want a papa here. Do you know who my papa is, *Signor* Luca?"

The boy's words pierced his heart. How to reply? What if he did know? He certainly wouldn't have the right to reveal him—at least not without Maria's permission. "I don't think so." Luca released a long breath. "But I wish I did."

Nico sidled into him. "That's okay, *Signor* Luca. When I'm big, I'll find him and bring him to meet you." Nico sat up. "Will you help me find my papa, *Signor* Luca?"

Luca swallowed hard. "Let's ask God to help you find your papa, all right?"

Nico gave him an emphatic nod.

Luca bowed his head. "Father in Heaven, please help Nico find his papa. Amen."

"Amen!" Nico shouted with a giggle. "I can't wait to tell Mama that God is going to help me find my papa."

Despair weighed on Luca's heart. Perhaps this was one prayer that might best go unanswered.

Chapter Twelve

Dawn trimmed the eastern sky in broad strands of purple and pink as Don Franco mopped up the last of the water from the schoolroom floor. He paused to wipe his brow with his cassock sleeve. He would need to cancel classes for today to have the roof fixed. By tomorrow, everything should be back to normal.

For the students, at least.

The storm had left him shaken. He'd come so close to losing the one thing that could serve as penance for his sin—the headmastership of the parish school. It was not a position he'd hoped for when he'd first become a priest. He'd had a much bigger dream in mind. Rome. A cardinalship. Maybe even the papacy.

But his stupidity had changed everything. Pursuing religious ranks would only endanger him even more. If his guilt were exposed, he'd surely face dismissal, and then defrocking. Those he could endure. But the awful judgment of God? That was another matter.

He replaced the mop and bucket in the utility closet and then left the windows open to air out the room before returning to the rectory. On his way, he'd stop by the home of Antonio Esposito, the village carpenter, to ask him to fix the school roof. Then, perhaps, he'd catch a few hours of sleep after the long, grueling night.

The wind had diminished, leaving in its wake a blanket of fallen branches, broken clay pots, and damaged shutters. The Monasteros' house lay in a heap of smoking rubble. The Taormina and DiMino houses, although still standing, were badly damaged by the fire.

How like his own life the village looked! Rubble everywhere. Charred and broken. Good only for the trash heap.

A few young men were up and about, removing debris from their property. Don Franco nodded as he passed by, too tired to stop and chat. Making his way through the damaged landscape, he wondered about Nico and Maria. Had they reached home safely? Had they been forced to take shelter somewhere? How could he find out?

Remembering that Maria now worked for Luca, he redirected his steps toward the tailor shop. If anyone in Pisano had news about Maria, it would be her employer.

With steady step, he climbed over piles of fallen branches and broken clay. The hem of his cassock caught on the jagged edge of a clay pot, nearly causing him to lose his balance. Catching himself, he proceeded across the square to Luca's shop.

"Don Franco." A woman's voice arrested his steps. He turned to find Teresa Monastero heading his way.

"Teresa, what are you doing out in this destruction?"

She stopped, breathless, directly in front of him. "I'm going to the pharmacist. Mama's heart medicine was lost in the fire, together with her prescription."

"I'm so sorry. What a tragedy for you and your family!"

"It is, indeed. But at least we're all alive."

"Yes, thank God for that."

She tilted her head. "What are you doing out, *Padre?*"

Should he tell her? He hesitated for a moment. "Actually, I'm going to Luca's tailor shop to inquire about one of my students, Nico Landro. He and his mother left the school during the storm yesterday, and I was concerned about whether they got home safely."

She raised an eyebrow. "Why would Luca know?"

Her question took him off guard. "Nico's mother works for him." He cleared his throat. "I guess I just surmised he might have some information."

Her narrowed eyes exuded suspicion. "*Padre*, perhaps I am overstepping my boundaries, but I'm concerned about Luca."

"For what reason?"

"Do you not recall an incident that occurred several years ago regarding Maria Landro, the boy's mother?"

Don Franco's stomach clenched as he shook his head in feigned ignorance.

"It seems she was involved in a scandal of seduction that shook the village and left her family ruined." She lowered her voice. "This is the same Maria Landro who is now working for Luca."

The fear of encroaching exposure gripped him by the throat. "Are you sure?"

"There can be no question. The age of Maria's child coincides with the incident, and, if you've noticed, Maria has no husband."

He'd noticed. He'd also noticed that the topic of Nico's illegitimacy had risen to the forefront of public interest. First the bishop; now Teresa. Who would be next? He would need to be more careful. "So, you are concerned about Luca."

"Very much so. Luca is falling for her, and I'm worried she will seduce him just as she seduced Nico's father."

Don Franco's muscles tensed. "But Luca is far too wise to fall into such a trap."

"Don't be too sure, *Padre*. Far better men than he have succumbed to a wicked woman's charms." Teresa laughed. "Please don't think me scandalous, *Padre*, but if I didn't know you better, I'd think Maria Landro could seduce even you."

Don Franco's blood turned to ice.

* * *

The sun had risen above the horizon when Luca opened the front door outward a crack to assess the damage. Yellow clouds covered the village. The strong wind had diminished to a moderate breeze, and the particles of sand now rested in random piles.

He'd hoped Maria and Nico would have left before dawn, but there was no way they could leave until he removed the fallen tree. He surveyed the toppled palm. Its trunk completely blocked not only the entire front of his shop but also that of Giacomo's barbershop next door. Their work was laid out for them.

As Luca pondered how best to handle the situation, Giacomo himself appeared. He was at least able to open his front door.

Luca called through the slightly opened door. "Good

morning, Giacomo."

"*Buon giorno*, Luca."

"I see we share a common problem this morning."

Giacomo laughed, stroking his graying beard. "What a storm, no? I haven't seen one this bad in all of my forty-three years in Pisano. And the sand is still blowing."

"But thank God not as bad as yesterday. It should fizzle out completely by the end of the day."

Giacomo rubbed his forehead. "Did you hear? We lost some fishermen at sea."

Luca tensed. Pisano was a fishing village, and sea accidents, although rare, did occur now and then. "Who was it this time?"

"Pierino Moffa and his two boys."

Luca's heart constricted. He knew them well. They were customers of his. He also knew firsthand the pain of losing loved ones at sea. "I am so sorry." He thought of Pierino's wife and the boys' mother. His heart swelled with compassion at their loss. He'd offer to do whatever he could to help the grieving widow.

"Life is tough, eh, Luca? Just look at this tree. We need to get it moved right away if we want to open for business today."

Luca nodded. "That's exactly what I was thinking. I have some heavy rope in my shop. We'll need two more strong men."

"My sons will help."

"I'll help too, *Signor* Luca."

Luca hadn't noticed Nico standing beside him.

Giacomo looked surprised. "Who's the boy?"

Luca tensed. "He's the son of my new seamstress."

Giacomo gave him a knowing look. "I see."

"Look, Giacomo. It's not what you think."

A puzzled look crossed Nico's face. "What does he think, *Signor* Luca?"

Luca placed a hand on Nico's shoulder. "Never mind." He tousled the boy's disheveled hair. "Looks as though you could use a barber." Luca smiled. "It so happens I've got one right here for you. Meet *Signor* Rizzo, Pisano's best barber."

"And the only one." Giacomo waved a hand at Nico from the other side of the fallen tree. "Nice to meet you, young man."

Nico smiled. "My mama cuts my hair."

Giacomo chuckled. "Well, she does a good job of it, if I say so myself."

"She puts a bowl on my head and cuts around the edges." Nico gestured the entire cutting process with his hands as he turned in a complete circle. "Do you want my Mama to show you? She's inside."

Luca caught the shocked look on Giacomo's face but said nothing.

The barber cleared his throat. "Maybe some other time, son." His gaze shifted to Luca. "Well, let's get this tree out of here, shall we?"

Nico tugged on Luca's sleeve. "Can I help, *Signor* Luca?"

Luca thought a moment. "I'll tell you what. Let *Signor* Rizzo and me remove the big part, and then you can help with the rest. How's that?"

Nico nodded emphatically.

Maria appeared behind them. "Oh, here you are,

Nico. I've been looking for you."

"Mama, *Signor* Luca is going to let me help him move this big tree."

Luca saw her face suddenly turn bright red as she noticed Giacomo through the slightly opened door.

Luca's gaze met hers. "Yes, Giacomo and I will remove the trunk, then Nico can help with the branches."

Luca moved aside as Maria pulled Nico toward her by the back of the shirt and hurried out of sight.

The look on Giacomo's face was a cross between sheer surprise and deep concern. "So, who is the woman?"

"She's the boy's mother."

A sly smile nipped at the edges of Giacomo's lips.

Luca recoiled, hating to admit how much his own thoughts resembled Giacomo's. "Things are not always what they appear to be, Giacomo. She's my new seamstress. She's been helping me with the overload of orders I've been getting from our men leaving for America. She and her son got caught in the storm last night and had no place to go."

"I see." Giacomo did not seem convinced. "Well, your business is none of mine."

Luca opened his mouth to explain further but decided against it. The less said, the better.
He rubbed his forehead. "I'll go get the rope."

"And I'll go get my sons to help us."

Within the hour, the tree had been removed from the shop entrances and rolled into the square for later disposal by village officials.

Giacomo extended a hand toward Luca. "Thank you, my friend. You're a good neighbor. Just like your father before you."

At the mention of his father, Luca's throat constricted. He could only nod in gratitude.

Giacomo pointed toward Luca's shop. "As for the woman and child, that's just between you and me, okay, my friend?"

Luca restrained his anger. "It's not what you think, Giacomo, I swear to you."

Giacomo returned to his barbershop without saying another word.

But despite Giacomo's promise to remain silent, Luca worried that the barber would spare no words with his customers.

* * *

Maria's face burned with shame. Would the ignominy never end? She hadn't expected to find Nico standing at the front door, nor to be seen by Giacomo Rizzo. With every intention to the contrary, she'd effectively ruined Luca's reputation.

Nico whined at her side. "Mama, why wouldn't you let me help *Signor* Luca?"

"I'm sorry, Nico, but moving that tree is work for big men."

"But I'm a big man."

She hugged him close to her side. "You're big on the inside, son. Someday, you'll be big on the outside too, and you'll be able to do the work big men on the outside do."

Before Nico could protest, Luca entered the shop. "Glad that's done. Now we can open for business."

Maria smiled weakly. "Nico, would you go upstairs for a few moments and play with the little wooden horse

Signor Luca gave you?"

"Okay, Mama." He climbed up the steps to the second floor, and as soon as he was out of earshot, she wrung her hands. "Luca, I'm so sorry."

"Sorry for what?"

"For embarrassing you before your friend."

"Well, I won't deny I was embarrassed. But Giacomo and I go back a long time. If he doesn't know me by now, then there's nothing I can do about it."

"But surely he was wondering what I'm doing here. I mean, he must know I spent the night." She wished she could decipher the unsettled look in his eyes.

"Maria, listen. Regardless of what Giacomo was wondering, we know the truth, don't we?"

His voice belied his words, as did the worried look on his face. "Nonetheless, I think it would be best if you and Nico leave as soon as possible now that the storm has passed."

She knew he was right, and she also knew the venom of vicious tongues. "I'm sorry for all the trouble I've caused you." She lowered her eyes. "Nico and I will leave immediately." She turned and hurried up the stairs to fetch her son. If she didn't need her job so badly, she'd quit on the spot. Now that Giacomo had seen her, there was no telling what gossip would fly.

She found Nico engrossed in play. "Look, Mama. I'm making my horse gallop faster and faster." The child galloped his horse up the side of the kitchen chair and onto the kitchen table.

"Nico, put the horse away now. We must go home."

"But we are home, Mama."

Oh, how she wished that were true! Tears stung her eyes as she drew him to her. "I'm afraid not." After the incident with Giacomo, there was not even the remotest hope of that.

She gently released her son. "Now go get your school bag."

"I don't want to go home, Mama. I like it here."

"Perhaps I can bring you to visit another time. Now we must go. Nonna is probably worried sick about us."

"Why can't Nonna come to live here, too? And Aunt Luciana, and Aunt Cristina, and everybody."

She chuckled at his precious innocence. "They want to stay at *Bella Terra*. That's their home."

"But Uncle Biagio is going to take *Bella Terra* away from us."

She started. How did Nico know that? He must have been eavesdropping on one of her conversations with her mother.

Nico rushed past her. "*Signor* Luca!"

Maria turned to find Luca standing at the entrance to the kitchen.

From the look in his eyes, she knew he'd heard everything Nico had just said.

"You're losing *Bella Terra*?" Concern tinged Luca's voice.

She blinked back hot tears and nodded.

"So that's the reason you need work." His voice softened.

Too embarrassed to speak, she nodded again.

"*Signor* Luca, will you tell Uncle Biagio not to take the farm from us?"

"Nico!" Maria looked at him sternly.

Luca put his hands on Nico's shoulders. "Don't scold him, Maria. He was only trying to help."

The hurt on Nico's face was like an arrow in her heart. "I'm sorry, Nico. *Signor* Luca is right. You were only trying to help."

Luca approached her. "We need to talk."

"But there's nothing more to say. Other than what's already been said."

"I disagree. There's a lot more that needs to be said."

She sensed a distance in his voice—a need to talk for his sake, not hers.

She watched as he walked with a determined stride to a small closet and removed a broom and a dustpan. "Nico, I need your help. Would you please sweep up the pieces of tree bark inside the front door while your mama and I talk?"

Nico's eyes lit up. "Yes, *Signor* Luca. I'm a good sweeper."

"I'm sure you are." Luca smiled and ceremoniously handed him the broom. "Please sweep the big pieces into the dustpan and then throw them in the trash."

"I will, *Signor* Luca." With a look as proud as that of one just promoted to a high honor, Nico set to his task.

Alone with Luca, Maria sensed his gaze upon her.

"What's going on with your Uncle Biagio?" He motioned her toward a chair at the kitchen table.

From where she sat, she could see the debris-strewn square as vendors arrived to assess the damage to their stalls.

Luca took a chair across from hers.

She drew in a long, deep breath and squeezed the arms of the straight-backed chair. "Uncle Biagio is my father's younger brother. When my father was alive, they never got along. Papa tried to reconcile before his death, but Uncle Biagio would have none of it. Anyway, Uncle Biagio has always resented that my father inherited *Bella Terra*, and he's been trying to take it from us ever since."

She tensed. There was something different between them.

Luca motioned her to continue.

"Recently, Uncle Biagio came to our house with a document he said was written and signed by my father on his deathbed. My father's been dead eight years, so the appearance of this document at this moment seemed quite strange to me. In any case, the document states that Uncle Biagio has the first right of purchase should we need to sell *Bella Terra*." As she thought of the whole situation, her stomach tied itself into a knot. "It looks as though we need to sell the farm. My reason for taking this job was to help pay off our debt. But despite your generosity in paying me a wage far above the norm, I very likely will not be able to earn enough money to pay off the debt in time."

If only his gaze were not so penetrating.

"I see."

How natural it felt talking to him! Her heart stirred at his expression of genuine interest.

He rubbed his chin with his hand. "This document you mention, is it legitimate?"

"I don't think so. Mama doesn't recall Papa's ever mentioning such a document. And it was unlike Papa to do anything major without telling Mama about it. I think Uncle Biagio is lying and forged the document for his own gain."

Luca nodded. "Far be it from me to judge another, but I think you're right."

His quiet strength made her keenly aware of the weight of the burden she'd been carrying alone. It comforted her to share it with him, although solving her enormous problem was solely her responsibility. "I've confronted Uncle Biagio and demanded proof of the authenticity of the document. So far he has given me none."

"Nor will he. That's my hunch, at least."

She moved to rise. "I plan to speak to my father's attorney about the matter. But now, I really must go. The wind has slowed, and Nico and I can walk without being knocked over."

Relief lined his face. "I'm sure you'll be glad to get home."

Her jaw slackened. "Yes. Yes, I will." She fumbled with the skirt of her dress. "Very well, then. Our things are ready. I'll call Nico."

She tensed as his piercing gaze hovered over her for a long moment.

Finally, he rose. "I'll call him for you."

As Maria followed Luca toward the door to fetch Nico, the shop bell rang. When the door opened, Maria stood face-to-face with Don Franco Malbone.

Chapter Thirteen

"*Buon giorno*, Franco." Luca spoke first in a quick attempt to spare Maria more embarrassment. He'd sensed that her earlier surprise encounter with Giacomo had humiliated her enough to last a lifetime. Now he wondered at the look of shame that had risen to her face the instant Don Franco appeared at the door. Was it a sign of her guilt, as were her twitching hands on Nico's shoulders while she held the child close in front of her?

"Come in." As he motioned to the priest to enter, Luca's mind whirled with a single question. Why was he here?

Don Franco walked in, his wide-brimmed hat clasped tightly in both hands. Deep furrows lined his brow. "Hello, Luca. I came to inquire about Maria Landro and her son Nico." He glanced at them. "I see they are safe and sound."

How did Franco know he'd find Maria and Nico here? Why would he care enough about them to stop by?

Luca gestured toward them. "Yes, thank God they are both well. They sought shelter here on their way home from school."

Don Franco's gaze shifted toward Maria and Nico. "Yes, yes, I see. I thought they might have done so, since Maria works for you." He cleared his throat and addressed

Maria. "I'm glad to see you are both all right." He hesitated. "When you left the school yesterday in the storm, I worried you would not make it home."

Luca's gaze flitted back and forth between Maria and Don Franco. Why would a rapist be concerned about the woman he'd raped? Was Franco's behavior merely a front to hide his guilt, or was he innocent of Maria's accusations? Had she actually seduced him?

"We were forced to take shelter here." Maria's voice broke through the awkwardness of the moment. "Luca was kind enough to take us in."

"Yes, fortunately they were still in the village when the storm hit. There would have been no place to find shelter on the road to *Bella Terra*." He might as well get it all out in the open right away. It would help stem the tide of gossip that had already begun with Giacomo, he was sure.

"I slept in Luca's big bed, *Padre*." Nico wriggled free from his mother's grasp and moved toward his teacher.

Don Franco raised an eyebrow. "I see." His hands fumbled with his hat.

"Mama slept there, too."

Maria's face paled.

Luca was quick to reply. "Yes. I gave them my bed and slept in the cot in the back room of my shop." Why did he feel the need to explain?

Don Franco nodded. "The damage has been extensive. The Monasteros' house has been destroyed by fire. Both the DiMinos's' house and the Taorminas' house suffered a good deal of fire damage."

Luca started. "How are Teresa and her parents?" As much as Teresa annoyed him, she was still a close friend, and he shared her loss.

"They have left for Ribera where they will be staying with her uncle until they can rebuild their house."

Luca shook his head. "I am so sorry. I did not know. I'll offer my help in the rebuilding."

Don Franco sighed. "It's going to take a lot of work to get back to normal."

"I'll help, *Padre*." Nico drew himself to his full stature.

Don Franco nodded. "Thank you, Nico. You are a good boy."

Luca watched the boy's face widen into a smile.

Don Franco lifted his hat to his head and looked at Maria. "Well, I'd best be going. I just wanted to be sure you were safe." He started to leave then turned back. "Oh, by the way, there will be no school today. The roof was slightly damaged by fire, and I'm having it repaired this morning. If all goes well, we'll resume classes tomorrow."

"No school today?" Disappointment filled Nico's voice.

"Surely you're not upset at a day off from school, are you, Nico?" Luca tried to lighten what had become a very tense moment.

"I like school." Nico took Don Franco's hand. "And I like you, Don Franco." The boy rested his head against the priest's sleeve. "Did you find my papa yet?"

Franco's face turned ashen.

So, Luca's suspicions were right. His gaze flew to Maria.

Her jaw squared as she bit her lower lip.

He wanted so much to take her in his arms. To

comfort her. But he still did not know the full truth. Had she been raped, or did she seduce his friend?

"Come, Nico." Maria's voice rang strong. "Don Franco must go take care of the school building so you can return to class."

"Yes. Yes, I must." The priest's voice halted. "We can't afford to miss too many lessons, right?" He reached down and patted the child's head.

Nico looked up at him and smiled. "Right, *Padre.*"

Luca studied Don Franco. "If you need any help, please let me know."

The priest nodded. "Thank you." Without saying another word, he left.

As he watched his childhood friend depart, Luca found himself doubting him more than ever.

* * *

Holding Nico's hand, Maria led the way through the village square, completely strewn with debris. Despite the now clear air, piles of sand covered the entire village.

The Sicilian sun beat hot on her head as they picked their way through the rubble. Seagulls swooped and lunged overhead, crying in unison as they searched for food. Stray cats roamed around the overturned fish stalls, looking for scraps, while here and there, people ventured out to assess the damage. A few shop owners cleared away fallen branches from their storefronts, and just beyond the square, a middle-aged woman swept away the thick layer of sand the storm had left on the brick sidewalk in front of her cottage.

Maria trod carefully over the fallen palm branches. In front of Luigi's café, the wind had overturned several small, umbrella-covered tables and blown some away. The only thing that remained of Angelo's fish market was the sign that had once hung over the front door.

Good thing the storm had lasted only a day.

"Be careful, Nico." She squeezed his hand more tightly. "I don't want you to get hurt."

"I'm being careful, Mama."

She led him around a mass of tangled rope that lay in their path.

"Mama, can we go back to live with *Signor* Luca?"

Maria softened her grip on his hand. "Why do you want to live with *Signor* Luca?"

"Because I like him."

Longing filled her. "I do, too." Her voice was barely a whisper.

"Well, if you like him too, let's ask him if we can live with him."

She chuckled. "It's not as simple as that."

He raised his gaze toward her, a puzzled look on his face. "Why not?"

She hesitated. How could she explain in a way he would understand? "We cannot live with *Signor* Luca unless he and I are married."

"Then why don't you get married?"

She smiled at the innocence of childhood. "Because *Signor* Luca has not asked me to marry him."

"Then I'll tell him to ask you."

Her heart lurched. "Oh, no, Nico! You mustn't!"

"Why not?"

"Because it would not be proper. If *Signor* Luca wants to marry me, he will have to ask me himself." She stopped in surprise. The words had come straight to her lips from the depths of her heart.

What would she say if Luca did, indeed, ask her to marry him?

She drew in a deep breath of salt air that blew in from the sea. Leaving Luca's house had made her realize even more how much she loved to be near him. And the way he'd handled Nico filled her with admiration. Her son needed a man in his life. There couldn't be a better man than Luca Tonetta.

"But why can't I ask *Signor* Luca to ask you to marry him, Mama?" Nico tugged on her arm. "Please?"

"It's hard to explain, Nico. When a man loves a woman, no one will have to tell him to ask her."

A stray dog diverted the boy's attention. "Mama, look. A dog. Maybe he's lost."
Nico pulled away from her grasp.

"Nico, stop!" She ran after him, but before she could catch him, the dog sprang toward him and sank his teeth into her son's ankle.

Nico screamed. "Mama!"

"Don't move, Nico." Maria rushed toward him.

The dog growled as he tore at the child's leg.

Maria grabbed the nearest fallen branch and struck the animal with a vengeance. "Get out of here! Go!"

But the dog refused to loosen his hold on Nico's ankle.

Nico screamed, his face contorting in fear and pain. "Mama, make him go away. He's hurting me."

With a physical strength she didn't know she possessed, Maria kicked the wild animal in the stomach while beating his head with the branch. The dog howled, then finally released the child and scrambled away.

Nico hobbled toward her, tears streaming down his face.

Maria knelt on the ground and examined his ankle. The dog's teeth had torn the skin. Blood oozed from the open gash. "I have to get you to the doctor right away."

"But I don't want to go to the doctor, Mama."

"We must go, Nico. The dog might have rabies. Here, let me carry you."

Taking a deep breath, she picked him up and carried him back to the village square. Doctor Raffaelli's office was at the far end of the square, only a few doors down from Luca's shop. She considered asking Luca to accompany her but thought better of it.

Out of breath, she entered the doctor's office and carried Nico straight up to the reception window. The waiting room was packed with people.

A young girl sat at a desk, writing in a ledger.

Maria approached her. "Please, *signorina*. My son has just been bitten by a stray dog. Is the doctor in?"

The young girl looked up. "Yes, he is, *signora*. But you will have to wait your turn. There are others ahead of you."

"But—"

"I'm sorry, *signora*. We have several injuries to tend to because of the storm. What is the patient's name, please?"

"Landro. Nico Landro."

The girl added the name to a long list. "I will call you when it's your turn."

"Do you know how long that will be?"

The young girl leaned forward and glanced around the waiting room. "Perhaps an hour."

Maria sighed. "Very well, then." She turned to find a seat, but there was none available.

An elderly man, noting her distress, stood up and offered her his seat.

She gratefully accepted.

Settling into the hard-backed chair, she adjusted Nico on her lap.

"Mama, it hurts." The child buried his face in her shoulder.

"I know, darling. Try to be patient. The doctor will see us soon." She caressed her son's hair and drew him closer to her heart. Fear clutched at her as the dog's wild-eyed look flashed before her face. What if he were truly rabid? A bite from a rabid dog was always fatal.

Her body shuddered with the terror that strangled her. She would not let her son die. She simply would not.

She looked around the room. There were at least seven people ahead of her. One young man had a bad bruise on his forehead. Another's arm was badly gashed. A third patient, an elderly woman, sat with her head bowed.

A nurse opened the door and called for the next patient.

Nico began to shiver in her arms.

She touched his forehead. It felt warm.

Her body tensed.

The hour dragged by. Finally the nurse appeared again. "Nico Landro?"

"Yes, that's my son." Gathering her whimpering child in her arms, Maria rose to the curious stares of everyone in the room.

The nurse held the door open for her and Nico. "This way, please."

Maria followed the nurse. She ushered them into a tiny whitewashed room at the far end of a long hallway. "I'll tell the doctor you're here."

Maria gently lowered Nico onto the examining table that lined one wall of the sterile room. Against the opposite wall stood a square table filled with vials of various colors and a container of bandages of different sizes. To the right of the table stood a straight-backed chair. A single tall window overlooked the square.

Nico clung to her neck, moaning in pain.

She smoothed the strands of hair on his forehead, damp with perspiration, then looked at his ankle. Blood covered the bruises that were now turning dark purple. "The doctor will be here soon, darling. He will make you all better."

"I want *Signor* Luca."

Nico's words echoed her own thoughts. But how could she impose on Luca once again after all he'd already done for them?

"Please, let's go to *Signor* Luca's, Mama."

"Perhaps afterward. Right now we must see the doctor."

Before Nico could respond, Doctor Raffaelli knocked and entered the room. He was a short, slender man with salt-and-pepper hair and a dark mustache. His stern demeanor fueled Maria's apprehension. He gave her a cursory greeting then turned his attention toward Nico. "So, you are the young boy who was bitten by a dog."

Nico nodded and rubbed a tear from his eye.

"Tell me what happened."

As Nico explained, the doctor examined his ankle and leg then glanced at Maria.

"Do you know anything about the dog?"

"No, Doctor. He seemed to be a stray. We came upon him as we were walking out of the village toward home. When we first saw him, he was rummaging through the debris left by the storm. Nico broke away from my hand and ran toward the dog. Before I could catch my son, the dog bit him."

The doctor look concerned. "Can you describe the dog to me? Did he seem wild or angry, and was he foaming at the mouth?"

The doctor's questions stirred fear in her heart. "He did seem angry." She hesitated as a lump formed in her throat. "But I don't recall seeing any foaming at the mouth."

The doctor shook his head. "Possibly a good sign." He sighed. "But we're still going to have to watch very closely for rabies, especially since your child has a slight fever."

Fear clawed at her throat. Every case of rabies she'd ever heard of had ended in death. If Nico died, she'd have no reason to live.

The doctor opened a cabinet above the table and withdrew a small vial of dark brown liquid. "If we can find the dog, I will use some of his own skin as an antidote. It's a method of cure based on Louis Pasteur's germ theory of disease. Meanwhile, however, I'm going to give your son an injection of a medication just in case. I can't promise you this will keep the child from contracting the disease, but it's the best we have." He faced Nico. "Please turn over on your stomach, son. I need to give you an injection."

"Mama, I'm afraid."

Maria forced a smile. "You're a big, brave boy, remember?" She helped him roll over and held his hand.

The doctor swiftly administered the injection. "We have to keep an eye on him for ten days, but I want to see him again in three days, do you hear? Meanwhile, it's imperative that you watch him for any symptoms of rabies, like fever, itching on the bite, or irritability. If the child experiences any of those symptoms, send for me immediately. Otherwise, I will see you in three days. Do you have any questions?"

How could she ask him the one question burning in her soul—was her son going to die?

She wrapped her arms around Nico. Never before had he been so precious to her. Never before had she experienced such haunting fear.

Never before had she needed Luca so desperately.

* * *

Luca struggled to concentrate on his work. Don Franco's appearance at his shop and Maria's reaction to the priest had unnerved him more than he wanted to admit. The truth was that Maria had stolen his heart, and he dreaded what that meant. If she were who Teresa said she was, then a relationship with Maria would mean the ruin of not only his business, but also his reputation. Perhaps now was as good a time as ever to go to America. No one would know the real reason he'd left. He could put Maria behind him and start a new life.

The shop bell clanged. He gulped down the rest of the water and went out to the front of the shop.

A sullen Teresa stood at the counter. "How is my favorite tailor today?"

Just what he needed right now. But guilt washed over him as he remembered that Teresa Monastero's house had just burned down. "Teresa, I'm so sorry to hear about your house. Are your parents all right?"

No flirtatious attitude or batting eyelashes today. "Mama is taking it hard." She sighed. "We lost everything, Luca. Everything. I've never seen Mama in such a state."

"I can only imagine her pain. And what about your father?"

"Well, you know Papa. He doesn't say much, but by the look on his face, I can tell he's devastated."

His stomach churned with compassion. Her parents and his had been friends for years. "I'm so sorry. Is there anything I can do? Perhaps help rebuild their house? Make new shirts or suits?"

Gratitude shone from her eyes. "Thank you. They may decide not to rebuild. Right now, we are planning on staying with my uncle in Ribera. We may even decide to settle there and not return to Pisano." She lowered her eyes. "It hurts too badly, if you know what I mean."

Luca remembered his own parents. "Yes. I do know what you mean."

She looked at him for a moment, as though expecting something more. But when he offered nothing, she continued. "I heard that Maria Landro and her son spent the night here last night."

Accusation, coming in the wake of offered

compassion, jolted him. "Yes, as a matter of fact, they did. They were fortunate to reach shelter just in time. Had they delayed a moment longer, they could have been seriously injured. Maybe even killed." He drew in a deep breath. "Where did you hear about it?"

"I have my sources." She gave him a knowing smile. Then, growing serious again, she looked him in the eye. "Luca, you've been a good friend for a long time. I don't want you to get hurt. Stay away from Maria Landro. She's no good. She comes across as sweet and innocent, but before you know it, she'll have you securely in her trap."

His jaw clenched. "Teresa, you don't know Maria the way I know her."

"Really?" Her voice rose. "What do you mean by that?"

Luca's body tensed. "I mean that she has been working for me for several weeks now, and every encounter we've had has been pleasant. Her work has been extraordinary, and my customers are more than satisfied."

"What do you mean by *encounter*?"

He wasn't surprised she'd latched on to that word and ignored all the others. "I mean that in all of my dealings with her, she has been nothing but most respectful and kind."

"Very well, Luca. You know how I feel about her. I will not warn you again. But when you find yourself and your business ruined because of her, don't come running to me."

Doubt reared its ugly head again. Was Teresa right? Should he listen to her? Was he being foolish to ignore her repeated warnings?

He hated that he didn't know the truth.

She played with the soft brown tendrils that framed her face. "I've spoken my piece. Now on to the reason for which I really came."

He waited for her to continue.

"I wanted to stop by to say farewell and to offer my good wishes for your future."

Suddenly he regretted all the times he'd mentally criticized her. "Thank you, Teresa. I wish you and your family well, too."

She smiled. "Thank you." She came around the counter, stood on tiptoe, and gave him a gentle peck on the cheek. "And remember. You have a standing invitation to dinner."

He noticed the tears in her eyes as she said good-bye. For the first time since he'd known her, he wished he had feelings for her. His life would be a whole lot easier. But he couldn't fabricate something that wasn't there, and there was no use trying. "Thank you. At some point, I plan to try my hand at tailoring in America. But before I leave, I'll take you up on that invitation."

Her eyebrows shot up. "Oh? I thought you were only *thinking* about going to America. I didn't know you had definitely decided to go."

"At the time we first spoke of it, I was considering the possibility. But the more I think about it, the more I think it's the direction God wants me to take." He hesitated. "At least at some point in the future."

She lowered her eyes. "Are you sure you're hearing from God, Luca? Or is it your rigid legalism that's leading you astray again?"

Her question troubled him. Legalism was a constant

battle in his life.

"If you go to America, I'll miss you."

He knew she was waiting for him to reciprocate with *I will miss you, too*, but he could not truthfully say it. "Thank you."

She fumbled with her purse. "Well, good-bye, Luca."

Before he could reply, the shop bell clanged. "Ciao, *Signor* Luca!"

Luca's gaze flew to the door where Maria stood with Nico in her arms.

"Nico, what are you doing here?" The look on Maria's face told him something was wrong.

"A big dog bit me, *Signor* Luca."

As Luca rushed to the child's side, he caught sight of Teresa's expression of disapproval but ignored it. "What happened, Maria?"

"We were walking up the hill toward home when Nico spotted a stray dog and ran toward it. Before I could stop him, the dog grabbed him by the ankle and bit him."

"Has he seen Doctor Raffaelli?"

"We've just been there." Her voice trembled. "Nico was asking for you, and since we were so close, I didn't think you would mind if we stopped by."

"I don't mind at all. In fact, I would have minded had you not come."

Ignoring the warning look on Teresa's face, Luca took Nico from Maria's arms and brought him to a chair in the waiting room. After placing the child on his lap, he looked at his bandaged ankle and his leg that had turned a dark shade of purple. "You got yourself a nasty bruise there, son. What did the doctor give you for it?"

"A needle, *Signor* Luca. This big." Nico placed his hands wide apart. "And it hurt."

Luca looked at Maria. "Is the dog still around? If so, he needs to be examined. If he is rabid, then we may have a serious problem on our hands."

Maria's face paled. "The doctor asked me to try to find the dog. He wants me to keep an eye on Nico for ten days and to bring him back for another examination after three days."

"Then you must stay here in case something develops during that time." He couldn't believe he'd offered, and in front of Teresa no less. He glanced toward her only to notice that her eyes had widened to the size of two spaghetti dishes.

"I cannot stay here, Luca." Maria's voice was firm. "*Bella Terra* is only two kilometers away."

In a strange way, her protest comforted him. It was the boundary he needed. Of late, he'd found himself becoming lax in his self-imposed rules when it came to Maria. "Yes. Yes, perhaps that would be a better idea. Nico will be more comfortable in his own bed. I'm sorry. I was just thinking of the child's well-being."

"But I like your bed, *Signor* Luca."

Maria broke in. "Nico, *Signor* Luca needs his bed to sleep."

"But you slept in it when we were here, Mama."

Maria's face turned a deep shade of red.

Teresa interrupted him. "I think Maria is right, Luca. It would not look good for her to stay here. After all, she already has a questionable reputation."

Maria flinched, but she did not defend herself.

Luca's chest nearly exploded with anger. "With all due respect, Teresa, I don't think it's any of your business what Maria does."

Teresa raised her chin. "Very well, then, Luca, I shall be on my way. Your life is in your hands." She strutted toward the door.

"No, Teresa. My life is in God's hands."

"Good-bye, Luca." She slammed the door without waiting for his reply.

So much for Teresa. He was sorry she'd left on bad terms, but he would not allow her to malign Maria. He turned his attention toward her. "Let's get Nico back to *Bella Terra*."

"I can manage myself, Luca. We'll just take our time. Besides, I didn't come looking for your help. You've done enough for us already."

He looked at Maria. "I know you didn't. But you certainly can't carry Nico up that hill by yourself." He smiled. "Wait here while I go borrow Giacomo's wagon. I won't be long."

Without giving her a chance to protest, he placed Nico in the chair, flipped the store window sign to the "Closed" position, and left, certain that his helping her take Nico home would cause wicked tongues to wag.

Chapter Fourteen

Don Franco held the bishop's latest letter in trembling hands. The bishop couldn't possibly have gotten his reply to his first letter yet. Why was his superior being so insistent? Why couldn't he drop the subject of Nico's father? Now His Excellency was threatening to dismiss the child from school if allegations of his illegitimacy proved to be true. Allowing an illegitimate child in the school did not serve as a good example of appropriate behavior among parishioners.

Don Franco let the letter fall to his desk and walked toward the window. So what if Nico was born out of wedlock? It wasn't the child's fault. Why punish him for the sins of his father?

The sins of the father are visited on the children till the third and the fourth generations.

He shuddered, remembering the words from Holy Scripture. Was innocent Nico to reap the results of his father's sin? Wiping the perspiration from his brow, Franco brushed aside the pang of guilt. Sin always demanded a price, but he hadn't considered that his son would have to pay it.

A sparrow flew to the window ledge, tilted its reddish-brown head, and peered at him. Don Franco watched it linger for a brief moment then fly away.

The bishop's persistence unnerved him. He'd just

have to put him off yet another time. But this time, he'd do it with finality. He would write to him and explain that all his efforts to locate Nico's father had been exhausted and there was nothing more he could do. Perhaps His Excellency would finally drop the matter.

Don Franco drew in a deep breath. He knew Bishop Fumo well enough to know that he would not drop the matter. Franco must do whatever it took to protect himself.

Grabbing his wide-brimmed cleric's hat, Don Franco left the rectory to check on the schoolhouse roof. The school was only a few paces away, on the other side of the church. A large palm tree separated the two buildings, its lower branches severed by the storm and now lying strewn on the ground. He'd have them removed later that afternoon.

A crew of men had worked steadily all morning repairing the fire-damaged building. One good thing about the men in the parish—they were always quick to lend a helping hand.

As Don Franco approached, Antonio Esposito waved to him from the rooftop. "We're finishing up the last few tiles, *Padre*. Thank God, the damage was not too bad."

Don Franco looked up, shading his eyes from the blazing sun. "Yes, thank God, indeed. That means we can resume school tomorrow."

Antonio climbed down the ladder from the roof and joined Don Franco. "Speaking of school, what's going on with the new boy? I think his name is Nico. My son said some of the older boys are bullying him. Something about the lad being a—excuse the expression, *Padre*—a bastard. My boy said they're giving him a pretty hard time."

Don Franco's blood turned cold.

Antonio wiped his sweaty brow. "What's the story, *Padre*? Is the boy really a bastard?"

Don Franco's jaw tightened. "I am not permitted to share private information about students."

Antonio's gaze remained steady. "So, he is then."

The hair at the nape of Don Franco's neck prickled. "I said I am not permitted to share private information about students."

A hard look crossed Antonio's face. "I don't mean to pry, *Padre*. I'm simply concerned about my son. The bullies seem to be getting out of hand."

"Rest assured, Antonio, that I am aware of the situation and that the matter is being handled appropriately."

Antonio nodded. "Well, if things get out of hand, let me know. I don't want my boy—or any of the children, for that matter—getting hurt."

Don Franco's stomach churned. "No one does."

Antonio's scrutinizing gaze remained on him for a long moment. Then, with a doubtful nod, the man left to gather his tools.

Unease gnawing at his stomach, Don Franco watched as his parishioner walked away from the building. How much longer before the veil of secrecy that had enshrouded him for seven years unraveled completely, leaving him naked in front of everyone?

* * *

The wagon crept at a snail's pace over the branch-strewn road to *Bella Terra* as Maria held a feverish Nico in her arms. She couldn't wait to get him home to his own bed where he could get the rest he so desperately needed.

She glanced at Luca. He hadn't spoken a word the entire trip. What was he thinking?

Her heart sank at having been discovered by both Giacomo and Don Franco. Despite his protests to the contrary, he'd been embarrassed at the appearance of impropriety her presence had conveyed to his friends. She'd never forgive herself for having agreed to spend the night at his shop. Not only had Giacomo surmised wrongdoing, but the look on Don Franco's face spoke of his own doubts about her behavior.

As if he had any right to judge.

Yet, if she were totally honest with herself, she'd wanted to see Luca and had used the storm as a good excuse. Not that she could have made it safely home to *Bella Terra*, especially with Nico. The winds had been violent. But her heart had been drawn to Luca's shop for shelter like iron drawn to a magnet. The time she'd spent with him had been the happiest of her life. The way he'd treated Nico—as a good daddy would treat his son—and the way he'd listened to her when she'd confided in him—

She blinked back hot tears. Being with him felt so right. But to cling to any false hope that Luca might ever feel the same about her was sheer foolishness. And even if he did develop feelings for her, his moral character would not permit a woman with a tainted reputation into his life.

How she hated Don Franco for having stolen not only her virtue, but also all hope of happiness!

She looked up at the large stucco house that overlooked the valley. Soon they'd have to sell it to Uncle Biagio—unless, of course, she changed her mind about marrying Lorenzo Mauro.

She shuddered at the thought. Yet, what right did she have to think only of her own feelings? Were it not for her, the family business would still be flourishing.

"We should be arriving soon," Luca broke the silence.

From where she sat, Maria could see the bell tower rising in the distance. Her grandfather had installed it to mark the hours of daily prayer when the family and all the servants would stop in unison to worship God. Her ancestors' faith had been strong despite difficult times. Why hadn't her faith persevered? Was she not their equal? Or perhaps her suffering was far greater than anything they'd ever experienced.

As the wagon slowed, she took a long look at the house she loved. Nothing could force her to leave it. Not even her uncle's manipulation. Fond memories warmed her soul as she remembered her happy childhood days there, roaming its many spacious rooms and gazing out the large windows that overlooked the village and the sea beyond. She'd been born in that house and been loved and cared for within its four walls. In the distance, she could see the fields where she'd picked peppers and squash side by side with her papa, mama, and younger sisters. She loved the rich smell of the earth, the balmy breezes, and the terraced hills that sloped into the nearby Mediterranean Sea. *Bella Terra* was who she was. To leave would be akin to suicide.

In the distance, the brilliant blue-green Mediterranean shimmered like liquid glass under the early morning sun. All around, the storm had left a thick layer of yellow dust over the once-lush green countryside, though the first rains would wash it away.

The storm had left its mark on the house as well. The

large weather vane that once sat on top of the roof—the weather vane her father had placed there when she was a little girl—lay bent and twisted on the ground. Several of the roof tiles had blown off, leaving gaping holes revealing the undersurface of wood. The large pink dogwood tree at the side of the house drooped sideways, its trunk severed from its thick roots.

She sighed. They'd need money for repairs. Money they didn't have.

Lorenzo's face rose to her mind. Accepting his marriage proposal would immediately solve her family's financial problems. Besides, it was obvious he loved her. What more could she ask?

The wagon came to a halt.

"Nico, we're home." Maria drew him close.

"No! No! No!" He shook his head forcefully. "Home is where *Signor* Luca lives."

The fever had made the child delirious. Lifting him gently, Maria handed him to Luca who had already descended and was standing by the side of the wagon. She gathered her skirts and climbed down the two wooden steps to the ground.

She motioned to Luca. "Come this way, please. We'll go in the back door."

Her mother rushed out to greet her. "Maria! *Figlia mia!* Thank God you're all right. I've been worried sick." Her mother embraced her and burst into tears.

"Mama, this is Luca Tonetta. He was kind enough to bring us home."

Mama nodded. "Oh, thank you, sir! You are a Godsend!" Her mother made the sign of the Cross and lifted her eyes to heaven.

Luca smiled. "I am happy to help."

Nico groaned in pain.

A worried look crossed Mama's face. "What's wrong with Nico?"

"He was bitten by a stray dog as we were walking home."

"Dear Lord, have mercy! Did you take him to the doctor?" Her mother touched her grandson's hand.

"Yes, we were there a short while ago. Doctor Raffaelli said I have to keep a close eye on him for ten days to make sure he has not contracted rabies."

As soon as they entered the kitchen, her younger sisters ran to greet her. Luciana gave her a tight hug. "We were so worried about you and Nico. Did you spend the night at the school? Oh my, what happened to Nico?"

Her mother raised a finger to silence Luciana's questions. "Nico was bitten by a dog. We need to put him to bed to get some rest."

They all followed Maria to Nico's bedroom, where Luca laid him gently on the bed.

Maria turned to Luca. "Thank you for bringing us safely home."

"It was my pleasure. If you need transportation later to the doctor, please send for me."

She nodded and smiled. "Thank you. If necessary, I will." She moved to usher him to the door.

He shook his head and raised his palm. "Please, don't bother. I can find my way out." Kindness tinged his voice. "Your son needs you now."

His understanding touched her heart. She nodded and

returned to her sick child's bedside. Nico's anguished face told her it was going to be a long night.

* * *

For all of Maria's cajoling, Nico would not be comforted. "Please, Mama, take me to *Signor* Luca."

The child had grown obsessive. It was the fever. She applied another cool wet cloth to his forehead. Although she too had hated leaving Luca's house, it was good to be back in her own home. She'd missed the comfort of her bedroom and of the large kitchen where her mother and sisters gathered to cook and to chatter. The events of the past two days had left her feeling like a wrung-out dishrag.

"Maria, I've brought you some chamomile tea." Her mother entered Nico's bedroom and placed a tray with two teacups on the dresser.

Maria took the cup from her mother's extended hand. "Thank you, Mama. I could use some right about now."

The middle-aged woman wrung her hands as she approached the bedside. "How do you feel, Nico?" She took her grandson's hand.

"I want to go to *Signor* Luca's." In obvious distress, he turned his head from side to side, repeating the words.

Maria sighed and glanced at her mother. "That's all he's been saying since we got home."

"He must have had a good experience there."

"It was new and exciting. Besides, Luca spoiled him with attention."

"I'm sure. From what you say, Luca is a fine man."

Maria read between the lines. "Yes, he is." She rose

and felt Nico's forehead. It was still hot with fever. "I'm going to send for Doctor Raffaelli in the morning." She folded her arms against her tense body.

"Why don't you get some rest?" Her mother placed a hand on her shoulder. "I'll sit with him for a while."

Maria hesitated. "Will you promise to call me if the fever rises?"

"I promise."

She embraced her mother then headed for her own bedroom, grateful for the chance to rest. As she crawled into bed, the weight of the day's troubles crashed in on her. Every muscle of her body ached with fatigue. Her mind drifted to Luca. Being with him had somehow made her burdens seem light. His confident demeanor, his inner strength, the quiet way he prayed before their meal—all revealed a man who knew his Creator in an intimate way.

For the first time in a long time, her mind turned to God. It had been so long since she'd talked to Him that she'd forgotten how. She shifted to her side. No, she hadn't forgotten. She'd just chosen to stop talking to Him. Why talk to someone who'd refused to help her when she needed Him most?

Her stomach knotted.

Perhaps she should ask Luca to pray for her son. Luca had a special relationship with God. One she wished she could have but never would.

Why would God want a relationship with a soiled woman? She could offer Him nothing worthy of His love.

Adjusting her pillow, she buried her face in its softness and let the hot, pent-up tears of despair finally flow.

Chapter Fifteen

His muscles taut, Don Franco watched Antonio's burly figure disappear into the distance. A man to be reckoned with, a man who would not let the matter of Nico's illegitimacy drop.

Don Franco shuddered. He'd have to act quickly. Maybe he should alter the church records. But would he really sink so low? And against the mother of his own child?

But he had to do something to dispel any suspicion. Once the ink dried, he'd breathe easily. There'd be no fear of further questions.

Squelching the weakening protests of his conscience, he opened the creaking door to the classroom. He made his way down the aisle, past the large bookcase to the left and the rows of student desks to the right. He stopped at Nico's desk. What would his son think of him if he knew the truth?

Don Franco stifled the thought.

He continued to the far corner of the room where the fire had charred a large section of the ceiling. He looked up. Surprisingly, except for a fresh coat of paint, the damaged area was indistinguishable from the rest of the ceiling. Antonio and his men had done an excellent job.

Satisfied with the repairs, Franco left the building. The sun had already begun its descent toward the western horizon. Splashes of orange and crimson vibrated against the evening sky, pulsating in the oppressive heat that had kept most people indoors. An eerie stillness pervaded the air that hung heavy with humidity. Don Franco took his handkerchief from his pocket and wiped his brow.

Something black flew across his face and startled him. A crow. The bird nearly stopped his heart. He paused. Crows were uncommon in Agrigento province. Was the black bird an omen of some sort, blown there by the hot winds? Were the winds and fire a sign of danger or death?

A warning from God?

A chill coursed through his veins.

He quickened his pace toward the rectory. He still had an hour before dinner to review Nico's birth records. With Rosa busy in the kitchen and Don Vincenzo hearing confessions, he could carry out his deception without interruption.

His stomach tightened.

Entering by the back door, he passed through the kitchen and greeted Rosa. The rich aroma of simmering tomato sauce struck his nose. "Something smells good." He feigned joviality.

"It's my special marinara sauce, *Padre*. Your favorite."

"Ah, yes. No one makes marinara sauce like you, Rosa. Although I must say, my late mother would have given you a run for your money."

The elderly housekeeper laughed then grew serious. "Your mother was a saint, *Padre*. She always had high hopes for you." She wiped her hands on her apron. "And you didn't let her down."

He tensed. What would his mother think of him now? Thank God she was no longer alive to witness what he was about to do. It would surely kill her.

"I'll be in my office, Rosa. Please call me when dinner is ready."

"I will, *Padre*. It will be about an hour."

He nodded then walked down the short hallway to his office, the aroma of tomato sauce lingering in the air. He stopped in front of his office door. A wooden cross hung there at eye level. His collar scratched his neck. His cassock seemed heavier than usual. Was God speaking to him?

Would God ever speak to him again if he—it didn't matter. In a final fight with his conscience, he silenced its warning once and for all and shut the office door.

The clicking of the latch resounded in his ears.

He headed straight to the parish vault at the far end of his office. Entering the combination, he then opened the heavy door and retrieved the large record book stored inside. His breath came in short gasps as he brought the record book to his desk. He blew off the thin layer of dust. The *scirocco* had reached even into the vault.

The book's ornate cover bore the diocesan emblem— a cardinal perched atop a crucifix. Inscribed within the book's pages were the baptismal records of all the members of his parish for the last fifty years. The latest entry was a baptism he himself had performed only a month earlier.

Turning the pages with care, he found the name Landro. His heart lurched at the sight of Maria's entry. Born January 18, 1868. Father, Samuele Landro. Mother, Concetta Taormina. Baptized January 19, 1868 with the witness of godparents Valeria and Francesco Vacante.

She'd been only seventeen when—

His stomach convulsed. He drew in a deep breath and proceeded to turn the pages. At the sight of Nico's baptismal record, his heart caught in his throat. Born January 13, 1886. Mother, Maria Landro. Father, unknown.

He swallowed hard as tears stung his eyes. Falsifying the document would render his paternity forever silent. His sin forever hidden.

His torment forever alive.

Nico's face rose before him. The child would never have proof of the truth. Would never know him as father.

Don Franco pressed his fingers against his pounding forehead.

Baptized: January 13, 1886. Godparent: Midwife Ornella Pellegrino.

His chest tightened.

No one would ever know if he inserted a fictitious name for Nico's father.

He placed trembling fingers on the page of Nico's baptismal record. Steadying his hand as best he could, he took a razor blade from his desk drawer and lowered it to the page. The razor hovered over the word "unknown." He would scrape it away and enter a random name in its place. Nico would have a father. And it wouldn't be he.

But the closer to the paper the blade got, the more Franco's hand trembled. As the sweat of crushing guilt dripped from his brow, his entire body broke into a paroxysm of tremors. Falling forward, he dropped the razor from his shaking fingers.

He lowered his head to the desk. "I cannot do it." The whisper rang in his heart. "I cannot do it."

As he stared at the page, he knew he'd met his limits. Depravity had taken him this far. He would not allow it to take him any farther.

* * *

Luca wavered between desire and doubt as he lit the gas lamp in his workroom. Two hours still remained before daybreak, yet sleep eluded him like a slippery fish. The little restless sleep he'd gotten served only to aggravate the incessant pounding in his head.

Thoughts of Maria chased after each other in his brain. He kept dropping stitches on the suit jacket he held in his hands. It was all he could do to keep from going mad.

He took another sip of hot coffee and resumed working on the alteration he'd begun the day before. A light rain tapped against the windowsill. Normally he loved the rain, but now its continual dripping drove him to distraction.

He adjusted the garment on his lap. He should not have allowed himself to fall for her. Despite Teresa's warnings, he'd let Maria's charm lure him into an emotional dilemma that now made withdrawal extremely painful.

Impossible, even.

Truth was, he'd fallen desperately in love with her. She was the missing part of him, the piece that made him whole.

Yet, withdraw from her he must if he wanted to maintain his integrity. Continued association with a woman rumored to be tainted would ruin everything his father had worked so hard to build—the family name, the business, and, most of all, a respected son.

But he couldn't just turn his back on her. What if she

were indeed innocent? What if she had no one to stand up for her? To protect her?

To love her?

Luca rubbed the aching muscles in his neck. This kind of inner conflict over a woman was new to him. Uncomfortable. Tormenting, even. A man should be able to fix things right away and move on with his life. Wasn't ambivalence a sign of weakness?

He took an unfinished pair of trousers from the shelf and began to measure the cuffs. It was mindless work, the kind he could do while planning his escape from temptation.

Self-hatred gnawed at him. He should have known better than to relax his boundaries, especially after falling into sexual sin seven years earlier. But, thank God, it still wasn't too late to stem the tide of love that had made its way into his heart.

Or was it?

He must leave for America right away. He wouldn't wait.

He searched his heart.

Is it time, Lord?

No words came in response.

His hand tensed as he stitched around the cuff. Wherever he turned, he saw her. Beckoning him. Enticing him. Running toward him, arms outstretched, a look of longing on her face.

He shook his head to drive away the vision. No, he would not give in to temptation. He would not pursue the soiled woman he loved.

Instead, he would avoid her at all costs.

Even if it meant part of him would die in the process.

Maria awoke with a start, her entire body cold with sweat. Throwing the blanket aside, she jolted out of bed and ran into Nico's room, her heart pounding. Her child lay fast asleep. In the rocking chair next to his bed, her mother slept soundly as well.

She breathed a sigh of relief.

Her mother stirred. "What is it, Maria?" The older woman's alarmed whisper sliced the air.

"I'm sorry for waking you, Mama. I had a bad dream, that's all."

Her mother sat up in her chair. "What did you dream?"

She didn't want to tell her she'd dreamed that Nico had died and she'd killed herself as a result. Her mother was superstitious and would read something into it that wasn't there. "It was nothing, really."

"You should always pay attention to your dreams. They speak to you."

Maria shuddered. "They could speak lies too, you know. Just because you dream something doesn't mean it's going to happen."

Her mother shrugged.

Nico stirred.

Maria lowered her voice to a whisper. "Oh, dear. I don't want to wake him up. He needs the rest."

Groaning, Nico mumbled. "I want *Signor* Luca. Please go get *Signor* Luca, Mama. Please."

Maria wrapped her arms tightly around herself. The child's insistent request troubled her. Why did he keep calling for Luca? Was her son delirious? Or did he simply need a father? If she were honest with herself, she too wanted *Signor* Luca. "Nico, darling, *Signor* Luca is asleep. I will send for him in the morning."

A slight smile crossed the boy's face. "Thank you, Mama. *Signor* Luca will make me all better."

Maria's mother took her by the elbow. "The child is delirious. We must send for Doctor Raffaelli right away."

Maria fought back the fear. "Dawn will break soon. I'll send for him then."

"Perhaps you should send for Luca as well."

Her mother's words surprised her. Yet, as she pondered them, she realized her mother was right. She would send for Luca, too.

The very thought of it brought deep comfort to her soul.

She wiped the perspiration from Nico's fevered brow. Since being bitten earlier that day, he'd taken a turn for the worse. Now, as she held vigil at his bedside, talons of fear dug deep into her soul.

What if Nico died?

The thought of losing the only child she was likely to have pierced her heart.

Nico stirred. "I'm thirsty, Mama."

She took the glass of water from the nightstand and held it to his lips.

He drank only a sip before resting his head back on the pillow. He looked at her with glazed eyes. "My leg hurts."

She took his hand. "Doctor Raffaelli said it would hurt for a little while, but before long, you won't feel any pain at all."

"I want *Signor* Luca, Mama. Will you go get him?"

"It's four o'clock in the morning, darling. *Signor* Luca is asleep." How she wished Luca were there with her! His very presence filled her with peace. "I'll tell you what. Tomorrow, when I deliver my sewing to *Signor* Luca, I will ask him to come visit you."

A smile lit Nico's flushed face. "*Grazie*, Mama." He shifted in the bed. "I like the way *Signor* Luca talks to God."

Maria's ears perked up. "When did you hear *Signor* Luca talk to God?"

"When I couldn't sleep the night we stayed at his house. I went downstairs to the back room of his shop. He was awake. We sat in a big chair, and *Signor* Luca asked God to help me find my papa."

Maria's throat constricted. She forced herself to remain calm. "Why did *Signor* Luca pray for that?"

"Because I asked him if he knew my papa. He said he didn't, but that God did. And *Signor* Luca said God would help me find my papa."

Dread grabbed hold of her heart. She wanted to ask God not to answer that prayer, for Nico's sake.

But what if God did answer Luca's prayer? What would she do then? How would she explain to her child the horrific event that resulted in his birth?

"Why do you want to find your papa, Nico?"

The child's lip quivered. "I want to show the bullies at school that I have a papa, too."

The ache inside her rose to the edge of unbearable. "Are the boys at school still teasing you about your papa?"

Nico's eyes brimmed with tears. "They tease me every day, Mama. They keep calling me *bastardo*. What does that mean?"

Maria's mother gasped.

Hoping to divert both his and her mother's attention, Maria picked up the glass of water. "Try to drink more water. It will help make your fever go away." She placed her hand behind his back and lifted him forward.

He took a single sip and then lay down again.

She felt his forehead. It was aflame with fever. Her soul shook. At daybreak, she would send for Doctor Raffaelli.

Nico struggled to speak. "What does *bastardo* mean, Mama?"

She swallowed hard. He'd have to know sooner or later, although she would much have preferred later. "A bastard is a child whose parents were not married when he was born. It is not a kind word."

He gave her a puzzled look. "But only married people have children."

She hesitated, carefully choosing her words. "Unfortunately, no, Nico. That's how it should be, but it doesn't always happen that way." She hoped he wouldn't ask any more questions. "Now try to go asleep. You need your rest to get better."

He fell into deep thought. "Mama, am I really a bastard?"

A knife twist to her heart would have caused less pain. "It's late, darling. We'll talk about this some other time."

"But I want to talk about it now."

"Nico, I said we'll talk about this another time. Now, please try to go to sleep." She didn't mean to be abrupt with him. She simply wanted to protect him.

He sniffled and wiped his eyes with the back of his hands. "All right, Mama."

In deep anguish, she watched him drift off to sleep.

The time had come to expose the truth.

The time had come to confront Don Franco.

Though it made her feel like a coward, she'd leave it to him to answer Nico's heart-wrenching question.

Chapter Sixteen

Don Franco stood before the altar, hands raised, head bowed, heart tormented. It had fallen to him to say the eight o'clock Mass on this weekday, the Feast of the Madonna of the Sea. For centuries, she'd been Pisano's patron saint, the one to whom the villagers prayed for safety at sea and protection from storms.

He wondered how many of their prayers had been answered.

Perhaps his sin had brought judgment to the village.

He tugged at his Roman collar chafing against his neck. He hadn't grown accustomed to the discomfort of wearing priestly garments in hot weather and probably never would.

A warm breeze blew in from the windows to the right of the sanctuary. He nodded as the young altar boy brought the sacred elements to the altar and then retreated to his position of service on the lower steps behind Don Franco.

The acolyte rang the communion bell, summoning the congregants to kneel. Don Franco waited till every knee was bent and the church was again silent.

He took a deep breath and extended his hands.

"On the night He was betrayed . . ."

The word caught in his throat.

Betrayed.

He was as guilty as Judas. He'd betrayed Christ, man, and himself.

His hands trembled as he picked up the sacred Host and continued.

"He took bread, blessed it, broke it . . ."

A whistling sounded in his ears as the sanctuary began to spin around him. Grabbing hold of the altar, he steadied himself, hoping no one had noticed.

An old woman began to travail in prayer, crying out, "Have mercy, O God! Have mercy."

Don Franco shuddered. He knew her prayer was for him, not for herself.

A long pause ensued. He could hear the people shifting in their pews.

Summoning every ounce of courage, he straightened himself to his full height and proceeded.

"And gave it to His disciples."

Hypocrite, his heart screamed. If he could do so without dishonoring the sacred Host, he would drop everything and run.

But he stood motionless, frozen in fear.

"*Padre,* are you all right?"

The acolyte's question startled him to clarity.

He drew on whatever remaining strength he could muster. "Yes, my son."

Don Franco completed the words of the Communion ritual then nodded toward the acolyte.

The boy followed him down to the altar to serve Communion.

One by one, Don Franco placed the Host on the

waiting tongues of the parishioners. In the purity of their eyes, he saw his own depravity and cringed.

His knees weakened. As he approached the last person, he fell forward. Blackness descended over his eyes, and the world disappeared.

The last sound he heard was the plaintive cry of an old woman.

"God, have mercy."

* * *

A banging on the door awakened Luca from a deep sleep. Shielding his eyes from the glaring morning sun, he bolted from his bed, threw on his robe, and hastened toward the door. A quick glance at the clock unnerved him. Nine o'clock. He'd overslept. Must be an angry customer.

Another forceful knock shook the door just as he opened it.

A middle-aged man dressed in the garb of a laborer stood before him.

Luca tied the belt of his robe. "I'm sorry. Were you waiting long?"

"Forgive me for waking you, *Signor* Tonetta, but I have an urgent message for you from Maria Landro. I am Salvatore, the Landros' former hired hand."

Luca's heart lurched as he motioned for the man to enter. "No apology necessary. I'm glad you woke me up. Not good for business when the owner oversleeps." He raked his fingers through his hair. "I should have opened my shop over an hour ago."

The man fingered his cap in both hands. "*Signorina*

Landro summoned me to fetch you. Her son Nico is sick with fever and has been calling for you all night."

Luca stiffened. Was Nico really calling for him? If he defaulted on his resolve, he feared succumbing to Maria's charms and ruining his life forever. Was it worth the risk?

Yet, the child was asking for him. He couldn't turn his back on the little boy who'd aroused deep paternal instincts within him.

He couldn't refuse the pleas of a sick child.

Luca motioned him inside. "Give me a moment, please. I need to get dressed."

The man smiled and nodded. "I will wait for you outside."

In a few moments, Luca found himself adjusting his stride to Salvatore's as the two men crossed the square toward the winding road leading to *Bella Terra*. The sun continued its upward arc, sharpening its splendor as they climbed the hill to the Landro farm. Robins fluttered back and forth on the low branches of eucalyptus trees, their voices welcoming the new day. The smell of freshly baled hay filled the morning air.

Luca gazed over the wide expanse of fields that lay barren in the distance, fields that, at this time of year, should have been bursting with wheat, oats, and barley. Instead, the land lay fallow, like a ravished maiden left to die.

He swallowed hard. Strange how the land mirrored Maria's account of her life.

He wanted so much to believe her. But how could he deny the counsel of two trusted friends? Friends he'd grown up with and who had no reason to lie to him.

Luca wiped his brow. Despite the early morning hour,

the sun was already hot.

"Looks like a beautiful day." Salvatore's words distracted him from his thoughts.

"Yes, a welcome respite after the *scirocco*."

As they turned the bend, Luca's breath caught at the magnificent sight before him. Stretched all the way to the horizon, the Mediterranean glistened like an emerald jewel. No wonder Maria didn't want to sell *Bella Terra*. The place was a treasure. Its majesty encompassed the hills, the valley, and the sea. It was paradise on earth.

He began to understand a little better the disgrace into which the Landro family had fallen. *Bella Terra* was not just their home; it was their identity, an identity carved by four generations of honest, hard-working Landros.

"There it is." Salvatore pointed to the large stucco estate at the top of the hill.

Edged in sunlight, it reminded Luca of a small-scale medieval castle, strong yet welcoming. Its thick walls covered a large expanse of land and seemed not to keep people out but, rather, to welcome them as it merged with the surrounding countryside. A large courtyard, burgeoning with white irises and purple bougainvillea, accented the front and back of the house. Its red tiled roof provided a striking contrast to its sand-colored walls. The only thing the house lacked was a moat surrounding it.

As he approached the house, Luca braced himself. A sense of excitement overtook him. He'd come for the child, he told himself.

For the child alone.

Yet, whom was he trying to fool?

He'd come because he could not say no to his heart.

He'd come because the woman he loved had sent for him, and he could not refuse her request.

Salvatore pointed toward the house then motioned for Luca to follow him.

Luca took a deep breath. The air seemed purer here atop the hill overlooking Pisano. The roses more fragrant. The sun more brilliant.

Luca followed Salvatore through the back courtyard, a lovely space with a fountain that once probably bubbled forth streams of water but now stood dry. A large fig tree grew in one corner, but it too showed signs of decay.

Luca's heart twisted. Maria had told him the farm needed repair, but he hadn't realized how much. He was glad he'd been able to offer her a job.

Salvatore stopped at a large wooden door and knocked on the brass knocker.

Taking a deep breath, Luca stood to his full stature and waited.

To his surprise, it was Maria herself who opened the door.

At the sight of her, his heart melted.

To his delight, she looked pleased that he'd come.

* * *

At the sight of Luca standing at her front door, Maria's heart warmed with longing.

"Luca. Thank you for coming. Nico has been calling for you all night. He wanted me to send for you at four o'clock this morning, but I told him you were asleep. I'm so glad you're here."

Heat rose to her face at the sudden rush of words that

poured out of her mouth. From the strained look on Luca's face, surely he thought her a bit too effusive. The heat in her face intensified.

Realizing to her dismay that she'd ignored Salvatore, she turned toward him. "And thank you, Salvatore, for fetching Luca."

The man bowed slightly then retreated.

Maria opened the door wide to allow Luca entrance then closed it behind her. "Come this way, please."

Without another word, she led him up the winding foyer staircase to the second floor, past two large curtained windows that overlooked the hillside. Luca was strangely silent as they followed the narrow hallway to Nico's room. Perhaps she'd offended him by sending for him.

She stopped and pointed to a doorway at the end of the hall. "Nico is in there." She looked at Luca. "I've prepared him for your visit."

Luca nodded. "I'll do my best not to excite him too much. I understand he needs to remain quiet."

A surge of gratitude flooded her heart. "Yes. We're hoping it's nothing more than an infection from the dog bite."

"I join you in hoping for the best."

"Thank you." Although her voice was barely a whisper, it held the depths of her heart. She never ceased to be amazed at the enormity of Luca's compassion and understanding. Yet, there was something strange in his demeanor today—a hesitancy, maybe even a reluctance, uncharacteristic of him.

She led him to Nico's bedside, where her mother was seated. "Mama, this is Luca Tonetta. Luca, please meet my mother, Anna Landro."

Her mother rose and warmly greeted Luca. She then pointed toward Nico.

The child was half asleep.

Maria touched her son's hand. "Nico, I have a surprise for you."

The boy stirred and opened his eyes. In a flash, they widened with joy.

"*Signor* Luca! *Signor* Luca!" Nico pushed himself up and threw his arms around Luca's neck. "I knew you would come, *Signor* Luca. I just knew it." He buried his face in Luca's shoulder.

Maria swallowed the lump in her throat. If only Nico had a father like Luca.

If only Nico's father *were* Luca.

She watched as Luca sat down on the bed and drew Nico to him. "How are you doing, my little friend?" He tousled the child's unkempt hair.

"I'm sick, *Signora* Luca. Mama says I have to stay in bed until I'm better."

"Your mama is very wise. You should listen to her."

Heat rose to Maria's cheeks.

"I try to listen to her, *Signor* Luca. Really I do." He lowered his eyes. "But sometimes I forget." He cast a guilty glance at Maria.

Luca patted the child's hand. "You're a good boy, Nico."

"You'll make me better, won't you, *Signor* Luca?"

Maria hesitated. How could she tell her son that he might not recover? That Luca wasn't God?

Luca answered her question for her. "Nico, I can't make you better, but God can."

"*Signor* Luca, will you ask God to make me better? The same way you asked him to find my papa?"

Maria wrapped her arms around herself as she caught Luca's cursory glance in her direction. Was he asking her permission to pray?

In his eyes she saw the faith she herself lacked. Instinctively, she responded with a nod.

She drew near as Luca laid his hand on Nico's head. "Father God, please make Nico better. I pray in the name of Jesus. Amen."

Her heart stirred as Nico embraced Luca.

The child clung to his neck. "Thank you, *Signor* Luca. God is making me better already."

Luca caressed his head. "God is faithful, Nico."

As Luca rose, Maria drew near to the bed and fluffed Nico's pillow. "It's time for you to get some rest, darling."

"I'm tired of resting, Mama. Can't I get up?"

She looked at his pale face and sweaty brow. "Maybe in a little while."

"But, Mama. Why do I have to stay in bed if God is making me better?"

She couldn't deny the boy's reasoning. Why, indeed? "Rest will make you better faster." It was as good an answer as she could give without denying the power of God.

Nico frowned but obeyed. He laid his head back on the pillow and was soon fast asleep.

Maria turned to Luca. "Thank you very much for coming."

"You are welcome." His voice was cool, his demeanor distant.

She'd certainly imposed upon him. "Luca, please

forgive me. Had it not been for Nico's incessant demands, I would not have sent for you. I did it for him alone."

Why did she say that? She knew the truth. She'd sent for him for herself as well. Because she needed his strength.

"I was glad to come."

But as she saw him to the door, she wondered at the emotional distance between them.

Then she knew.

Someone must have been gossiping to him about her.

Chapter Seventeen

Shortly after Luca's departure, Doctor Raffaelli arrived. Maria let him in and thanked him for coming.

"How is the boy doing?"

As she led the doctor upstairs to Nico's room, she described his restlessness during the night and his high fever. She also recounted Nico's obsession about summoning Luca.

Doctor Raffaelli nodded. "Fever will do such things. Your son must have a special affection for Luca."

"He deeply loves him."

The doctor looked at her. "That's not surprising. Luca Tonetta is as fine a man as they come this side of heaven."

The doctor's words fanned a fragile flame within her heart. "Yes, he is truly a good man."

Nico was sitting up in bed when they entered the room.

The doctor approached the bedside. "Well, young man, you're looking better than I'd expected."

"*Signor* Luca asked God to make me better."

Doctor Raffaelli cast a questioning glance at Maria then proceeded to examine the child. A perplexed look crossed the doctor's face. "I was almost certain this was a case of rabies, but it seems to be nothing more than an infected wound."

Maria breathed a long sigh of relief. "Thank God."

"One never knows with a dog bite. Fortunately, the wound was causing the fever. Just keep the area clean, and your son should be fine in a couple of days."

The doctor placed a hand on Nico's knee. "You're going to be all right, son." Doctor Raffaelli smiled. "And next time you see a stray dog, don't chase after him."

By evening, Nico's fever had broken. Maria smiled for the first time in several days. "You look better, Nico."

"What did you expect, Mama? *Signor* Luca asked God to make me better."

The depth of his childlike faith not only struck her but shamed her as well. Didn't Jesus talk about the faith of little children? The kind of faith that created miracles?

She'd had that kind of faith at one time, but a priest no less, the supposed representative of God, had shattered it. Could she ever regain it?

Nico pushed the covers off his legs. "May I get out of bed now?"

Her heart warmed at the sight of her little boy longing to escape the prison of his bed. "I suppose so. But let's not overdo it." She took his hand and helped him climb down from the bed. "I'll take you downstairs to the kitchen. Nonna made you some chicken soup."

Upon standing, he wobbled a bit but then stood firm on his feet. "See, Mama. I told you. I'm all better."

The smile he gave her could have melted the hardest rock.

"Nonna will be surprised to see you up so soon."

She led him down the long hall to the stairway. Holding his hand, she descended one step at a time until they reached the landing. At that point, Nico let go of her hand and took off in a run.

"Nico. Wait. Take your time."

But her words fell on deaf ears.

She hurried to the kitchen and found Nico sitting on his grandmother's lap. She was showering him with kisses.

Maria caught her mother's eye. "Nico wanted to come down for your delicious soup."

Her mother laughed. "I see. I was all ready to bring it up to him, but his wish is my command."

Maria laughed. "Of course, Mama. What are grandmothers for but to cater to their grandchildren's every whim?" She gave her mother a peck on the cheek. "But spoiling him will only make his life difficult."

Her mother grew serious. "His life is difficult enough already."

Maria swallowed hard. Her mother was right. For a six-year-old child, Nico had already endured much suffering.

Nico pinched his grandmother's cheeks. "My life isn't difficult, Nonna. My life is fun."

Maria watched as her mother squeezed her grandson to her heart. "You are a precious little boy, Nico. A precious, precious little boy." The older woman's voice quivered.

He pulled back from her embrace. "I'm a big boy, Nonna. A brave, big boy. Mama said so."

Maria's mother turned toward her and smiled. "Your Mama is absolutely right, Nico. She is absolutely right."

Her mother's vote of confidence was the final spur Maria needed to proceed with the plan she'd been formulating in her mind.

Tomorrow she would arrange to confront Don

Franco.

And she would ask Luca to go with her.

* * *

Maria slung the large bag of altered garments over her shoulder and carried it through the square. It was time to deliver her finished work to Luca and to pick up more jobs.

It was also time to begin executing her plan to confront Don Franco. With Luca by her side, she'd ask Don Franco to make a public confession in the square, in full view of the villagers of Pisano. There, with all eyes upon them, she would draw from him the admission of his crime against her, and she would be exonerated. *Bella Terra's* former vendors would resume buying produce from her, and the farm would be saved.

The sound of the bubbling fountain caught her ear, echoing the surge of joy bubbling in her heart. For the first time, she saw an end to her suffering, a solution to her family's financial ruin. Most of all, she saw the restoration of a good name for Nico.

But she wasn't so foolish to assume that Don Franco would confess without a fight. She shifted the garment bag on her shoulder as she passed a small group of men engaged in subdued conversation in front of Giacomo's barber shop.

"Rosa said he barely escaped death."

The mention of Rosa's name caught her attention. Everyone in Pisano knew that Rosa was the rectory housekeeper. But who had barely escaped death?

Reluctant to intrude, Maria slowed her pace to catch more of the conversation.

"He was serving Communion when it happened."

220

Her chest tightened. Only priests served Communion. She slowed down and listened some more.

An old man leaned into the group. "Something's been bothering Don Franco for a long time now. Whatever it is, it's killing him."

"I heard he may not last the week, poor soul," someone mourned.

She came to a full stop. Don Franco couldn't die now. Not when she was so close to being set free.

She quickly covered the few remaining paces to Luca's shop and grabbed the doorknob. Her whole body shook. She struggled to catch her breath. If Don Franco died before confessing his guilt . . .

She must not wait any longer to confront that horrid man.

She opened the door.

The bell clanged and Luca emerged from the back of the shop. At the sight of his smile, her whole body warmed. Everything about him radiated goodness.

Unlike Don Franco.

"Maria." Luca's eyes shone.

She slipped the garment bag off her shoulder and placed it on the counter.

He drew the bag toward him. "I see you've been quite busy."

"I'm doing my best to keep up with the orders."

He pulled out a pair of trousers and held them up to the light. "You're doing a fine job. A very fine job."

His words gave her the courage to proceed. "Luca, have you heard?"

"Heard what?" He took out a linen shirt and nodded

approvingly as he inspected the repaired shirt pocket.

"Don Franco." She took a deep breath. "On my way over here, I overheard that he suddenly took ill. He almost died."

Luca's face paled as he put down the shirt. "I had not heard."

"It must have just happened."

"Where is he?"

"At the rectory, I assume."

"I must go right away."

He quickly grabbed a pile of clothing from the shelf behind him and placed them on the counter. "Here. For tomorrow." He slid the clothes toward Maria. "Forgive me, but I must run. Don Franco and I are childhood friends."

Luca's words struck at her resolve. Would confronting Don Franco hurt the man she'd grown to love?

Maria hesitated. "May I go with you?"

A surprised look crossed Luca's face.

"I've wanted to do this for a long time. I need to confront him about his crime against me. I need him to confess his guilt . . . and my innocence."

Luca frowned. "Do you think now is the right time?"

Maria's stomach twisted. "If not now, when? He might die at any moment."

Luca's face darkened as his gaze held hers. "You do realize, don't you, that he may be in no condition to grant your request, or even to talk with you."

She nodded. "I'm willing to take that risk. Besides, it would mean a lot to me if you were there with me."

Did she read ambivalence in his eyes?

"Let me grab my key." He removed his leather apron

and placed it over the back of a chair. Then, taking his key ring from the cubbyhole behind the counter, he walked toward the door. After Maria exited, he reversed the sign to the closed position then locked the door.

Maria quickly fell in step with him. How easily the pace of her gait matched his, the same rhythm, the same stride! She felt alive at his side, fully woman.

Eyes began to stare as she and Luca made their way across the square toward the small dwelling that for decades had served as home to Pisano's priests.

Luca did not speak but hurried faster toward the rectory.

Her muscles tense, Maria increased her pace to keep up with him. The heat of judgment and condemnation scorched her as she read the minds behind the staring eyes.

What's a good man like Luca doing with that whore? She'll be the ruin of him. Maybe we'd better warn him before it's too late.

Maybe Luca's not the man we thought he was. Maybe he's already involved with her. Maybe she's seduced him, too.

She squared her jaw.

Whispers. Mumbled words.

Lies. And more lies.

Her neck stiffened against the bitter juice of wicked gossip. She raised her chin and, keeping her eyes straight ahead, she threw her shoulders back and planted each foot squarely in front of her. No one could steal who she was. No venom could poison her unless she took it in.

And no one could force her to drink it.

She wiped her brow. The slight breeze blowing in

from the sea was not enough to relieve the oppressive weight of the moisture-filled air. Just ahead, above a nearby palm tree, seagulls swooped and squawked, then sailed upward again toward the beating, afternoon sun. Their agile wings carved fluid arcs across the azure sky.

She longed to share in their freedom.

In the distance, dark clouds approached like giant ants looking for food to devour.

They neared the rectory. Maria's skin crawled. The morning's *panino* caught in her throat. She hadn't stepped inside the small stucco dwelling since that fateful day seven years earlier. Despite the intense heat, a cold sweat seeped from her pores.

She glanced at Luca, his hands stuffed in his pockets and his gaze focused on the stone pathway before them. Thank God he was here. With her. Not only would he give her moral support, but he'd also serve as a witness to Don Franco's confession.

She drew in a deep breath. Rosa would be there. She'd be surprised to see Maria. The old woman had expressed belief in her innocence and had even come to visit her shortly after Nico's birth, but their relationship had cooled over the years. Perhaps Rosa just couldn't bring herself to believe that Don Franco was a rapist. Maria wouldn't have believed it herself if she hadn't experienced the horror of his throwing her on the bed and . . .

She shuddered. Priests stood only one step lower than God, if even that much lower. Far easier—and less dangerous—to believe a priest than a parishioner.

Luca knocked on the heavy rectory door.

At the sound of shuffling footsteps, Maria clenched

both fists, bracing herself for her first meeting with Rosa after several long years.

The door creaked open. Rosa's eyes fastened themselves first on Maria's. Shock, then gladness, skittered across her face. "Can it be? Maria? Is that really you?"

Maria entered first. "Yes, Rosa."

The old woman hugged her close. "O God, thank You for this answer to prayer."

Maria stiffened. Answer to prayer? What prayer had Rosa been praying all these years?

For a long moment, Maria remained in the old woman's embrace. Rosa's bones protruded from her spine. Her shoulder blades poked through her house dress. Maria felt the passage of time. Her old friend had grown frail.

Rosa drew back and, holding Maria's hands, looked closely at her. "You've grown into a beautiful woman." There was no condemnation in her voice, no indicting judgment.

Only love.

Warmth soothed Maria's soul. She realized how much she loved this woman who'd been her mentor and a second mother to her.

Rosa turned to Luca. "Forgive me, Luca. I was so astounded to see Maria that I neglected to greet you. Won't you come in?" She took Luca's hand and shook it.

"Greetings to you too, Rosa. We're here to visit Don Franco. How is he?"

Rosa's eyes creased into a worried frown. "Not well, I'm afraid. We nearly lost him during Mass this morning. It was quite a shock, to be sure. He's so young." She clasped her hands then made the sign of the cross. "He's resting."

"Can he have visitors?" Luca spoke in a whisper.

"I think so. Come this way, please."

An eerie solemnity hovered over the house as Maria followed Rosa down the familiar hallway to Don Franco's room. So many memories flooded her mind. Memories of the last time she'd run down this hall. Of the way she'd fled from Don Franco's room, terrorized, disheveled, and forever shaken. Of the dreadful shame and humiliation that had ensued.

Her pulse quickened as they approached the room. She wheezed, coughed, couldn't get enough air. Struggling to compose herself, she focused on the echoing of their footsteps on the ceramic tile floor. Each step pounded against her memories, stirring them to the surface, shaking any stability she'd managed to develop since the horrible crime. The day she'd dreaded, yet had hoped for, had finally arrived. In a few moments, she'd confront the man who'd wronged her, the man who'd ruined her life and her hope. In a few moments, redemption would be hers, sealing her family's future.

So why did she feel like a criminal walking to her execution?

She shook it off. She needed to be strong, confident, in control.

Rosa stopped at the doorway and faced them. "I'll tell him you're here."

Maria glanced at Luca standing at her side. His face looked grave, solemn, as though expecting the worst. Yet, his presence gave her strength and inspired courage.

Rosa reappeared at the door. "You may come in now. Don Franco will see you."

Luca motioned for Maria to enter first. How she wished she could grab hold of his hand to draw from his calmness! To drink from his strength.

To lean on his peace.

The head of the wooden bed faced the stained glass window opposite the door, just as it had when—

Maria's throat constricted, and her stomach heaved.

Rosa motioned them toward the bedside then patted Luca's arm. "I will leave you now. Please remember to keep your visit short. He cannot take too much conversation."

Luca nodded. "Of course."

Taking the lead, he walked to Don Franco's bedside.

Marie followed close behind.

The room smelled of camphor and wilted roses. A small vase of them drooped on a large mahogany dresser opposite the bed. The tapestried curtains had been drawn to keep out the light and cast a somber shadow over the beige stuccoed walls. At the far end of the room, a Baroque-style armoire stood with its door slightly ajar.

Don Franco lay half asleep, his head propped up on a pillow. Beads of perspiration dotted his forehead. A light multi-colored quilt covered him up to his chin. His lips, parched with fever, parted in low moans.

He turned slowly toward them.

Maria started. His face bore the ashen pallor of death. His eyes lay sunken within their sockets, drawn tight with the shadows of sickness.

An unexpected twinge of compassion tugged at her heart. She hardened herself against it.

Luca took his friend's hand. "Franco, I am so sorry."

Don Franco's voice was no more than a whisper.

"Luca." His gaze then shifted to Maria. He sighed a deep, long sigh.

Maria's heart pounded. Don Franco seemed in no condition to talk. Yet, she must confront him about his guilt. He could die at any moment. She might not have another chance.

She swallowed hard. Despite her bitterness, seeing him near death overpowered any lasting desire for vengeance. She wished him no harm. She wanted only justice for herself and her family. "Don Franco, I am sorry about your illness."

His gaze remained fixed on her. His dark eyes held fear.

She clasped her hands at her waist. "Don Franco, I must make a request of you."

He stared at her, the fear in his eyes turning to terror, as though he'd been expecting this moment for a long time.

She began again. "Don Franco . . ." The words caught in her throat. "I should have done this a long time ago." Despite the trembling of her body, she squared her shoulders and fixed her gaze on him. "With Luca as my witness, I ask you to admit that you raped me, that you are the father of my son, and that I am innocent of all wrongdoing."

Don Franco's mouth twitched violently. His dark eyes shot bullets of fire. A purplish tint crept into his face as his breathing came in short gasps.

Was he on the verge of apoplexy?

He raised himself on one elbow, his face contorting into a scowl as he pointed a shaking finger at her. "I did not rape you!" He rasped through clenched teeth. "You seduced me!"

The blood drained from Maria's face. Her limbs weakened as her whole body grew numb. She must be having a nightmare. She had not heard him correctly. Surely he'd misunderstood.

Don Franco sank back onto his pillow.

Maria stood motionless, fixed to the floor in disbelief. Nausea swept through her.

Then a scream welled up inside her and escaped from her imprisoned soul. "You lie! You raped me and you know it!"

"Maria." Luca stood at her side. "Please. The man is dying, can't you see?"

Fire exploded in her veins. She turned on Luca. "Can't you see that I too have been dying? For seven long years? Surely you don't believe him!" She grabbed Luca by his jacket lapels and pounded his chest. "I'm innocent, I tell you! I'm innocent!"

She broke into convulsive sobs.

Luca stood before her like a stone wall, his hands at his sides.

Shaking uncontrollably, she buried her face in his chest and sobbed.

But instead of comforting her, he pulled away and left the room.

* * *

Maria staggered out of the rectory, her heart pounding and her throat aflame as she ran through the square toward the road to *Bella Terra*. The people, the shops, the vendor stalls—everything blurred before her. Hot tears stung her eyes and rolled down her cheeks. She needed to get a hold of herself. For her safety. For her own sanity.

But especially for Nico.

Her mind reeled as she struggled to catch her breath. Luca hadn't even bothered to wait for her. He'd nodded to Rosa before storming out the door. The old woman, stunned by their quick departure, stood bewildered as Maria flew past her.

What to do now?

There was nothing left.

No truth. No future.

No hope.

Why had she ever thought Don Franco would speak the truth? Why would he do something against his own best interest? Why would he risk losing everything by confessing his guilt?

She'd been a fool.

A naïve fool.

She stumbled over a fallen branch. Its jagged edge scratched her arm, drawing blood.

Her vision blurred. She could end it all. If she killed herself, stabbed herself in the heart, the stench of her humiliation would die with her, no longer holding power over her family. The villagers might have mercy then. Finally.

Breathing hard, she dragged herself up the hill toward *Bella Terra*, grabbing hold of the lower branches of drooping almond trees. The scalding heat lay like a heavy haze over the countryside. Not far from her feet, a field mouse scurried to take cover under a rock.

If only she had a rock to crawl under.

The world spun around her in a dizzying frenzy. Each

step was a nail in the coffin of hope. Each breath, a death knell to her dream.

She looked up toward her house, now only a few feet away. Within its walls lay her life. All she loved. All she owned. All she was.

But now Don Franco's lie had irrevocably stolen it from her forever.

Numb with the shock of it all, she fell to the ground and buried her face in her arms. Why had she assumed that a man who'd harbored hypocrisy for seven long years would suddenly admit his guilt? Not even the prospect of imminent death had softened his hardened heart.

A pang of guilt struck her own conscience. Was not she, too, guilty of a hardened heart? Had not she, too, allowed sin a stronghold in her life, planting a root of bitterness to strangle her? Had not her hatred for the man who'd wronged her demanded vengeance?

For a long moment she lay there, despair consuming her, as her life drained away like water from a broken jar.

Suddenly, Nico's face appeared before her, pure and smiling. She would not forsake him. The precious one born of her pain. The innocent child born of her shame. She would not allow her hopelessness to steal his hope, nor his future.

No matter Don Franco's sin against her, she had no right to take vengeance. Vengeance belonged to God. To her belonged only to forgive.

But how? How could she forgive the man who'd destroyed her family? The man who'd betrayed her, destroying all hope for her future and that of her son?

The man who was her only means of salvation?

I am your Salvation!

She started at the Lord's words. Tears stung her eyes. Yes, He alone was her salvation. Not Don Franco. Not *Bella Terra*. Not even Luca.

She dug her trembling fingers into the rich soil of the ground beneath her. "Oh, God! My sin is great before You! I have harbored hatred in my heart. I have desired vengeance which belongs only to You. Please, forgive me!"

Hot tears flowed from her eyes, washing away all bitterness of heart. When she'd released the last wrenching sob, she stood to her feet, ready to face whatever life would bring.

Chapter Eighteen

Luca paced the confines of his little shop, his fists clenched with grief. He was a coward. A dastardly coward. His despicable behavior in abandoning Maria at the rectory would have made his father turn over in his grave. Papa had raised him better than to be rude to anyone, especially one in distress. Sinner or saint--all deserved the milk of human kindness.

A heavy weight pressed against Luca's chest, choking the breath out of him. Learning the truth about Maria hadn't brought relief. Instead, it had augmented his agony to the point of despair.

In no frame of mind to deal with customers, he'd left the closed sign in place and pulled the shades. Maria's face filled every crevice of his mind. There was no place he could go that she wasn't already there, reaching out to him. Beckoning him with her deep, ebony eyes.

Was this the same powerful allure that had seduced Franco?

Yet, as she'd pounded Luca's chest in utter despair, her eyes had shouted her innocence in the midst of the world's denial.

And Luca's callousness.

He raked his fingers through his hair, his mind

bouncing back and forth between what Franco had said and what Luca wanted to believe.

Where was the truth?

No use trying to work. His mind riveted on Maria. In accusing her of seduction, Don Franco had confirmed Luca's worst suspicions.

His stomach twisted with regret. Why hadn't he listened to Teresa? One woman knows another, just as one man knows another man. Teresa had been right all along.

He rubbed away the tears stinging his eyes. He couldn't even consider asking Maria to marry him now.

Yet, why couldn't he shake the niggling thought that the truth was not what it appeared to be? That Don Franco was lying, and that Maria was innocent? Hadn't Don Franco been the one to grow angry at her question? If he had nothing to hide, why the rage? If Maria had something to hide, why the confrontation?

Was she telling the truth? Would Don Franco, his lifelong, loyal friend and highly revered parish priest, perpetrate such a crime and then lie about it?

Luca dropped into a chair. Far better to live in the false hope that Maria was innocent than to have no hope at all.

He shook his head in dismay. No. Far better to live in the truth that set one free.

He'd find out the truth for himself. He'd go back to the rectory alone.

Before it was too late.

* * *

Don Franco took a sip from the water glass Rosa held to his mouth. His parched lips both craved and resisted the cool liquid. His body still trembled from his encounter with Maria. She'd finally done the thing he'd dreaded for seven long years. She'd finally found the courage to confront him.

He lay back on his pillow and stared at the ceiling. Visions of that dreadful day seven years earlier appeared before his eyes, tormenting him with their horror.

Rosa placed a damp cloth on his forehead. "You must drink more water, *Padre*, to bring down the fever."

He ignored her words. He didn't want to bring down the fever.

He wanted to die.

Self-loathing filled him as he pondered the baseness to which he'd fallen. Only hell awaited him now. The hell he'd deliberately chosen, and the hell he deserved.

He groaned.

Rosa removed the cloth from his forehead. "What is it, *Padre?*"

"Please leave me now, Rosa. I want to be alone."

A worried look crossed the old woman's face. "But, *Padre*—"

He raised a feeble hand. "No need to worry. I will be fine."

Another lie.

Was his life filled only with lies?

Was his life nothing but a lie?

"Very well, *Padre*." Her voice held concern. "Will you promise to ring the bell if you need me?" She took a small bell from the bed stand and placed it on the mattress within his reach.

Don Franco wrapped his fingers over the bell. "I promise."

His words didn't seem to satisfy her. "I will be back a little later to check on you."

The lengthening shadows of the afternoon sun crept across his bed, covering him in despair. With Rosa gone, the specter of loneliness preyed more heavily upon him than ever.

He longed for, yet dreaded, the death that would put an end to his earthly misery but only begin his eternal one.

A sharp pain shot through his chest.

Guilt unconfessed becomes a stronghold.

Strange that his mother's words should surface to his mind. He was six years old again. Nico's age. He'd stolen a peach from his neighbor's peach grove and eaten it. Ridden with guilt, he'd rushed home to confess to his mother.

He could still see the look of sorrow on her face. He could still hear the anger in her voice. "Franco, what you did was wrong. You sinned before God by breaking one of His commandments. You must confess your sin in order to be right with God again. And you must confess to our neighbor and pay him for the peach."

Confess his sin. It was as easy as that.

And as difficult.

Why could he not admit his guilt? What kept him from turning to God in repentance and asking for the forgiveness that would surely come? What demonic hubris held him captive in its strangling grip?

Was not the fear of hell sufficient to move him? Had his soul been so utterly possessed by the devil himself that God had abandoned him? Left him to his own devices?

Give me your will. I want your will.

He heard the words as clearly as he heard the sparrow pecking at his window.

But instead of heeding God's voice, he hardened his heart against it.

* * *

The blazing sun descended its arc as Maria staggered toward her house. A new resolve filled her heart, invincible in its dependence on Christ.

As she rounded the final bend in the road, she stopped short. Uncle Biagio's horse and wagon stood in the courtyard.

Could things get any worse?

Beyond the wagon, on the veranda, her uncle was engaged in an animated conversation with her mother. He held a sheaf of papers in his left hand and kept hitting them with his right.

Maria approached the veranda and caught her mother's eye.

"Maria!" Her mother rushed toward her. "What happened to you?"

Maria looked down at her skirt. It was covered with dirt from her fall. Spots of blood from her injured arm dotted the fabric.

"Nothing serious. I tripped over a fallen branch on the road." She brushed the dust off her skirt. "I'm fine. Really." Now was not the time to tell her mother about her encounter with Don Franco.

She shifted her gaze to her uncle. "What brings you

here?" She already knew—the scoundrel—but the question would give her leverage.

His smile singed her soul. "I've come to alert your mother that I will be assuming ownership of *Bella Terra* in the very near future. I have the legal papers here for your mother to sign." He waved the papers in her face. "These documents prove that I have the right of first purchase, as your father desired and expressed to me on his deathbed."

The smugness in his face turned her stomach. "What if Mama won't sign them?"

Her mother averted her gaze.

"Mama, you must not sign the papers!"

Mama placed a hand on her arm. "We have no choice, Maria." Tears welled up in her mother's eyes.

Maria's heart could sink no farther. What more could she say? What more could she do? Don Franco's lie had destroyed her last possible means of saving the farm.

Maria looked at Mama, shook her head, and went inside. Her heart lay like a leaden ball within her chest.

Uncle Biagio had won.

Nico sat on his knees on a chair at the kitchen table, drawing a picture. At the sound of the opening door, he turned.

"Mama! Mama! Look what I drew for you." He slid off the chair and ran toward her open arms, stopping short just as he reached her.

She quickly dabbed her tear-filled eyes with the back of her hand, knelt down on one knee, and reached for him. "Nico, darling."

The child took her tear-stained face in his chubby little hands and grinned. "Mama, I see the sun in your eyes."

A sob rose to her throat and lodged there. Those were her father's words. How did Nico know? She'd never told him.

Maria squeezed her son to her heart, buried her head on his little shoulder, and wept.

Her son stroked her hair. "It's all right, Mama."

It's all right, Maria.

Hope coursed through her as God's voice spoke in the depths of her spirit.

Yes. Everything was all right. She still had her beautiful Nico to live for. Everyone else had abandoned her. Her child had not.

Nor had her God.

Chapter Nineteen

Luca found himself knocking at the rectory door for the second time that day.

"Rosa, I must talk with Franco, please. For only a moment. It's extremely important."

The housekeeper nodded and ushered him in. "After you and Maria left, his fever rose. I tried to get him to drink some water, but he took little." She dabbed a handkerchief at her eyes. "I think he's lost the will to live."

Luca's heart clenched. He could only nod in response.

She straightened and composed herself. "You know where his room is. Just knock before you enter."

"Thank you."

A sense of foreboding filled the air as Luca followed the short hallway to Don Franco's room. He knocked softly then entered.

"Franco. It is I. Luca."

The priest turned his head. His eyes were like burning coals in their sockets; his facial muscles, taut with a grief unlike anything Luca had ever seen on a human face.

"Luca." The name came forth haltingly. Painfully.

Luca approached the bed. "Franco, what's wrong?"

The priest's eyes darted away from him. "Nothing. Nothing is wrong."

"But you are not the Franco I knew. The boy I grew up with. The young man who loved life. What has happened?"

A low moan escaped Don Franco's lips. "Have you come only to torment me?"

Taken aback, Luca took a moment to get the question out. "Franco, did you rape Maria Landro?"

Don Franco's face contorted into a paroxysm of terror as a loud wail erupted from the darkest depths of his soul. Turning away from Luca, he buried his face in his pillow and broke down in violent sobs, from which came forth the word *yes*.

Luca's eyes filled with tears. He finally had his answer.

And it ripped the very heart out of him.

He loved Franco. He loved Maria. And he was caught between the two.

Luca rested a hand on his friend's shoulder. "You have done right to admit your guilt. Now I pray you'll confess it before God and receive His forgiveness."

The solemnity of the moment demanded Luca's departure. After he left, Don Franco's sobs lingered long in his ears.

* * *

Don Franco opened his eyes then blinked several times as they adjusted to the dimness of the room. Perspiration drenched the pillow and sheets beneath him. Lying helpless on his bed, he shivered under a woolen blanket. In his clenched fists, he held a small wooden crucifix.

The sharp pain in his chest had subsided considerably, but the ache in his heart had grown worse. Despair held him in unrelenting jaws. Death had never looked more inviting, nor more horrifying.

He drew in a deep breath then raised himself slightly on one arm and lifted his head. Disoriented, he gazed around the darkened room to get his bearings. A lone candle flickered on the dresser, casting a white circle on the wall behind it. In its light, he saw Rosa sitting by his bedside, a black rosary dangling from her clasped hands, her lips moving rapidly in whispered prayer.

"Rosa, it is time."

"Time for what, *Padre*?"

"Time for last rites."

The old woman rose instantly. "I will call Don Vincenzo."

A spasm shook Don Franco's body. Yes, he must have last rites. He must not die in sin. He must not risk going to hell.

She hastened out of the room, her rosary still dangling from her fingers.

The sick room fell deathly silent. Dark shadows of fear descended upon Don Franco, grabbing him by the throat. He gasped for air but could find none.

No. He could not die. He must not die. Not before DonVincenzo administered last rites.

Vivid images of the demon-infested bottomless pit tormented his mind. The agonizing cries of damned souls who had lost all hope reverberated in his ears and tore at his entrails, driving him to the edge of madness. Souls eternally separated from God. Eternally condemned to a fiery furnace of unending torment.

Souls eternally imprisoned in their willful sin.

They'd chosen to be their own god, and now they had no god to save them.

He groaned in anguish.

Rosa came running in, followed by Don Vincenzo. She rushed to Franco's side. "*Padre*, what's wrong?"

Don Franco saw the worried glance she exchanged with Don Vincenzo. The associate priest immediately uttered the opening words of the ritual: "*Pax huic dómui. Et ómnibus habitántibus in ea.* Peace to this house, and to all who dwell herein."

Don Vincenzo turned toward Rosa. "Please prepare the table."

She quickly covered the small bed stand with a white cloth in preparation for the administration of the sacrament.

"Hurry, *Padre*. I don't think he has much time left."

Don Franco moaned. "Yes, hurry."

Don Vincenzo thrust open the black leather bag in which he carried the items for administering last rites. With quick motions, he placed a small vial of extra virgin olive oil, blessed by the bishop, on the white cloth together with six small pellets of cotton to wipe the places of the body he would anoint. Next he took a wax candle standing in a candleholder and set it on the table next to a linen cloth with which to cleanse his fingers.

Rosa hurriedly brought a small bowl of water filled from the water pitcher on the dresser and placed it next to the candle.

Finally, Don Vincenzo placed a tiny bottle of holy water on the table and handed Don Franco a small crucifix to hold during the administration of the sacrament.

His hand shaking, Don Franco reached for the crucifix and, bringing it to his lips, kissed it reverently. His blood ran cold at the gravity of his sin against a holy God. He held the crucifix to his chest and followed Don Vincenzo's every motion. Franco knew the ritual by heart. During his decade as parish priest, he'd often administered last rites to the sick. Now it was his turn.

Dressed in surplice and purple stole, Don Vincenzo took the bottle of holy water and sprinkled it over Don Franco, over the room, and over Rosa, forming the sign of the cross, all the while reciting the antiphon *Asperges me, Domine. Cleanse me, O Lord.*

The words reverberated in Franco's heart as he recited them silently with the ministering priest.

After completing the prayer, Don Vincenzo turned toward him. "Franco, do you wish to confess your sins?"

The icy grip of guilt choked Franco. Pride and shame beckoned him to remain silent. But the fear of hell constrained him to confess.

"Yes." The word left his lips on the wings of his heart.

Don Vincenzo drew closer as Rosa retreated. Bending his ear toward Franco, Don Vincenzo encouraged him to begin.

With all the strength that remained within him, Franco strained for courage.

"I raped Maria Landro."

Don Vincenzo's face turned white.

Franco drew in a deep breath. "I hid my guilt for seven long years and caused an innocent woman to suffer because of my hypocrisy and deceit. I fathered a child and abandoned my duties toward him." A sob broke from his throat. He turned away from Don Vincenzo. "I do not deserve forgiveness, yet I plead for it. May God have mercy on me."

Don Vincenzo straightened from his bent position and lifted up his hand to form the sign of the cross. "Don Franco Malbone, I absolve you from your sins. In the Name of the Father, and of the Son, and of the Holy Ghost."

A long sigh of relief escaped Franco's lips. For the first time in seven years, he was ready to die.

Don Vincenzo reminded him of the power of the sacrament to forgive sins, to strengthen the soul, and, to heal the body. Then, extending his right hand over Don Franco's head, he recited the prescribed words: "In the name of the Father, and of the Son, and of the Holy Ghost. May all the power of the devil over you be destroyed by the imposition of our hands."

Don Vincenzo took the vial of olive oil and poured a few drops onto his thumb. Then,
placing the oil on Don Franco's forehead, he formed the sign of the cross on his eyes, his ears, his nostrils, his mouth, his hands, and his feet.

Don Franco trembled under his colleague's sacramental touch. A sensation like the balm of warm oil coursed through Franco's veins. He felt strength coming back into his body.

Don Vincenzo gave him a final blessing then left the room.

But despite receiving the sacrament, Don Franco still did not have complete peace. One thing yet remained undone.

He must confess his sin to Maria Landro and publicly exonerate her of all guilt. And in order to do that, he must get well. Death would be the easy path now, for Don Vincenzo could never reveal Maria's innocence because he had learned of it in confession.

The responsibility for a public confession rested with Franco alone. But first he would confess to his superiors.

* * *

For the first time in seven years, Maria awoke refreshed after a good night's sleep. Strange how outside circumstances had gotten worse, but inside, peace reigned in her heart.

She slipped into her cotton robe and went down to the kitchen. The aroma of freshly brewed espresso filled the air. Her mother and Nico sat at the kitchen table, deep in conversation.

She kissed her mother's cheek. "Good morning, Mama."

Her mother looked up and smiled. "Good morning."

Nico giggled. "Mama, Nonna said you're a sleepyhead."

Maria feigned anger as she pulled up a chair and sat down. "Mama, what secrets are you telling my son about me?"

Her mother's eyes twinkled. "No secrets at all. Just look outside. The sun has already traveled halfway through its arc."

Maria followed her mother's gaze. "It can't be noon already."

"Not yet. But close to it. It's 11:20."

"I can't believe I slept this late."

Nico slipped out of his chair and came to Maria's side. "All that crying last night made you tired, Mama. I'm glad you slept 'cause now you're not tired, and now you won't cry anymore."

A lump rose to her throat. The blessed innocence of childhood. How sad that one lost it so easily!

She lifted him on to her lap and squeezed him. "Today is a day for smiles, right, Nico?"

"And laughing." He proceeded to giggle at the top of his lungs.

Luciana walked into the kitchen. "What's all the racket?"

Nico clapped his hands. "I'm laughing. Do you want to laugh with me?"

Maria's heart warmed at the sight of her younger sister laughing with Nico. Soon Cristina entered the room and, before long, everyone was laughing.

How precious her family was! How could she have fallen into despair when she had so much to live for?

A sharp knock on the door silenced the laughter.

Maria's mother rose to open the door.

There, with a smug look on his face, stood Uncle Biagio, with that wretched sheaf of papers in his hand.

Before she opened the door, Mama turned to Maria. "By the way, I could not bring myself to sign the papers yesterday."

Maria's heart soared.

Chapter Twenty

"Don Franco, His Excellency is ready to see you." The receptionist motioned for him to follow her.

The one-hour train trip from Pisano had been uneventful, except for the trembling of his body. After receiving last rites, Don Franco's strength had miraculously returned. God had answered Don Vincenzo's prayer.

Franco's heart pounded as he shuffled down the long narrow corridor that led to the bishop's office. On either side of the hallway hung large faded tapestries dating back to the Middle Ages and depicting battles waged in the name of Christianity.

Those battles were nothing compared to the battle he'd waged in his heart.

He drew in a deep breath. Beneath his feet, the cold ceramic tile echoed his every step, like a ticking clock counting down the minutes to his destruction. Images of criminals on their way to their execution flashed across his mind. His collar chafed against the rivulets of perspiration that streamed down the sides of his face and neck.

He paused to catch his breath, but only briefly, so as not to arouse the curiosity of the receptionist.

Upon reaching the bishop's office, she motioned him to enter.

Franco nodded and froze at the threshold.

"Are you all right, *Padre*?"

He wiped his brow with his handkerchief. "Yes. Yes, I'm fine."

She gave him a doubtful look then returned down the long corridor from which they had come.

Fear clutched at Franco's throat. Today he would make his confession. Today he would reveal to the bishop the identity of Nico's father.

Today he would face his destiny.

He reached for the doorknob and turned it. The creaking sound of the massive oak door as it opened startled his already taut nerves. Like a vise, his jaw tightened, and his mouth grew dry with fear.

A shaft of bright light from a far window cast a shadow in the vestibule, darkening it.

"Is that you, Franco?" The bishop's voice boomed from the far end of the room.

Franco closed the door behind him and entered the main part of the office. The room was large and square, with dark paneled walls and built-in mahogany bookcases lining three of the four walls. On the fourth wall, a broad casement window reached from ceiling to floor and displayed a magnificent view of a courtyard burgeoning with yellow roses. In front of the window, a bespectacled Bishop Fumo, wearing his clerical robe, sat at his massive oak desk amid stacks of papers.

He rose to greet Franco. "Well, well, dear Franco. It is good to see you." The bishop extended a welcoming hand. "Please, sit down." He motioned to a leather Queen Anne chair opposite his desk then sat down again.

Franco sank onto the edge of the chair, his hands tightly clasped on his lap. Cold spasms shook his body.

The bishop leaned forward. "So, my dear man, to what do I owe the pleasure of your visit?"

Franco swallowed hard. He was only a confession away from total destruction. Of his reputation. His career. Perhaps even his life. He could still keep silent.

No. He'd come too far to turn back now. *God, help me!*

He met the bishop's steady gaze. The encouraging look in his superior's eye prompted him to continue.

"I know the identity of Nico's father."

The bishop smiled broadly. "Glory to God! I knew if anyone could find out, you could. So tell me, Franco, how did you discover this wonderful piece of information? Where is the child's father? And how did Nico react to the good news? That boy is an amazing little chap, isn't he? So inquisitive. So perceptive. So absolutely delightful."

The bishop's words twisted the knife already piercing Franco's heart. Fear clutched at his throat, rendering speech impossible.

"So who is the fortunate man who calls himself Nico's father?"

The room began to spin as Franco groped for the words. He grabbed his chest to allay the intensifying suffocation that threatened to rob him of all breath.

Concern spread across the bishop's face. "Franco, is something wrong?"

He forced the words out of his mouth. "Your Excellency." His voice caught. "I am Nico's father."

The blood instantly drained from the bishop's face.

He sat mute, his horrified eyes glaring at Franco in shock.

Like the pall of death, dark silence hung in the air. The silence of disbelief. The silence of impossibility.

The deafening silence of betrayal.

Franco shifted in his seat, his heart no longer pounding.

His Excellency leaned forward. "I am sure you are aware of the seriousness of what you have just told me."

"Yes. I am aware."

"And of the consequences that must ensue."

Franco's throat constricted.

"Yes. I am aware of the consequences as well."

The bishop rose and, forefinger to his chin, began pacing the floor. "I must take the matter to the archbishop, who will then take it to the Vatican." He turned abruptly. "Are you prepared for the reprimand of the pope himself?"

Franco's muscles tensed. "I am prepared, Your Excellency, for whatever punishment is meted out to me."

"Very well, then." The bishop returned to the chair behind his desk. "Do you want to tell me how this happened?"

Franco grasped for the right words. "The mother is Maria Landro, former housekeeper at my rectory."

The bishop raised an eyebrow.

"I violated her against her will yet forced her to bear the shame and ignominy alone for seven long years. I threatened her with God's wrath--and more--if she were to expose my guilt." Hot tears stung Franco's eyes and spilled over onto his cheeks. A sob caught in his throat. "Because of the shame I inflicted upon her, her family's reputation suffered as well as their business. Now the family is on the verge of bankruptcy." He drew in an anguished breath. "All because of my sin."

"Have you made your confession and asked God's forgiveness?"

"I have repented before God and asked His forgiveness. I have confessed to Don Vincenzo who gave me last rites, and I will ask Maria's forgiveness this very day. There remains only my public confession."

"Yes. A public confession in this case is, indeed, in order." The bishop took a deep breath. "You are aware, Franco, that you will be discharged from your priestly duties."

A spasm of remorse shook Franco's body. "I supposed as much."

"To allow you to continue in your duties would be to mock the cause of Christ."

"I've mocked His cause already. May He forbid that I should ever mock it again."

The bishop remained silent for a long moment. "There is nothing more to say at this point. I will inform the archbishop of the matter. He will very likely want to meet with you himself to discuss what steps are to be taken to dismiss you from the priesthood." The bishop paused. "Have you considered what you will do or where you will go?"

Franco shook his head, sorrow weighing like lead on his aching heart. "I suppose I could leave Sicily and start a new life elsewhere. Perhaps England or America."

The bishop cleared his throat. "Well, whatever you do, I wish you well."

Don Franco did not miss the catch in his voice.

"Very well, Franco, you may go now. I will refer your

case to the archbishop. I am certain he will summon you soon."

Franco rose. "Thank you, Your Excellency. I must ask your forgiveness as well."

The bishop stood. "Forgiveness granted, Franco. Go in peace."

Nodding, Franco left the bishop's presence, the fragrance of forgiveness hanging in the air between them.

He hoped the archbishop and the pope would be as forgiving.

* * *

Maria stood as Uncle Biagio entered the kitchen through the back door.

She nudged Nico toward the same door. "Nico, go outside and play."

"All right, Mama."

Biagio's eyes gloated with the pride of victory.

Maria squared her shoulders and raised her chin. "Hello, Uncle Biagio."

"Hello, dear Maria." He took her hand and planted a cold kiss on each of her cheeks then greeted her mother and sisters.

Maria clenched her jaw. The nerve of him. The outright gall.

He held papers in front of her. "I'm sorry to say the time has come for me to take over *Bella Terra*." He turned toward Mama. "Anna, I give you one last chance to sign these papers. If you do not, you will fall into bankruptcy."

Maria glanced at her mother. Anxious lines etched the

older woman's face.

"Oh, really, Uncle? You're *sorry* to say?"

A warning look crossed her mother's face. "Maria, your uncle is doing us a great service."

Maria spat at his feet. "That's what I have to say to your great service."

Her mother gasped. "Maria!"

Her uncle's face hardened. "So that's how you respond to my generosity, is it?"

Flames coursed through Maria's veins. "What generosity? Do you call it generosity to rob your brother's wife and children of their inheritance? Do you call it generosity to lie about my father's deathbed desire that his wife and children keep *Bella Terra*? Do you call it generosity to steal what does not belong to you?" Rage burned within her. "You know nothing of generosity. You are nothing but a scoundrel."

Her mother grabbed her by the arm. "Enough. This is a disgrace."

Maria looked deep into her mother's eyes. "Mama, you know I'm speaking the truth."

Biagio narrowed his eyes. "So—the whore of Pisano has questioned my generosity?"

Like a viper, the word struck its mark, piercing her heart in a place she thought had long hardened against the stinging pain of false accusations.

She blinked back hot tears. "You're just like the rest of the villagers. You think I'm guilty. You've always thought I was guilty, haven't you?" Her voice rose. "Did you ever think I might be innocent? Did you, Uncle? Did you ever think that maybe I was raped?"

His face showed no emotion. Only the unflinching hardness of a heart whose opinion was set in stone.

Maria fixed her gaze on her uncle and lowered her voice. "I promise you, Uncle, one day you will eat your words when you discover I am innocent."

Tears streamed down her mother's face.

"I'm sorry, Mama. I mean no disrespect. I want only the truth to prevail."

She gathered her two younger sisters in her arms. "I'm sorry you heard all of this. But I refuse to give up. *Bella Terra* belongs to us, and I will fight until my dying day to keep it."

Her sisters' quiet sobbing unnerved her. Gently releasing them from her embrace, she turned and, with a heavy heart, left the room in silence.

As she left, she heard Mama say, "Biagio, I cannot sign the papers."

* * *

The sun had nearly completed its descending arc when Don Franco's carriage reached *Bella Terra.* He'd come directly from the bishop's office to ask Maria's forgiveness. His heart pounded as he stood at the large oaken door of the main entrance. Perhaps no one had heard him sound the brass knocker. He knocked a second time. The sound of approaching footsteps made his pulse race. He took a deep breath and squared his shoulders.

A young girl of about fourteen answered the door. She resembled Maria, but with lighter coloring.

"Yes, *Padre*? May I help you?"

Don Franco nervously fingered his wide-brimmed

hat. "I'm here to speak with Maria. Is she home?"

The girl's eyebrows knit into a question. "Yes, I'm her sister Luciana. Come in, *Padre*. I will go get Maria for you."

He entered the large foyer, lifted his eyes, and looked around. The winding mahogany staircase led from a white marble floor to a wooden landing. In the center of the foyer, a cut-crystal chandelier hung majestically from a ceiling painted with angelic figures in the style of Michelangelo. On either side of the foyer, two large drawing rooms revealed a bank of large windows that overlooked the panoramic view of the hills and the sea.

He'd heard much of *Bella Terra*, but it was even more magnificent than he'd imagined. Throughout the many years the Landro family had held membership in his parish, never once had he visited them.

A pang of guilt cut his heart. He'd also never visited his son and the mother of his son who lived here.

O God! What a miserable wretch I've been! Help me to make it up to them.

Luciana returned. "Come this way, *Padre*. My mother is in the kitchen and welcomes you there while I fetch Maria."

He hesitated. "Would it be possible first to speak with Maria alone?"

Luciana wrinkled her nose. "I suppose so, *Padre*. But surely you'll join us for coffee afterward." She smiled. "I'll be right back."

Her sister did not know.

His mind raced. Before making a public confession, he owed Maria a private one.

He scanned the foyer once again. The front door beckoned. His heart rose to his throat. He could turn back now and never have to face her again. Maria would never know why he'd come.

His breath came in short gasps. He walked toward the door and turned the knob.

My grace is sufficient for you.

His whole being relaxed as he received the words into his spirit. He released the knob.

"Don Franco."

At the sound of Maria's voice, he froze, then turned around.

"You are here to see me?" Her voice betrayed no anger. Only curiosity--and deep pain.

He swallowed hard. "Yes, Maria. There is something I must say to you."

She stood before him, her hands clasped in front of her, her head high, her eyes waiting.

He opened his mouth to speak, but the words died on his lips.

Chapter Twenty-One

Luca   hastened   toward   *Bella Terra*. Don Franco's shocking confession had left him numb with disbelief at his friend's crime and with grief for the woman he loved. How could he have doubted her innocence? Even for one second? To think she'd suffered such public ignominy and pain for seven long years and suffered it alone and without cause.

Shame filled his soul at the way he'd treated Maria. He'd been cold and unfeeling. Too quick to believe she was guilty. Too self-righteous to discern her pain. Too blind with false assumptions to see the truth. He wouldn't be surprised if she never wanted to see him again. She'd trusted in him, and he'd failed her.

Failed her miserably. He hoped his failure was not beyond repair.

Like a flaming arrow, remorse pierced his soul. Could she find it in her heart to forgive him?

And Don Franco. The friend he'd looked up to ever since he could remember as an example of holy living. Of godly righteousness. Of purity and honesty. This blow was worse than discovering the truth about Maria. To discover guilt after assuming one's innocence was far more painful than to discover innocence after assuming one's guilt. The latter was cause for rejoicing; the former cause for despair.

His anger flared at the injustice of it all.

Yet, who was he to condemn his friend? Had not Luca himself been guilty of sexual sin, albeit by mutual consent?

You've never told Maria about your past.

The Lord's words jolted him, piercing his conscience.

"O, God! How can I?"

How can you not?

Yes. How could he not tell her? If he kept it hidden, it would be an unspoken wedge between them forever.

No, he would not hide the truth. He would come clean on a sin that, left unconfessed, could end the most beautiful relationship of his life.

As he rounded the bend that brought *Bella Terra* into full view, the setting sun cast soft coral shadows over the tiled rooftop and open courtyard. Splashes of brilliant pink and orange formed a magnificent backdrop to the centuries-old structure. In the distance, the Mediterranean shimmered in sun-kissed shades of emerald green and midnight blue.

Luca drew in a long breath of the refreshing salt air. It had a deeper freshness at this altitude, untainted by the earthy smells of the village below. Everything about the place seemed finer, purer.

As he approached the house, he noticed a horse and wagon parked behind the veranda. Perhaps he shouldn't have come. The family had guests. He considered turning back, but his conscience would not allow him to do so. No. He must set the matter straight with Maria. It was the right thing to do.

Quickening his pace, he climbed the last several hundred meters of the road and reached the veranda at the back of the house. Through the open kitchen screen door, he heard the voices of a man and woman engaged in conversation. He recognized the voice of Maria's mother, but who was the man?

Luca hesitated then climbed the few steps to the veranda and the back door. As he drew closer, he heard the name Biagio. Of course. Maria's uncle. The one she'd spoken about.

The one who was trying to steal the family's fortune.

Luca stopped. Had God brought him here for a reason beyond asking Maria's forgiveness?

Taking a deep breath, he knocked on the door.

Expecting Maria's mother to answer, he found himself standing, instead, face to face with Biagio Landro.

Luca stood at eye level with Uncle Biagio. The older man's demeanor demanded respect, but a respect rooted in a belief that he was superior to most men—and more powerful.

Luca saw right through it.

"I'm Luca Tonetta, Maria's employer. Is she in?"

Biagio's eyes narrowed and scanned Luca from head to toe. "So, you are the famous tailor Maria works for."

Luca bristled at the belligerent sarcasm in Biagio's voice. Maria was right about him. He was up to no good. "I wouldn't call myself famous. Perhaps *well-established* would be a better term."

Biagio broke into an icy smile. "Come in, won't you?" He acted as though he owned the place.

Luca tensed. Maybe he already did.

Luca stepped inside.

Biagio pointed to his sister-in-law. "*Signor* Tonetta, this is Anna Landro, Maria's mother. And, of course, my sister-in-law."

"Yes, we've already met."

Maria's mother approached him with an outstretched hand and a gentle smile.

"Hello, *Signor* Tonetta. Welcome again to my . . ." She hesitated and looked at Biagio. "I should say, my brother-in-law's home."

Luca started. So the transaction had taken place. The conniving thief. Luca was too late.

Biagio cleared his throat. "Yes, technically mine, Anna. But we must sign the papers to make it official."

Ah, there was still hope. Luca straightened his shoulders. "It's a pleasure to see you again, *signora* Landro."

The older woman nodded and smiled. "Likewise."

"Your Maria is an outstanding seamstress. I'm blessed to have found her."

Signora Landro's face beamed. "She is blessed to have found you too, *signor* Tonetta. Thank you for offering her a job."

"I can assure you the gain was mostly mine." Luca smiled at her, then shifted his gaze toward Biagio. "I see you are occupied, so I won't take your time. I'm here to speak with Maria. Is she at home?"

Biagio cleared his throat. "It seems everyone is looking for Maria today."

Luca raised an eyebrow. "Everyone?"

"Yes, Don Franco Malbone is even now awaiting her in the foyer."

What an interesting and unusual turn of events! A flash of inspiration struck Luca. If he could get Franco to vindicate Maria in Biagio's presence, the farm could be saved.

Luca prayed silently for wisdom. "How coincidental! Don Franco is an old friend of mine."

The old woman smiled, obviously unaware of the truth. "Well, in that case, I will go get him and tell him you are here."

Without waiting for a response, she left abruptly for the foyer, leaving Luca alone with Biagio.

The older man pulled out a chair. "Have a seat, young man." He eyed Luca suspiciously as he took a seat across the table. "May I get you an *aperitivo*?

Luca shook his head and sat. "No, thank you." He studied Maria's uncle. Guile seeped from Biagio's dark eyes. Tense fists rested on his crossed legs. One foot swung backward and forward in obvious annoyance.

"I assume Maria has told you about the family's need to sell the farm."

"Yes. And she also told me you've offered to buy it."

A proud smile smeared Biagio's face. "It's the least I could do as next of kin. Besides, it was my brother's— Maria's father's—deathbed wish that prompted me to do so. He expressed concern that his wife and children would find it too burdensome to manage the farm. As his younger brother, I feel a grave responsibility to carry out his wishes."

The lying skunk. Even if Maria hadn't told otherwise, Luca read the lie in Biagio's eyes. The deathbed-wish excuse was obviously nothing but a fabrication. An attempt to wrench the farm from the hands of its rightful owners.

To steal his brother's legacy.

Luca took in a deep breath. Maybe God had sent him

here at this precise moment to thwart Biagio's wicked plan. But how?

"So you see yourself as the family's savior."

"Exactly."

Luca kept his thoughts to himself. Though he really wanted to give this uncle a piece of his mind, it wasn't his place to criticize Uncle Biagio. But it was most certainly his place to do whatever he could to save Maria and her farm.

He glanced at the kitchen doorway. At any moment, Don Franco would appear. Luca would urge him to set the record straight once and for all.

* * *

Maria didn't really care how long she had kept Don Franco waiting, but now that she stood before him, she expected him to speak. What gall prompted him to come to her home uninvited? Especially after his horrendous accusation at the rectory. Hadn't he stabbed her heart often enough and then struck the death blow by lying about her guilt and his innocence? Had he come now to twist the knife?

She clasped her hands in front of her, her heart pounding, her stomach churning. *Please, Lord, don't let me be sick in front of him.*

Franco cleared his throat. "Maria." He hesitated. "Maria, I have come to ask"—a sob caught the edge of his words—"your forgiveness."

His eyes revealed the deep sorrow of true repentance.

She froze in disbelief. Could it be? Was the man who'd ruined her life actually asking her to forgive him? She must be dreaming.

But how could she trust him? He'd betrayed her once. What proof did she have that he wouldn't betray her again?

His eyes pleaded with her.

No, she didn't want to forgive him. To be kind toward him. After everything he'd done. What about *her* pain?

Silence hung in the air as she strained to grasp the reality of what she'd just heard. For seven long years she'd hoped against hope for this moment. Now that it was here, she wavered between compassion and hatred. Could she indeed forgive him?

Would forgiving him minimize the atrocity of his crime? Set him free with no punishment? Keep her forever a victim of his whims?

The questions hung heavy in the air. For the first time, she held his life in her hands.

Her pulse raced as the large grandfather clock in the hall ticked away the seconds. Power wrestled with pity as she gazed at the broken man standing before her. This could be her crowning moment. The moment where she could return an eye for an eye, a tooth for a tooth. She could watch the beast who'd destroyed her grovel at her feet. And the revenge of it all would be oh, so sweet.

Nico burst into the foyer. "Mama! Mama! Signor Luca is waiting for you in the kitchen."

"Luca?" She hadn't been expecting him. Why had Luca come?

"Mama, hurry up."

She gave her son a stern look. "Nico, you must be polite and wait. I am talking with Don Franco. Please tell *Signor* Luca I will be there momentarily."

A remorseful look crossed Nico's face. "I'm sorry,

Mama."

She looked at her son and then at his father. She was the permanent link between them. What she did to one would affect both of them for the rest of their lives.

Compassion began to tug at the edges of her heart as Nico nestled into her long skirt. She drew him toward her and held him close. Then, taking a deep breath, she faced Don Franco and swallowed hard.

"Yes." The words came hard. "Yes. I forgive you."

A heaviness lifted from her soul.

Don Franco's face spoke relief. "Thank you. I will be forever grateful to you." He turned to leave.

Maria's mother hurried into the foyer and stopped short. "*Padre* Malbone." She gave Maria a questioning glance, but Maria did not reply.

"Maria, Luca Tonetta is waiting to see you."

"Will you join us for coffee?" Maria's mother addressed Don Franco.

He shook his head. "No, thank you. I really must be going."

Nico grabbed the priest's hand. "Please, *Padre?* Please stay for coffee."

Maria read the need in Don Franco's eyes. "Yes. Please stay. Luca is here, and I would like you to meet my Uncle Biagio." Perhaps Franco would confess his guilt to her greedy uncle.

Nico pulled Don Franco by the hand. "Yes, *Padre,* you will stay. I won't let you leave. Not until you've had your coffee."

While Nico dragged Don Franco toward the kitchen, Maria took her mother by the arm. Later, she would finally tell Mama the whole story without fear of harm. But for now, Maria would wait to see if Franco had the courage to confess before the entire village.

* * *

Luca rose as Nico entered the kitchen with Don Franco in tow. Maria and Mama followed close behind.

Luca's gaze caught Maria's. She looked different, as though a weight had lifted from her shoulders. Then his gaze shifted to Don Franco. He, too, looked different. Relieved. At peace.

Forgiven.

Luca instantly knew. Franco had asked Maria's forgiveness, and she had granted it.

Luca's heart warmed. Now Don Franco must speak the truth to Uncle Biagio.

Mama slipped her arm out of Maria's. "*Padre*, surely you remember my brother-in-law, Biagio Landro."

The family patriarch stepped forward, his head cocked, his face plastered with a fake smile. "Well, well, *Padre* Malbone. I seem to remember you from way back, when my dear wife—God rest her soul—used to attend the Church of the Holy Virgin." He shook Don Franco's hand. "You were the new priest in the parish back then, if I recall. Isn't that right?"

Don Franco nodded. "Yes, many years ago, about ten. You have a good memory."

Luca sensed his friend's discomfort and strode toward him. "Franco, what a pleasant surprise to find you here!"

Don Franco smiled. "I can say the same of you. What

brings you here?"

Luca hesitated then glanced at Maria. "Actually, the need to ask for Maria's forgiveness."

An awkward silence settled over the room.

The priest's voice broke the silence. "Interesting. That's what brought me here, too."

Luca's soul stirred. "Franco, we both owe Maria more than an apology." He faced Biagio. "Her uncle Biagio here is about to buy the farm out from under them. All because he thinks Maria is guilty of sin when she is not."

Biagio rose to his full six feet. "How dare you defend my niece?"

Blood engulfed the veins of Luca's neck. "How dare you *not* defend her?"

"It is my duty to preserve the integrity of the Landro name and to save the farm."

Luca moved closer. "But it is not your duty to condemn your niece without proof and to steal the farm out of her hands."

Biagio's eyes narrowed. "The farm is none of your business, *Signor* Tonetta."

Don Franco stepped forward. "But it is mine." He touched Luca's arm. "Allow me, please."

Luca stepped aside, his gaze resting a moment on Maria, whose eyes were glued to Don Franco.

The priest held up a hand and turned toward Uncle Biagio. "*Signor* Landro, there is something you must know. Your niece is absolutely innocent of all wrongdoing. The blame for the failure of the farm rests entirely on my shoulders." He paused and took a deep breath. "Maria is a victim of my abominable selfishness and sin. I am not only a criminal but also a coward. I hid the truth from my parish, my superiors, the public, the vendors, and, worst of all, from myself." He lowered his head then raised it again. "I wish to confess publicly that Maria is innocent, that my despicable actions ruined her reputation and that of her family, that the loss of the farm income resulted from the fact that, in a moment of rage, I violated an innocent young woman." His voice caught. "I alone am to blame."

Luca released the long breath he was holding.

Uncle Biagio stood speechless, his brow furrowed in dark lines.

Luca's gaze followed Maria as she approached her uncle and attempted to take the papers from his hand. "You won't need these any longer, Uncle."

He pulled back with a violent jerk. "Wait just a minute. How do I know you're telling me the truth? How do I know this visit wasn't planned?" A wicked sneer crossed his face. "I find it peculiar that the two of you showed up at the same time. What proof do I have that this whole scenario is nothing more than a setup to get me to relinquish what is rightfully mine?"

Maria moved toward him. "You want proof? I'll give you proof."

Maria walked to the back door and called Nico.

The child quickly appeared. "Come inside, Nico."

Maria took her son by the shoulders and stood him next to Don Franco. "Here is your proof, Uncle. Look at them together."

Biagio's face paled. For a long moment, he said nothing. His face softened with remorse. "It seems as though I, too, owe Maria an apology. Since it is a day for confessions, I will add my own." He lifted the sheaf of papers in his hand. "You were right, Maria. These documents are a forgery."

Maria cast a knowing glance at her mother.

"My brother did not sign them, nor did he draw them up. They are entirely my fabrication for my own self-interests." He sank wearily into a nearby chair. "When I learned that Maria had disgraced the family name, I wanted to wrest it from my brother's line and bring it into my own. It was a selfish act, but one done with the lofty purpose of protecting the Landro good name. That fact does not make it less despicable." He raised his eyes toward Maria. "Will you forgive me?"

She drew in a deep breath. Yet again, she was being asked to forgive.

How much more can I take, Lord?

Seventy times seven, dear one.

She drew in a deep breath. "I forgive you, Uncle Biagio."

Difficult work, this forgiving. It demanded a total dying to the self. A self that resisted dying.

Only by Your grace can I do this, O God!

You have finally understood, dear one.

She sensed the Lord's smile upon her as her gaze shifted to Don Franco, still standing by Nico. The priest had come through for her after all. "Thank you for telling the truth."

His eyes brimmed with tears. "Maria, if you would allow me, I'd like to do more than tell the truth." He placed a hand on Nico's shoulder. "I'd like to help you rebuild the farm."

His words took her by surprise. Had he spoken them a few days before, she'd have spat in his face. But God had changed her heart.

"What about your parish and school?"

He hesitated. "I've been dismissed from both duties."

Maria let out a long, slow breath.

"After confessing my sin to God, I confessed to my superiors. You can imagine how shocked and dismayed they were. Although they forgave me, they also defrocked me, as you can see." He glanced down at his clothing. "I am no longer permitted to perform priestly functions."

Of course the church would dismiss him. The flock had to be protected, even if the wolf in sheep's clothing happened to be the priest.

But hiring the wolf to work on her farm? Only a fool would do that. Forgiving was one thing, but forgetting was quite another. Plus, forgiving did not require that she continue communication with the one who had harmed her. To have a constant reminder of the rape in the continued presence of the man who'd raped her—well, that lay beyond what she could bear.

But he seemed truly repentant, and she could certainly use the help. Perhaps his presence on the farm would also provide a way for him to get to know his son.

Maria looked at her mother. "How do you feel about this?"

"The question is, 'How do *you* feel about it?'"

No. The real question was how did God feel about it?

Maria turned and walked toward the window. Before her lay her father's legacy. But it was not only her earthly father's legacy. It was her heavenly Father's legacy as well.

What do You want me to do, Papa God? This is Your land, entrusted to my care.

She listened for that voice she'd grown to love so deeply.

Accept his offer.

But how do I know I can trust him, Papa?

You can trust Me, My child.

Maria turned away from the window. Her gaze shifted to Nico. The child stood at Don Franco's side, holding his hand. Compassion for man and boy filled her heart. To deny them each other would be cruel.

Nico's voice interrupted her thoughts. "Can I tell you how I feel about it, Mama?"

His question took her by surprise. She should have known he'd been listening to the whole conversation. She hesitated. Such an enormous decision should not be made by a child. There was too much at stake.

Ask him, dear one.

"How do you feel about it, Nico?"

"Well, since Don Franco can't be my teacher at school anymore, he can be my teacher at home."

The child's logic made sense. She could hire Don Franco to work on the farm and to be Nico's tutor as well.

She looked at Don Franco. "Very well. You're hired. But I must warn you that I can pay you nothing until we regain the trust of our vendors and start selling to them again. It will take a while to rebuild *Bella Terra*. At least one planting and one harvest."

His face grew determined. "I will help you regain the trust of the vendors. I will make a public confession before them in the town square and encourage them to resume doing business with you."

Truly God was at work, making her life new. Healing her broken heart.

Giving her beauty for ashes.

Just as He had promised her in His Word.

Don Franco continued. "All the vendors will be gathered as usual in the square early tomorrow morning. I will be there at eight o'clock. May I ask that you be there as well?"

Maria's heart twitched. It was hard enough simply walking through the square. To stand there in front of the villagers while Don Franco confessed his sin—well, that was another matter.

Chapter Twenty-Two

Luca lingered behind after Don Franco and Biagio left. Maria's mother and her sisters had gone upstairs to work on a quilt. Nico had accompanied them to play with a puzzle. Only Maria remained in the kitchen.

Luca turned toward her. "Would you like to sit outside? It's a beautiful evening."

She nodded without speaking.

He followed her out onto the veranda. The night was warm and balmy with a star-studded, indigo sky overhead. Luca's heart raced as he mentally rehearsed the words of his confession. First, he'd apologize for having betrayed her at the rectory. Yes, betrayed her at a time when she'd needed him most. When she'd had no one else to protect her. To fight for her.

To believe her.

Then he'd confess his failure to remain pure until marriage. A confession even more difficult.

Guilt threatened to suffocate him as the full realization of his sin struck him with crushing force. Could she forgive him?

Could he forgive himself?

Luca looked into her eyes. "After you left yesterday, I returned to the rectory and questioned Don Franco. He told me the truth."

Her gaze met his, tears lacing her eyes. "Yet, when I told you the truth, you did not believe me. No. You believed him instead of me."

Her words indicted him and left him without excuse.

She lowered her eyes. "You're just like everyone else. You believed a priest over a woman. A pastor over a violated parishioner." A tear trickled down her cheek. "A so-called saint over a so-called sinner."

He felt the weight of her condemnation and absorbed it.

Her gaze rested on him. "A priest would never commit such a heinous crime, would he?" Sarcasm edged her voice. "No, a priest is above reproach."

Her accusation struck the mark as the rebuke in her voice signaled the intensity of her deep, deep pain.

Maria sighed. "So, you want to ask my forgiveness? You who took the priest's word over mine? You who defended a criminal? You who were quick to judge without seeking the truth?"

"'Maria, I am so sorry. So very sorry for doubting you."

The look of hurt in her eyes sliced through his heart. He drew in a deep breath. "There's more."

"More? What more could there be? Isn't what you've done enough?"

Luca took her hands in his. "Maria, I have a terrible confession to make."

* * *

She fixed her eyes on his. Not another confession. How much more could she take?

Luca leaned forward, his face taut, his eyes somber. "What I'm about to tell you is something that could change our relationship forever." His eyes reflected deep sorrow. "Something that could even destroy it."

Her stomach knotted. What could be so awful that it could destroy their relationship?

She looked deep into his eyes, now filling with tears. Fear rose in her heart. He'd met another woman. He didn't love her anymore. He'd never loved her.

"Shortly after my parents' death, I met a girl."

Maria's breath caught.

"The grief of losing my parents was so fresh and so agonizing that I sought comfort in the girl's arms. One thing led to another and, before I knew it, I'd—I'd lost my virginity."

His words crashed into her heart, splintering it into a million pieces. She recoiled and pulled away from him.

"Maria, can you forgive me?"

Images of Luca in another woman's embrace suffocated her, like an avalanche of runaway boulders roaring down a mountainside, crushing her under their enormous weight.

A sob caught in her throat. She'd forgiven Don Franco. She'd forgiven herself. But forgive Luca for this?

Impossible.

She'd been brutally forced to lose her virginity. He'd surrendered his without thought and of his own free will.

A tear trickled down her cheek.

My grace is sufficient for you.

But Lord.

If you do not forgive others, My Father will not forgive you.

Lord, this is different.

Not different, dear one. More painful, yes. But not different.

Repentance gripped her. How could she not forgive Luca when she herself had been forgiven of so much?

Luca repeated the words. "Maria, can you forgive me?"

She lifted her gaze toward the man she loved more than anyone else in the whole world. The remorse in his eyes cracked the last vestige of hardness within her. "Yes, Luca. I forgive you."

He rose and drew her to himself, enveloping her in his arms.

She fell into his embrace as he held her close.

"I love you, Maria Landro, the Madonna of Pisano." He found her lips and kissed them.

Tears of joy overflowed on to her cheeks. Luca loved her. Luca loved Maria Landro.

* * *

Don Franco arose long before dawn. He fell to his knees on the *prie-dieu* next to his bed. "Father, thank you for healing me and giving me the opportunity to make amends to Maria. In obedience to You, I am going to the square today to make a public confession of my sin. You know this is a very difficult thing for me to do. I will be standing before people who have known me all my life. People who have trusted me.

Confided in me. Looked to me for spiritual direction. And, yet, I have failed them, Father. Failed them miserably. My shame is great, Father. But no greater than the shame Jesus endured for me on the cross. Give me strength, Lord, to go through with this. I pray that as I exonerate Maria of all guilt, You will vindicate her and move upon the vendors' hearts to resume business with her farm. Restore Maria and her family. Help me to help them rebuild *Bella Terra*. I ask all these things in Jesus' Name. Amen."

Don Franco remained kneeling for a long time. His mind filled with thoughts of Nico. His love for the boy ran deep, deeper than he'd expected. The thought of watching him grow up filled him with hope. No matter how hard the public confession would be, he would do it. Not only for Maria, but for Nico as well.

He rose slowly. A tap on the window caught his attention. He moved toward the casement window just as a sparrow rapped its beak against the glass.

A lump formed in his throat.

I did not come to condemn the world, but to save it. As I watch over the sparrow, so do I watch over you.

This same loving Savior who came to save the world would now be with him as he confessed his guilt and helped set Maria free.

Don Franco took his small, leather-bound New Testament from his desk and, with trembling hands, placed it in his pocket. Then he closed his office door behind him, left the rectory, and headed steadfastly toward the village square.

The sun had just begun its upward arc from the eastern horizon. Long ribbons of purple-gray light melted into brilliant strands of yellow-gold. The lowing of cattle in the distance signaled a new day.

As he approached the square, vendors from the surrounding countryside made their way into the village, hauling carts filled with eggplant, peppers, and squash. Fishmongers, back from a night of fishing, brought in the sea's harvest of tuna, squid, and baby octopus. Middle-aged women carried baskets on their heads filled with freshly baked breads and pastries they would sell in the square. These were his people, his roots, his flock.

How he'd wronged them!

"Good morning, *Padre*."

Don Franco's heart sank. Soon that term of respect would carry the ignominy of sin. He nodded, his spirit faltering. Could he go through with it? Could he expose to these people who he really was? A dastardly hypocrite?

Early morning crowds began gathering in the square. Women dragging recalcitrant children to shop for the day's groceries. Men setting up card tables for their daily game of *scopa*. Old women shuffling across the square toward the Church of the Holy Virgin to hear the Mass that Don Vincenzo would now celebrate in Franco's stead. The routine of daily life, soon to be interrupted.

His jaw stiffened, pulling taut the muscles in his neck and shoulders. He could still turn back. Leave the public confession undone.

Spare himself the public humiliation.

No. He must follow through with his decision.

He looked around for Maria. Perhaps she'd decided not to come. He couldn't blame her. She'd suffered enough public scrutiny already.

Whether she came or not, he would confess anyway.

Wagons laden with oranges, lemons, and limes rumbled into the square, their roughly hewn wheels kicking up dust. Others bore lettuce, broccoli, and kale. Some pieces fell by the wayside, where blackbirds devoured them.

Several of the vendors greeted him as he passed by.

When he reached the center of the square, he stopped and waited.

The pounding of his heart reverberated in his head. His hands grew cold, and sweat seeped from his brow.

His resolve wavered.

God, help me.

I am your strength.

In the near distance, Maria appeared with Luca at her side. Franco's gaze flew to her, and his courage revived. He owed it to her. And to Nico. He owed it to Pisano. He owed it to God to set the record straight once and for all.

Most of all, he owed it to himself.

Maria stood before him.

It was time.

Lifting his head, he shouted into the crowd. "Fellow citizens of Pisano, hear me, please."

His voice barely carried over the noise of the crowd.

"Citizens of Pisano, hear me, please."

One by one, the chattering voices subsided. All eyes turned toward him.

He fastened his gaze on Maria. "Citizens of Pisano, I have a public confession to make." His mouth was dry. His hands trembled. His heart pounded.

A death-like stillness settled over the square. A lone seagull swooped over the crowd and soared back up into the azure sky.

"You all know me as a man of God, a man of honor, and a man of integrity. I am here to tell you today that I am a criminal of the first order."

A deep hush settled over the crowd.

"I am a liar, a hypocrite, a coward, and a thief." He pointed to Maria. "I robbed this young woman standing before me, Maria Landro, of her virtue, her respect, and her good name. In an ignominious fit of rage, I violated her, raped her, and fathered a child with her. Then, for seven long years, I hid the truth from all of you."

Gasps of horror floated through the crowd. Old women lowered their eyes. Old men narrowed theirs. No one uttered a word.

"For seven years, Maria has suffered shame, humiliation, and the near bankruptcy of her farm as a result of my crime against her. And she has suffered alone." He paused. "You vendors refused to buy produce from her because of what you unjustly considered her loose and sullied reputation. You women scorned her and condemned her. You men leered at her and lusted after her. And all because of me." Don Franco raised his right hand toward heaven and raised his voice. "But I tell you before God that Maria Landro is innocent of all wrongdoing. She fought my advances, but I overpowered her. She is guiltless, guileless, and good." He lowered both his hand and his voice. "And I plead with you today, as her *paesani*, to help her family recover from their shame and financial loss by accepting her once again as a fellow citizen of Pisano and by buying produce again from her farm."

The crowd stood motionless, all eyes glued on Don Franco and Maria standing before him.

The sun burst full upon Maria, illuminating her in its radiant light.

Don Franco wiped his brow with his handkerchief. "Moreover, I must tell you that I have been defrocked by the Church and am no longer permitted to perform the duties of a priest. Nor do I feel worthy to do so." His voice broke. "Finally, I ask that you would find it in your hearts to forgive me. I have wronged you and betrayed you. You deserve far better than I." His knees weakened. Grabbing hold of Luca's arm, he stood face to face with Maria.

Her eyes brimmed with tears.

Looking her in the eye, Franco said, "May you now go in peace into the future God has prepared for you."

Taking his leave, he pushed through the crowd, avoiding the eyes of the stunned villagers. He needed to be alone.

Alone with his God.

Chapter Twenty-Three

Maria found herself immediately surrounded by villagers and vendors offering apologies. Many wept. Others expressed regrets. Still others offered her hope and encouragement.

"He's covering for her," a young woman murmured behind Maria. "It would be just like Don Franco to protect her."

Maria flinched at the insult but let it pass. There would always be those who refused to believe the truth. No. She would choose to rejoice at this display of repentance and remorse. Her long night of suffering had turned into day, and hope rose anew in her heart.

A fruit vendor approached her. "*Signorina* Landro, I am one who withdrew my business from your farm because I believed the lie about you. Will you forgive me?"

The sorrow in the man's eyes was genuine.

She took his proffered hand. "Yes, I forgive you."

How freeing it was to forgive, and how enslaving it was to withhold forgiveness!

The man nervously fingered a worn hat in his calloused hands. "As soon as you are ready for business, I would like to resume purchasing my peppers and squash from your farm." He smiled sheepishly, revealing a gold front tooth. "Yours are by far the best vegetables in the whole countryside."

Gratitude swelled in Maria's heart, crowding out the loneliness, the sorrow, the fear she'd had for so many years. These were the people she'd grown up with. The people who'd worked side by side with her father and with the generations of Landros before him. The people whom she'd loved like family but from whom the lie had estranged her. How great the power of truth to reconcile and restore!

"Thank you."

Another vendor approached. "*Signorina* Landro, I would like to start purchasing again from *Bella Terra*. Your zucchini are the best."

She laughed. "Especially deep-fried in olive oil and bread crumbs, right?"

The vendor returned the laughter.

Then a third and a fourth approached her. Soon a large crowd of vendors surrounded her, all asking forgiveness and pledging to buy their fruits and vegetables from *Bella Terra* again.

Maria smiled. "You have no idea what your business means to me and to my family."

Overhead, a trio of seagulls squawked and swooped in a graceful acrobatic dance, as though rejoicing with her.

She glanced at Luca. The look on his face told her he was eager to be alone with her.

She bid farewell to the few remaining people who still lingered and then excused herself. Her step was lighter, and her heart even more so. "Thank you, Luca, for your moral support. I couldn't have done it without you."

He smiled. "Oh, yes, you could have." He took her

hand. "By the grace of God, you've achieved your dream of saving *Bella Terra*."

"Yes. By the grace of God. Now al that remains is to restore her to her former glory." She smiled. "And that, too, will be done by the grace of God."

Luca nodded in agreement. "And now, I must get to work. My customers will be knocking down my door if they don't find the shop open." He held on to her hand a moment too long then released it.

She smiled. "I will stop by this afternoon with my latest batch of sewing."

"Very well. I will see you then."

She watched as Luca returned to his shop, her heart wondering what would come next.

* * *

A light drizzle fell on the square as Luca checked his pocketwatch. Maria would be arriving in ten minutes to drop off her sewing. Now that all had been settled regarding her reputation, and now that he'd confessed his gross sin to her, he could proceed with asking her to marry him.

He'd been thinking about it for a long time. Now at last he had total peace.

At the sound of the tinkling bell, he looked up from his work. "Maria."

She smiled and walked toward the counter, her canvas bag in hand. She hoisted it up to the counter and emptied its contents. Two pairs of trousers and three shirts. All mended and pressed, ready for delivery to their owners.

Luca no longer needed to examine her work. It was

impeccable. Confident that all had been done with excellence, he took her by the hand and led her into the back room.

Smiling, she asked, "Where are we going?"

"I need to talk with you privately."

"But no one is here."

"Yes, but a customer could walk in at any time."

He motioned her to a chair next to the small table and sat down next to her. "Maria, now that all has been settled with Don Franco, there is something I want to ask you. It's been burning in my soul for a good while now, but the time was not right."

He read the expectant look on her face.

His heart pounding, he cleared his throat. "Maria, will you marry me and go to America with me?"

* * *

Luca's words were like boulders knocking her off a steep cliff. A gasp caught in her throat then made its way down into her soul, bursting into fireworks of a joy the likes of which she'd never known. But in a single moment, her heart plunged from the heights of ecstasy to the depths of despair. Luca had just spoken the words she'd been longing to hear ever since she'd met him. But he'd spoken other words as well. Words about leaving *Bella Terra*. Leaving her family.

Leaving her beloved homeland.

Her heart halted between love and duty. Between the man she loved and her debt to her ancestors. Between the man to whom she was knit in spirit and the family to whom she was knit by blood.

To marry Luca would mean to leave *Bella Terra*. And that she would not do.

She could not do.

She looked into Luca's deep blue eyes, eyes filled with love and yearning. "Luca, I'm sorry. I cannot marry you."

His gaze dropped.

"It's not that I don't love you. The truth is I love you with all my heart, and I want to be your wife." She took his hands. "But now is not the right time for me to leave everything to go to America. I cannot leave *Bella Terra* just when the farm is getting back on its feet. Mama can't handle things by herself, and my sisters are still too young to run the farm. The lot falls to me to get *Bella Terra* up and fully running again. To do so, I will have to remain here. My duty is here, with my family."

He remained silent for a long moment.

She wanted to wrap her arms around him, to hold him close to her heart and never let him go.

She looked into his eyes. They were deep and penetrating, touching the farthest reaches of her soul. "I knew I was in love with you the night you offered Nico and me shelter from the storm. You risked your reputation for us, and I will never forget that. I've kept my feelings to myself all this time, for fear that you were not at all interested in me. Marrying you would be the fulfillment of my greatest dream. Yet—" She fumbled for the right words. "Yet, marrying you would mean moving to America." She lowered her eyes. "And that is something I cannot do right now."

Maria studied the broken man before her. He'd

counted on her acceptance of his offer. But her allegiance to her family—her allegiance to her dream—demanded that she remain.

Besides, if Luca wanted her so badly, why didn't he remain in Sicily? He had a flourishing business right here in Pisano. Why did he have to go to America?

He answered her unspoken thoughts. "Were it not that I sensed God's leading to go, I would remain in Pisano."

Her heart constricted. Would God bring them together only to separate them when they needed each other most?

Luca took her into his arms.

She laid her head on his shoulder and breathed in the musky scent of his manliness. His strong arms harbored her like a vessel that had finally reached its port.

They held each other for a long moment, his touch making her every nerve vibrate.

When at last her heart could bear no more, she drew back from his embrace. "Let me know how you are faring in the promised land."

He stroked her hair. "And you, let me know how you are faring in the restored land of *Bella Terra*."

She nodded as hot tears slid down her cheeks. Rising, she bid him farewell then left.

Dark clouds hung low over the village square. She crossed it and began the ascent on the road to *Bella Terra*.

Her heart ached. Would she ever see Luca Tonetta again?

Chapter Twenty-Four

The shop bell clanged. His heart shattered, Luca rose quickly and positioned himself behind the counter.

"Luca Tonetta." Teresa entered with a flourish and gave him a broad smile. Rain dripped from her silk head scarf and covered her long cotton dress.

She came up to him and gave him a peck on the cheek. "So, how's my favorite tailor?"

"Teresa Monastero, what a surprise to see you!" For the first time in his life, he did not feel annoyed upon seeing her. "What brings you to Pisano?"

He greeted her with a brotherly embrace.

She arched an eyebrow, flashed an engagement ring under his nose, and smiled. "I'm to be married next month to a wonderful man from Ribera."

Luca's heart warmed. He was truly glad to hear the news. "Your fiancé is a blessed man."

"Well, *he* seems to think so, and that's all that matters, I guess."

Did he detect a hint of reprimand in her voice?

"I'm back for only a short visit. Do you have a few moments?"

"Yes. Yes, I do. Who knows? If I don't take the time now, I may never see you again."

"And would that matter?"

He tensed. "Teresa, look. Let's let bygones be bygones."

She flashed a melancholic smile. "You're right. There are certain things I choose to forget. It makes life easier to live."

Motioning toward a chair, he nodded in agreement but made no verbal reply.

She took a seat across from him, removed her head scarf and placed it squarely on her lap. "So, I hear the big news in Pisano is Don Franco's confession."

She hadn't changed. As always, she got straight to the point.

He raked his fingers through his hair. "News travels fast. How long have you been back?"

"My train arrived in Pisano around noon. I took the first available coach here. The driver had already heard the big news and was making sure all of his passengers heard as well." She smiled demurely and straightened a fold in her skirt. "It's the talk not only of Pisano but of the entire province of Agrigento."

Luca let out a long breath. "And no doubt it will soon be the talk of all of Sicily."

Teresa leaned forward. "So, tell me. What happened?"

He saw the sincerity in her eyes. She wanted to know not for the sake of gossip, but because she was genuinely concerned about her former parish priest.

"Don Franco finally confessed. Maria is innocent of all wrongdoing." He looked away. "Don Franco raped her." The muscles in his jaw tightened as his gaze returned to hers.

"Nico is their child."

As she listened attentively, he recounted the entire story of Don Franco's admission of guilt, his public confession in the square, his exoneration of Maria, and his dismissal from the priesthood. He even told her that Maria had offered Don Franco a job as foreman of *Bella Terra*.

Teresa listened intently. "It sounds like a miracle."

"I believe it is a miracle."

She leaned forward. "Luca, I owe you a profound apology. I misjudged Maria." She sighed. "And it looks as though I misjudged Don Franco too." She touched the back of his hand. "Will you forgive me?"

"Of course, I forgive you." He hesitated. "It goes to show that only God really knows the human heart."

"Yes." She smiled. "And thank God for that. What a mess we humans make of things!"

"You're right about that." He shifted in his seat. Now that she was engaged, he didn't have to worry so much about his time rule. "Tell me about your fiancé."

A broad smile lit her face. "Oh, Luca. He is simply wonderful. Meeting him was well worth the wait." She leaned forward. "His name is Sergio, and he owns a jewelry store in Ribera." She showed Luca a brilliant diamond bracelet dangling from her right wrist. "He travels to Roma and Milano to purchase the best jewelry in all of Italy."

"He sounds like someone who will be well able to support you."

"Is that all you men think about?"

"Of course not. But it is, after all, a major responsibility a man has toward his wife."

"What about you? Who is the fortunate woman who

will capture the impenetrable heart of Luca Tonetta?"

"*Scusa?* What do you mean by *impenetrable*?"

She laughed. "You know very well what I mean. All of my attempts to win your heart backfired. I never could get through to you."

"Teresa, we simply were not meant for each other."

"And who was meant for you, Luca?"

He looked her straight in the eye. "Maria Landro."

Her gaze penetrated his soul. "You've always loved her."

Luca swallowed hard. "Yes. From the moment she first stepped foot in my shop."

"Then you should marry her." Her tone was matter-of-fact. As though nothing more needed to be said.

Luca's heart constricted. "I've asked her to marry me, but she refused. She said she cannot leave *Bella Terra* to go to America with me."

Teresa screeched. "Go to America with you? Are you crazy? She's just been given a clean slate that has resurrected her farm. How could she leave now? The farm needs her. Her family is depending on her." Teresa stood to her feet and pointed a finger at him. "You are a *cretino*, Luca Tonetta! A complete idiot! Have you lost all common sense? Why do you want to go to America if you're in love with Maria? If you ask me, Maria is the only one acting like a mature adult around here." She jabbed her finger into his chest. "If you're the kind of man I've always thought you were, you need to give up your silly dream of going to America and marry Maria."

She'd always spoken her mind regardless of how it affected the hearer.

"I think your dream was misdirected, anyway. For goodness' sake! You have a thriving business right here in Pisano. People know you. Your father before you established a reputation that you've carried on. Who knows you in America?" She waved a dismissive hand at him and crossed her arms. "Besides, you can't even speak English."

Was she right? Had he allowed a false notion to get in the way of common sense? Pride to drive out humility?

Ambition to crush love?

Yes, he'd wanted to make his fortune in America. So many villagers had sent letters from the promised land describing its riches and its unlimited opportunities. They'd stirred his sense of adventure.

But he'd wanted something more. He'd wanted to know that Maria would follow him to the ends of the earth. That she really would give up everything for him.

Yet, did that really matter? No. What really mattered is that he would give up everything for her. That *he* would follow *her* to the ends of the earth. And for him, the end of the earth was right where he was.

Teresa rose and moved toward him. "Luca, I've never lied to you, and I won't start now. Before meeting Sergio, I'd hoped that one day you'd consider marrying me. But I discovered I was wrong. You've loved Maria ever since you first set eyes on her." She lowered her head. "I just didn't want to admit it to myself." She drew in a deep breath and raised her chin. "But one can't help falling in love with someone, right? Even when that someone loves someone else." She put her hands on her hips. "Now get off your high horse and go tell Maria you're not going to America after all. Otherwise, you risk losing the greatest gift of your life."

Luca rose, too. He took her hands into his own. "Teresa, you are a wonderful friend."

"And so are you."

"I wish you many blessings in your new marriage. Perhaps some day I will get to meet your future husband."

"Perhaps someday." She turned to leave. "Luca?"

"Yes?"

"Take good care of Maria."

"I will."

"And give her my best wishes."

He nodded.

Teresa left without looking back.

Luca had a strange feeling he would never see her again.

* * *

Twilight filled the sky as Maria drew back the white lace curtain. From the large window in her bedroom, she watched the storm drop torrents of rain on the countryside. Like the sound of horses' hooves, the rain beat hard against the tile rooftop and splashed loudly against the windowpanes. Large puddles dotted the dirt road leading to the village. Here and there, a fallen palm branch lay broken along the winding road. Even after an hour of heavy downpour, the rain gave no sign of letting up.

Over and over, her mind relived Luca's marriage proposal. He'd been so tender. And so nervous. Had she done the right thing in refusing him? Should she have left everything and followed him to America? Was she giving up the best opportunity of her life?

And what about Nico? Was she thinking of his well-being or only of her own? If she'd said yes, Luca would have become not only her beloved husband, but also her child's father. All it would have taken was a single word from her.

A single word she could not utter.

Thoughts of doubt tormented her. Would Luca meet someone else in America and marry her? Would she remain a spinster for the rest of her life?

Would she never see him again?

How she missed him! Every moment spent in his presence filled her with life. What would she do when he left for America without her?

Yet, how could she marry him now? Her family needed her to help get the farm back on its feet. She was the firstborn in a family of only women. To leave now would be to betray not only her mother and her sisters but also her roots.

The rain beat against the casement window. Rivulets of water slid down the glass, racing each other to the bottom. Her heart raced with them.

She turned from the window and knelt by her bed. This was supposed to be the happiest day of her life, the day Don Franco exonerated her. Yet, sadness prevailed in her heart.

Had God restored *Bella Terra* to her only to take it away again?

It didn't make any sense.

She bowed her head in prayer. "Lord, show me Your will regarding Luca. Your thoughts are higher than my thoughts, Lord, and Your ways are higher than my ways. Help me to hear Your voice, Lord, and no other."

A deep peace settled over her spirit. She arose,

knowing exactly what she had to do. She would remain at *Bella Terra*. She would complete the task before her.

She would be true to herself and to her dream.

* * *

Luca could not cover the road to *Bella Terra* fast enough. Immediately after Teresa's departure, he'd closed his shop for the day. He needed to tell Maria that he'd decided not to go to America after all. Teresa had been right. His place was beside the love of his life.

The rain had stopped, and a brilliant sunset had taken its place. Upon topping the hill, he found Maria on the veranda with Nico.

"Signor Luca! Signor Luca!" The child ran toward him with outstretched arms.

Luca picked him up and placed him on his shoulder. "How's my big, brave boy?"

"I'm fine, Signor Luca." Nico laughed. "I'm bigger and braver than yesterday."

"Indeed, you are!"

Maria descended the steps of the veranda to greet Luca. "Why, hello. How nice to see you again, and so soon."

Her smile melted Luca's heart.

He took Nico off his shoulder and put him on the ground.

Nico turned to Maria. "Mama, I think you and *Signor* Luca should get married."

Maria's face turned crimson.

Luca tousled Nico's hair. "Funny you should say that, Nico. I'm here to tell your Mama the same thing."

Maria gave him a questioning look while Nico jumped up and down, clapping his hands. "Nico, would you go inside with Nonna for a few minutes. *Signor* Luca and I need to talk."

"Okay, Mama."

Luca drew near and gently took her by the shoulders. "Maria, I've decided not to go to America."

She gasped. "Oh, Luca, are you sure? Far be it from me to steal your dream."

He drew her to his heart. "You are my dream, Maria. My place is by your side" He lowered his voice. "I want you to marry me." He nestled his face into her hair.

She smiled. "Is that an order?"

He laughed. "Yes, it's an order. If, that is, you will still have me."

She gazed into his eyes. "I will gladly have you, Luca Tonetta." She drew in a deep breath. "For the rest of my life."

Chapter Twenty-Five

Don Franco put the final items in his trunk and fastened the lid. The wagon would be arriving soon to take his belongings to *Bella Terra*. Maria had assigned him quarters in a large room at the far end of the barn. From there, he would oversee the hired hands as they worked together to bring the farm back to its former prosperity.

With mixed feelings, he surveyed the now bare bedroom that had been his for the last ten years. The room that had marked his triumph upon being appointed to the pastorate immediately upon leaving seminary. And the room that had been the place of his downfall when he'd committed his heinous crime against Maria.

Although God had washed away his guilt, he still sorrowed at the memory of it.

The room's white stuccoed walls had grown dingy and gray. The area around the casement windows had chipped and flaked from rainwater that had seeped through over the years. On the windows themselves, the latches had rusted.

He rose and walked to the window. His legs no longer kicked against the long flowing garb of a cassock. The privilege of wearing it was no longer his. Instead, he'd donned an old suit that had once belonged to his father. The jacket was worn at the cuffs, and the trousers were a bit short, but they suited him well for the new life he was about to enter. A life of manual labor, far different from the life to which he'd grown accustomed. Yet, it held a certain fascination for him by virtue of its very difference.

Although he'd miss the warm, familiar surroundings of the rectory, he was glad to leave a place marred by the scars of his past. Despite his misgivings, a new future lay before him. Certainly not the future he'd envisioned for himself, but a future full of the promises of God. He would work hard. He would prove himself faithful. And most of all, he would be a father to Nico.

He marveled at the depth of God's grace. Like the mother of Moses, he'd lost his son only to regain him in a far better way.

What Satan had meant for evil, God was turning for good.

"*Padre*, your wagon is here." Rosa's voice sounded through the closed door.

He moved to open it. "Thank you, Rosa. I'm ready. Please send the driver in to help me with my trunk."

The housekeeper nodded and left.

He sensed the anguish in her heart. She'd served him faithfully for ten years. She'd seen him come in victory and now leave in defeat. Yet, she'd uttered not a word of judgment or reproof.

Grace.

Rosa understood grace.

And now he finally understood it, too.

A sparrow tapped its beak against the window.

A lump caught in Don Franco's throat.

This time, he had not frightened the bird away.

* * *

Having completed her daily rounds of the farm, Maria made her way up the narrow path back to the house. Things were coming along well. In the short time since Don Franco had publicly exonerated her, business had taken a major turn for the better. Now that the vendors had agreed to buy produce from them again, she'd be able to pay off all of the family's debts. A very good situation indeed, but one that required careful planning and organization.

Don Franco was proving to be a capable foreman. Under his careful leadership, the workmen had tilled the fields in preparation for the spring planting. Rows of peppers, squash, and cucumber plants lined the terraced hillsides surrounding the farm. Closer to the house, orange and lemon groves had been pruned and cleaned, and new trees had been planted.

She'd made a wise choice in hiring him, albeit a difficult one. Since coming to *Bella Terra*, the former priest had changed tremendously. He exuded peace and serenity, so different from the Don Franco she once knew. And being close to his son had given him a new lease on life. Nico adored him and spent hours working in the fields by Franco's side and being tutored by him at home. Still, their son did not know Don Franco was his father. That would come later, when the boy was better able to cope with the news.

Meanwhile, *Bella Terra* was coming to life again, and Maria was glad.

She whispered a prayer of thanks for all the blessings God had brought her way.

* * *

The day she'd long awaited had come. Maria twirled in front of the full-length mirror. The long satin skirt of her wedding dress spun gracefully and caught up with her. She placed her hands on her hips. "Oh, Mama. It's beautiful!"

Her mother stood behind her. The twinkle in her eyes and the broad grin on her face heralded her pleasure. "I loved every minute of making it for you."

Maria gave her mother a hug. "You are a magnificent seamstress, Mama. Most of all, you are a magnificent mother."

The older woman blushed as she took her daughter in her arms. "I have waited for this day for a very long time." Her voice caught. "I have waited for my Maria to be happy again. To laugh again." She wiped the tear that rolled down her cheek. "To love again."

Maria too had waited a long time. Many times she'd wondered if she would ever be happy again. If she ever would laugh again. She swallowed hard. If she ever would love again. But God had had mercy on her, and she had Him to thank for everything.

A rap on the door interrupted her thoughts. Before she could answer, the door opened.

Luciana and Cristina stopped short and gazed at their sister.

"Oh, Maria." Luciana gasped. "You look like a queen."

Cristina fingered Maria's gown. "And the most beautiful queen in the whole wide world."

Maria approached her sisters and embraced them.

"Are you almost ready?"

Luciana spoke first. "Yes. I just have to take off my robe and put on my dress. Then *Signora* Pina is going to curl my hair."

Cristina patted her curly head. "My hair is already done."

Maria smiled. "And it looks beautiful."

Maria lifted Luciana's chin and looked into her deep, dark eyes. "Are you nervous?"

Luciana's eyes filled with tears. "Not nervous. Just a bit sad."

"Sad?"

"Yes, at losing you."

Tears welled up in Maria's eyes. She'd been so caught up in the joy of wedding preparations that she hadn't considered the effect her marriage might have on her little sisters. Maria took Luciana's hands. "Oh, darling. You are not losing a sister. You're gaining a brother."

Luciana's eyes brightened. "A brother?"

"Why, yes. Luca will be your brother-in-law."

A smile beamed on Luciana's face. "Why didn't I think of that? It will be fun having a brother for the first time."

Cristina giggled. "Yes. Lots of fun."

Relief flooded Maria's heart. "Yes, we could use a brother in this family, don't you think?"

Luciana nodded. "And Luca is the best brother we could ask for."

The elder *Signora* Landro joined her daughters. "Come now, girls. We can talk about brothers later. Right now we need to finish dressing. We have less than an hour before the ceremony."

Maria's heart fluttered. In less than an hour, she would become *Signora* Luca Tonetta.

Then, she and Luca would take a honeymoon trip to the beaches of Taormina before returning to *Bella Terra* to set up house in a wing that had been closed when her father died.

Maria rested a hand on her mother's arm. "Mama."

"Yes, dear."

"I want to thank you for all you've done for me. You've been there for me all along, and that means so much to me."

Her mother sighed. "As your papa used to say, we are family. And family always sticks together."

Memories of her father filled Maria's heart. If only he could be here today. How proud he would have been of his firstborn daughter! As it was, her Uncle Biagio would be giving her away. A practice dictated by family tradition when one's father was deceased.

And by the forgiveness she'd learned to embrace as a key to life.

Her mother patted her arm. "We really must be going. The carriage is waiting outside to take us to the church."

Maria gave her mother a quick peck on the cheek. "I'm ready except for my veil. Will you help me put it on?"

Maria gently picked up the organza veil that lay across her bed. Her mother had worn it on her own wedding day. Maria lifted it carefully and laid it on her head as her mother began to pin it in place.

Goosebumps covered Maria as she studied the white veil and the white wedding dress. Although her body had been violated, she could rejoice, for she was pure in God's eyes.

She caught her mother's admiring gaze.

"You are lovely. Simply lovely." The older woman gave her a hug. "Now we really must be going."

Maria took a deep breath. "Yes, it is time."

Chapter Twenty-Six

The melody of "Ave Maria" rang from the small choir as Maria entered the Church of the Holy Virgin. Escorted by a repentant and forgiven Uncle Biagio, she walked down the long aisle toward the lily-decked altar. Her eyes searched for Luca's and instantly found them.

Her pulse raced as she approached the man of her dreams. Her feet could not walk fast enough. Her heart could not soar high enough. Her spirit could not sing loudly enough.

At last, she faced her beloved.

He took her by the hand, and together, they approached the altar. On one side stood Mama, Luciana, and Cristina, their eyes brimming with tears. On the other side stood Don Franco, his face beaming with joy.

And next to him, holding his father's hand, stood Nico.

Her heart exploding with joy, Maria smiled at her son.

He smiled back and whispered, "Mama, I see the sun in your eyes."

Her heart stirred.

And I, My precious daughter, see the Son in your eyes.

END OF BOOK ONE

COMING SOON: *A Sicilian Farewell*
Book Two in *The Italian Chronicles Series*

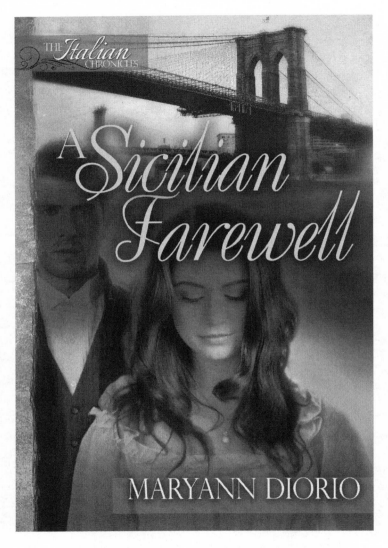

*A young woman, a new land, and a dream that
threatens to shatter all she holds dear . . .*

COMING SOON: *Return to Bella Terra*
Book Three in *The Italian Chronicles Series*

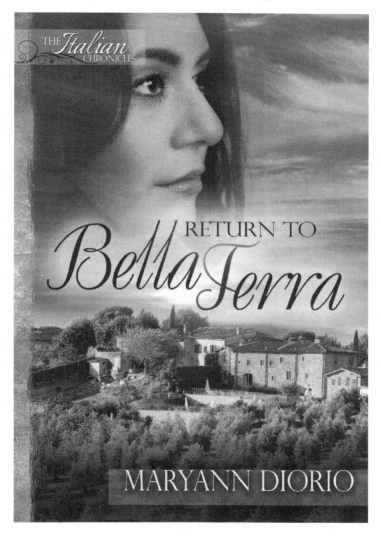

THE *Italian* CHRONICLES

RETURN TO *Bella Terra*

MARYANN DIORIO

A mother, her son, and the man who comes between them . . .

Questions for Group Discussion

NOTE: These questions may be used in a variety of ways, including book club or reading group discussions, in Bible study groups dealing with the topic of forgiveness, and for personal meditation.

1. Maria struggled with forgiving the man who raped her. From a human standpoint, her struggle was understandable. Yet, God commands us to forgive. What enabled Maria finally to forgive Don Franco? Can we forgive in our own strength?

2. Is forgiveness a challenge for you? If so, why? Why do you think forgiveness is so difficult for many people?

3. When a person refuses to forgive, how is her soul affected?

4. For a long time, Don Franco refused to confess his guilt out of fear of exposure. What are some other reasons people refuse to admit their guilt and seek forgiveness? What does the refusal to forgive or to ask forgiveness do to the human heart?

5. Does forgiving mean forgetting? Does forgiving mean trusting again the person who hurt you?

6. Maria chose to prove her forgiveness of Don Franco by offering him a job on her farm after he was defrocked. Does forgiveness mean maintaining a harmful relationship? How can you determine if you should continue or end a relationship with the person who hurt you?

7. Luca could not discern who was telling the truth: Maria or Don Franco. What should one do when one cannot

determine the truth in a given situation? Consider King Solomon and the two women claiming to be the mother of the same child (I Kings 3: 16-28).

8. Although Maria wanted to marry Luca, she chose to remain true to her dream of restoring *Bella Terra* to solvency. Should duty supersede one's personal desires? If so, when? How important is it to stay true to one's dream?

9. Is there someone in your life you need to forgive? Is there someone of whom you need to ask forgiveness? Is there something holding you back? If so, what is it?

10. Will you make the decision now to forgive that person or those persons who deeply hurt you? Will you make the decision now to ask forgiveness of the person or persons you deeply hurt?

Excerpt from A Christmas Homecoming:

Sonia put the finishing touches on the German chocolate cake she'd baked for Christmas Eve dinner. If Ben didn't want to join her, she'd take the cake to old Miss Hattie, a shut-in who lived next door, and share it with her.

As Christmas carols played softly in the background, Sonia sang along with Silver Bells, hoping to put herself in the Christmas spirit. A ring of what sounded like the doorbell interrupted her. No. It must be the sound of bells on the CD. It sounded again, but she ignored it a second time. But when the ring sounded a third time, she turned off the CD to listen. Yes, it was the doorbell.

She carefully put down the frosting-laden spatula and wiped her hands on a kitchen towel. Then she hurried to answer the front door. Probably the mail carrier or the FedEx man. Who else could it be? She wasn't expecting anyone, especially not on Christmas Eve.

She reached for the door knob and opened the door. Her heart froze at the sight before her.

Excerpt from Surrender to Love:

Dr. Teresa Lopez Gonzalez screamed, stumbled, and stifled a sob with her hands. "No! It's not true!" She gasped for air as the tragic news sucked the life out of her. "You're talking about the wrong person. It can't be my husband. Roberto is at work."

Trembling, she grabbed the edge of the kitchen counter to keep from falling.

This couldn't be happening to her. Surely it was all a dream. A bad dream. She would awaken soon to discover all was well.

The police officer lowered his head then lifted it again. Compassion filled his glistening eyes. "Ma'am. I'm sorry. So very sorry." He reached into his belt pouch. "We found this in your husband's shirt pocket."

Teresa's stomach clenched.

About the Author

MaryAnn's passion, as her registered trademark states, is to proclaim *Truth through Fiction*® because only truth will set people free (John 8:32). A widely published author of non-fiction, MaryAnn responded to God's call a few years ago to write fiction and has since published two novellas for adults, *A Christmas Homecoming* and *Surrender to Love* She hopes her stories will entertain and point readers to Jesus Christ, the Truth Who alone can set them free.

Dr. MaryAnn holds the PhD in French and Comparative Literature from the University of Kansas. She lives in New Jersey with her husband Dominic, a retired physician. They are blessed with two lovely grown daughters, a wonderful son-in-law, and five rambunctious grandchildren. In her spare time, MaryAnn loves to read, paint, and make up silly songs for her grandchildren.

How to Live Forever

Eternal life is a free gift offered by God to anyone who chooses to accept it. All it takes is a sincere sorrow for your sins (contrition) and a quality decision to turn away from your sins (repentance) and begin living for God.

In John 3:3, Jesus said, "Unless a man is born again, he cannot see the Kingdom of God." What does it mean to be "born again?" Simply put, it means to be restored to fellowship with God.

Man is made up of three parts: spirit, soul, and body (I Thessalonians 5:23). Your spirit is who you really are; your soul is comprised of your mind, your will, and your emotions; and your body is the housing for your spirit and your soul. You could call your body your "earth suit."

When we are born into this world, we are born with a spirit that is separated from God. As a result, it is a spirit without life because God alone is the Source of life. You may have heard this condition referred to as "original sin." Why is every human being born with a spirit separated from God? Because of the sin of our first parents, Adam and Eve.

I used to wonder why I had to suffer because of the sin of Adam and Eve. After all, I complained, I wasn't even there when they ate the apple! Yet, as I began to understand spiritual matters, I began to see that I was there just as a man and woman's children, grandchildren, great-grandchildren, and so on, are in the body of the man and woman in seed form before those descendants are actually born. In other words, in my children there is already the seed for their future children. In their future children will be the seed of their future children, and so on.

Now, as a parent, I can pass on to my children only what I am and what I possess. For example, if I speak only Chinese, I can pass on to my children only the Chinese language. I possess no other language to give them out of my own self. The same was true with Adam and Eve. Because they disobeyed God, their fellowship with

God was broken. Therefore, their spirits died because they were severed from God. As a result, they could pass on to their children only a dead spirit—a sinful spirit separated from God. And Adam and Eve's children could pass on to their children only a dead, sinful spirit. And so on, all the way down to you and me.

We said earlier that your spirit is the real you—who you really are. So what does it mean when your spirit—the real you—is separated from God? It means that unless you are somehow reconciled to God, you will go to hell after you die. Hell is a real place of real torment resulting from separation from God.

Now God is a holy God and He will not tolerate sin in His Presence. At the same time, He is a loving God. Indeed, He IS Love! And because He loves you so much, He wanted to restore the broken relationship between you and Himself. He wanted to restore you to that glorious position of walking and talking with Him and enjoying the fullness of His blessings.

But there was a problem. Because God is infinite, only an infinite Being could satisfy the price of man's offense against God. At the same time, because man committed the offense, there had to be Someone Who would also be able to represent man in paying this price. In other words, there had to be a Being Who was both God and man in order that the price for sin could be paid.

Since God knew that there was nothing man could do on his own to pay the price for his sin, God took the initiative. In the writings of John the Apostle, we learn that "God so loved the world that He gave His only-begotten Son, that whoever believes in Him shall not perish but have eternal life" (John 3:16).

What glorious GOOD NEWS! God loved you so much that He sent His own and only Son, Jesus Christ, to take the rap for your sins. Imagine that! Would you give your son to go to the electric chair for someone else? Well, that's exactly what God did! The Cross was the electric chair of Christ's day, and God gave His own Son, Jesus Christ, to go to the Cross for you!

In dying on the Cross for you, and in rising from the dead three days later, Jesus paid the price for your sins and repaired the breach between you and God the Father. Jesus restored the broken relationship between man and God. He provided mankind with the gift of eternal life.

So what does all of this mean for you? It means that if you accept Christ's gift of eternal life, you will be "born again." In other words, God will replace your dead spirit with a spirit filled with His life. "Therefore, if anyone is in Christ, he is a new creation. Old things have passed away; behold, all things have become new" (2 Corinthians 5:17).

If I offer you a gift, it is not yours until you choose to take it. The same is true with the gift of eternal life. Until you choose to take it, it is not yours. In order for you to be born again, you must reach out and take the gift of eternal life that Jesus is offering you now. Here is how to receive it:

"Lord Jesus, I come to You now just as I am—broken, bruised, and empty inside. I've made a mess of my life, and I need You to fix it. Please forgive me of all of my sins. I accept You now as my personal Savior and as the Lord of my life. Thank You for dying for me so that I might live. As I give you my life, I trust that You will make of me all that You've created me to be. Amen."

If you prayed this prayer, please write to me to let me know. I will send you some information to help you get started in your Christian walk. Also, I encourage you to do three important things:

1) Get yourself a Bible and begin reading in the Gospel of John.

2) Find yourself a good church that preaches the full Gospel. Ask God to lead you to a church where you will be fed.

3) Set aside a time every day for prayer. Prayer is simply talking to God as you would to your best friend.

I congratulate you on making the life-changing decision to accept Jesus Christ! It is the most important decision of your life. Mark down this date because it is the date of your spiritual birthday. Be assured of my prayers for you as you grow in your Christian walk.

God bless you!

Dr. MaryAnn Diorio

Other Books by Dr. MaryAnn Diorio

A Christmas Homecoming
When Sonia Pettit's teenage daughter goes missing for seven long years, Sonia faces losing her mind, her family, and her faith.

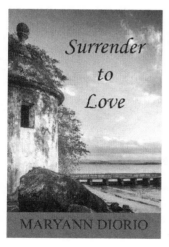

Surrender to Love
When young widow and life coach, Dr. Teresa Lopez Gonzalez, travels to Puerto Rico to coach the granddaughter of her mother's best friend, Teresa faces her unwillingness to surrender to God's will for her life. In the process, she learns that only by losing her life will she truly find it.

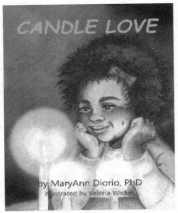

Candle Love

Four-year-old Keisha has a new baby sister. But Keisha doesn't want a new baby sister. Keisha is afraid that Mama will love Baby Tamara more than Mama loves her. But when Mama shows Keisha three special candles, Keisha learns that there is always enough love for everyone because the more one shares love, the more love grows..

Who Is Jesus?

Introduce your child to the true Jesus of the Bible.

.

Toby Too Small

Toby Michaels is small. Too small to be of much good to anyone. But one day, Toby discovers that it's not how big you are on the outside that matters; it's how big you are on the inside.

Do Angels Ride Ponies?

A handicapped boy discovers the power of faith to achieve the impossible.

You may find Dr. MaryAnn on the following Social Media Sites:

Website: www.maryanndiorio.com
Blog (Matters of the Heart):
http://www.networkedblogs.com/blog/maryanndiorioblog
Amazon Author Central:
http://www.amazon.com/author/maryanndiorio
Facebook: http://www.Facebook.com/DrMaryAnnDiorio
Twitter: http://Twitter.com/@DrMaryAnnDiorio
Goodreads:
http://www.goodreads.com/author/show/6592603
LinkedIn:
http://www.linkedin.com/profile/view?id=45380421
Pinterest: http://www.pinterest.com/drmaryanndiorio/
Google+: http://plus.google.com/u/0/+DrMaryAnnDiorio
YouTube: http://www.youtube.com/user/drmaryanndiorio/

TopNotch Press
A Division of MaryAnn Diorio Enterprises, LLC
PO Box 1185
Merchantville, NJ 08109
Tel.: 856-488-3580
FAX: 856-488-0291
Email: info@maryanndiorio.com

37599121R00202

Made in the USA
Middletown, DE
02 December 2016